KILLING CORTEZ

A.L. DENOVA

This is a work of fiction. The events depicted in this novel are fictions. Any similarity to any person living or dead is merely coincidental. Names, characters, businesses, places and events and incidents are either the products of the author's imagination or used fictitiously. Any resemblance to actual persons, living or dead, or actual events is purely coincidental

ISBN: 978-0-9995666-1-9

For more information please visit: AlDeNovabooks.com

The Dark, Disturbing Story of Love and Murder by Mexican Organized Crime

To my wife and children.

1

MEXICO IN THE MIRROR

Tecate Port of Entry
International Boundary
United States/México
Date: Thursday July 14, 1988
Time: 11:30 p.m.

THIS WAS THE WAY THEY HAD ALWAYS DONE IT. JC SQUEEZED
Carmen's hand and pulled her warm, fragrant form to him
across the sticky vinyl expanse of the 1966 Chevelle. Long,
dark, and sleek, Juan Carlos was aroused just looking at the
tight sexuality of the Chevelle. Carmen was fun when he
floored her.

"Cariño," JC smiled as he touched his warm lips to her
perfumed neck, "This is so simple we'll be swimming on the
beach in Coronado in two hours." He gunned the engine,
the roaring V-8 music to his ears. This was a trip he made so
many times in his 25 years and even in his mother's womb.
The drive across la frontera, one half mile from the dusty
sage brush of Tecate, Mexico, through the Port of Entry at
Tecate, United States.

The ease of border crossing was never wasted on JC. Within the hour he had been in another country with different laws, a different language and a more nuanced morality. Certainly, Mexico had laws. He grew to manhood learning that those laws could be dodged with the suggestive word or a less subtle stack of cash from a well-placed relative. He had many cousins who enforced Mexican laws. These same cousins, through family money and connections ensured such laws did not collide with JC. He lived only in Mexico but was glad he held his citizenship to the north. His parents had been too smart to let an accident of birth limit his future opportunities.

In the hot July air JC tasted the sage brush, dust and gas fumes. The air itself toasted out temperatures beyond 105°. More fragrant was his passenger for the night, Carmen Sophia Ruiz de Quintana. She was glued to him through her body heat on the gold vinyl car seat. As he approached the border north, he tried to slow his burning chest and racing pulse.

He rehearsed in his head all that he done so many times before, what Uncle Ramon Aguilar Santiago, "El Gordo" had drilled into his head: "Go through Tecate. At that place only the American casts-offs work there. You have nothing to declare, you are a U.S. citizen visiting your abuelita with your girlfriend and are returning to San Dimas where you live with your cousin. You own the car. Have Carmen flash a smile and show some skin," Ramon had confided. "You have nothing to worry about." It was for the family, for their business. They needed the delivery tonight for a deal later in the week. "In Tecate, make a call at the gas station. We'll give you directions from there. I will be waiting for your call."

JC had used those lines to his girlfriends at times, "I'll be waiting for your call." JC knew in his bones that Ramon really was waiting for that late-night call and that his own bones could be snapped if the right calls were not made on schedule. Nothing ran on time in Mexico except the drug smuggling.

Uncle Ramon had provided the encouragement that was needed, "El gringo flojo, the lazy American inspector, will be so much more interested in Carmen than you, the Chevelle, or the 1000 kilos of cocaine in the trunk." JC was no virgin to this enterprise. Even so, he made sure to tell Ramon that the girl, Carmen, knew nothing of the cocaine. JC watched American TV and he saw the "War on Drugs" commercials with Ronald Reagan and his wife, Nancy. They told him to, "Just say no." But the open border, said "Yes." They had the money and cops, but Americans let drugs pass through by the kilo and the ton.

JC tuned the radio dial to his favorite English station, slowed the car and pressed his tongue deep between Carmen's welcoming lips as a preface for what would come later that night. He turned up the volume of the techno chords pulsating through the metal of the muscle car.

JC had every belief that this was going to be a lucky crossing and a very lucky night in oh so many ways. The yellow international boundary line appeared into his rear-view mirror and he slowed to a stop at the primary inspection booth welcoming JC and Carmen into The United States of America.

A grizzled ex-Marine, pressed, thin and erect in a blue United States Customs uniform, a cigarette dangling from his lips, greeted JC by stooping at the driver's window of the Chevelle.

"Good evening," the U.S. Customs inspector told JC.

"Hi," JC replied, in perfect, unaccented English. JC was not much of a student but his family paid a driver to cross him and his five school age siblings Monday through Friday for thirteen years of public education in Chula Vista, California. The results were now in, he could speak American like the native that he was. And he crossed the border like the professional border crosser that he had been schooled to be.

"Where you coming from?" asked the inspector.

"Tecate," replied JC.

"Where are you going?"

"San Dimas."

"Who owns the car?" asked the inspector.

"I do," responded JC.

"Let's see the registration," demanded the inspector. JC opened up the glove box, pulled out a standard white business-sized envelope and removed the 1988 registration for the inspector. The registration showed an address in San Dimas, California. The inspector handed the registration back. JC could see the inspector's name on the blue uniform: Stewart. "Inspector Stewart?" asked JC.

Stewart shook his head, continuing "And what is your citizenship?"

JC smiled and told the inspector in perfect English, "U.S."

"Let's see your identification," Inspector Stewart demanded.

JC unbuckled his seat belt. He bent forward and slid out a nylon surfer's wallet. He pulled out his smiling California driver's license which revealed his grey eyes, ruddy complexion, perfect teeth and dark hair that fell to his shoulders.

Stewart looked at the driver, scanned the photograph on the driver's license and then glanced up in time to see the young couple kissing. Stewart shrugged, yeah, Mexican passion, typical. Stewart cleared his throat then smiled as he saw a flash of cleavage from the young Latina in the front seat. He nodded to Carmen.

"Miss, do you have ID?" Carmen opened up her red purse, pulled out a red wallet, found her current California driver's license depicting a luscious 23-year-old girl (herself) in a halter top, with long dark hair, abundant make-up and irreverent eyes. Stewart wondered about the rest of the body that was not shown in the ID.

The inspector peered at her license. "Is that you miss?" asked Stewart, in his most passive grumble.

"Yes," Carmen nodded.

"Citizenship?" asked Stewart.

"USA," Carmen responded. "Bringing anything in from Mexico?" queried Stewart.

"No," said JC. As the driver, he answered for the two of them.

The routine of the job comforted the inspector after twenty years in the Marines. "Then you kids have a safe drive home." Stewart winked at JC and waved his hand to permit entry.

JC fingered his Jesus Malverde pendant underneath his collared cotton shirt. He mouthed the words "gracias," as he knew gratitude in the thrilling moment of entry.

Together, they passed through the Tecate Port of Entry, with a smile and an effortless wave into the land of opportunity.

Another 1,000 kilos of cocaine crossed. That was money in his pocket tonight, at the latest tomorrow. Not bad for one hour of driving. Sweeter still with Carmen by his side.

2

LA LINEA

"Jesus Malverde." Again, JC kissed the gold pendant hanging from a 24-carat chain on his lean chest. He thanked his patron saint of smugglers for another successful crossing. He smiled with the easy confidence of a young man who was promised a handsome profit and had a beautiful, willing woman by his side. He had crossed 1,000 kilograms of cocaine in the trunk. He was a made man now with the cartel, with his uncle and with Carmen.

JC shook his head with the only logical conclusion. Lots of people wanted those drugs, and his family made sure their orders were filled. Metal signs, with the words "International Boundary, United States," had been scattered across this dry frontier at irregular intervals. These signs were the size of stop signs. They were more like surveyor's markers than boundaries of sovereignty. JC was not blocked by a barrier of concrete nor a wall of virtue.

"That was simple," JC repeated aloud. He squeezed Carmen's hand. She felt his warm palm moist with sweat.

"Why is it so easy?" Carmen asked.

"This is such a joke," JC declared. "This border, la linea.

They never stop us." Carmen stroked his arm. He felt his blood rise even with her light touch. "Cariño, the answer is clear. They do not mention the obvious here, not in Tecate, Tijuana, San Diego, or Los Angeles."

She wanted the relationship and the benefits, so she asked, "Mention, what?" There was no commitment or ring from him.

"Because they want it this way- we disappear and nobody asks questions," JC said. Carmen nodded, beginning to connect his words to what she had seen growing up in Tijuana.

"Just like the bodies that were piled in the trash outside my family's shop. No questions were asked."

"That's right," JC said, "We cross our product in trunks, spare tires and engine compartments. Nobody asks questions. There's just a big profit and no taxes. Those who do ask questions are dumped in your family's Tijuana trash can."

Carmen stared at the black curtain of the desert horizon which was dry and fragrant with sage. The smell was both alluring and untrustworthy like JC. She fought to distinguish the terrain from the sky. She knew she wasn't missing much even in the dark. "So, anybody who wants to travel north just crosses?"

JC nodded. "There is nothing from the ocean east through these hillsides and cactus. Nothing. That sign we just passed, I have pissed on it so many times when it's late and there is nobody is here."

JC pulled to the side of the road and shoved the car into park. He jumped out. Deftly, he unzipped his tight designer jeans. He was an expert at undressing anyone including himself. He thanked the United States with a warm flood of gratitude on the boundary sign. He paused to admire his dripping admiration of America. He dashed back to the car and his girlfriend for the trip. He had proved his manhood again.

JC turned to Carmen and half laughing said: "La migra, they are the joke with their uniforms and questions. They never stop us," purred JC returning a light stroke to her arm. "$15,000 a kilo, becomes $30,000 a kilo, becomes $150 a gram. 1000 grams in a kilo. That's a $150,000 per kilo for the family. A profit of $135,000 a kilo." JC repeated this arithmetic rosary for sustenance.

This promise was her ultimate aphrodisiac.

A low white building jutted out of the desert. In faded neon, "Discount Gas" lit up the deep night. Leaving the engine running, he pulled into the closed gas station. "Cariño," JC offered, "I am calling them, to tell them we are crossed."

He left the car door open and dashed over to a solitary pay phone near the gas station office. A flock of cigarette butts punctuated the blacktop. He kicked the white debris with the toe of his running shoes. He then plunged his right hand into his tight jean pocket. He retrieved a fistful of American change. Quickly, he dropped each quarter in the narrow slot. He held his breath, as if he was feeding coins to a slot machine. JC tingled with the thrill of the payout. From memory, he dialed the country code on the black rotary dial, 4-8-4 he repeated to himself. There would be no misdial. No mistakes, not tonight.

He dumped in 10 US quarters. The dial was sticky with the residue of the region. He never brought a paper with his uncle's number north with him. He heard the familiar ding and click and a saccharine female voice announcing: "You have $2.50." He listened for one shrill ring then a second followed by a deep bass voice that said:

"Bueno."

As instructed, JC answered in Spanish: "We are going to the beach. She does not know."

The reply was, "The pier at the usual time." Both parties hung up.

3

NO SPARE

UNCLE RAMON WAS NO DUMMY. HE WAS A PRACTICAL businessman. "See here nephew," Ramon had said while exhaling his cigar, "We are both cheating in our marriage, Mexico and America." He snapped his thick fingers for emphasis. "We are good Catholics so we understand we will be forgiven. We cross drugs, we cross people. They want both. We only offer what gringos desire. Like any business we are filling a need. The Americans cheat too by letting us in."

JC nodded in agreement as Uncle Ramon continued, "They buy what we have, but they lie. They act in secret as if Jesus is blind. But we see. Our mistresses bear us children and come to our funerals. Their girlfriends live in shame. And it is the same here." Uncle Ramon poured out the tequila and the border cotillion, "Trade one language for another. Spanish, English." Ramon, swept his left hand. "And one land where laws, lawyers, and judges are bought and paid for- Tecate, Mexico for another country - San Diego, USA. Nephew, the border does not change the desires of men."

JC nodded in silence as the smooth tequila lubricated the flow of conversation.

"It is our connections and our families." Ramon smiled wider and put a finger to his lips in pantomime. "We are proud of this tradition and heritage." JC had been told of the illustrious accomplishments of his family, the Santiago family. Border crossing for the Santiagos was a proud family trade which was perfected over generations.

Uncle Ramon recounted tales of their great grandfather in the bootleg liquor days and then the marijuana and now the cocaine. Those gringos with their Puritan background were always making some form of sin illegal. The Santiago family stood ready to profit by supplying the banned transgression.

JC never forgot Uncle Ramon's words of advice, "Supply and demand. Limit supply and the price rises, be it gin or cocaine." Those gringos paid dearly for Prohibition, they outlawed booze. Fortunes were made in those years from 1920 to 1933 for the bootleg liquor sold to Americans. They paid dearly for the prized cocaine. The Santiagos stood ready when Americans made fun illegal. With each decade, his family's landholdings grew as did their influence and their indulgent, night-long carne asadas.

His whole life, JC had passed anything and everything and anyone through the border. Politicians, prosecutors and judges on both sides of the border joined together to binge on women and alcohol in high end ocean front hotels. Who were they fooling? Not the Santiagos but maybe some gringos on the east coast.

"The US border is a paper towel," JC would say to his compadres after a successful crossing, over Mexican beer with lime. How they would laugh, and drink on the beach in Coronado, looking south.

Carmen listened more closely to the sloping waves on the gentle beach, adjacent to the U.S. Naval Seal training center. The coastal air was perfection; warm, but not hot. The fine sand between her toes so soft. The beach was breathtaking and deadly at the same time.

She waited for JC's touch after his latest conquest crossing what the cops called contraband. He laughed: "For $20, cocaine can make any place Palm Springs, and make you feel better than the Marlboro man."

"What do you get when you mix equal parts of the Catholic Church, conquistadores, cronyism and just perfect weather?" Each time, JC answered his own question, "San Diego."

And then he would roll back laughing on the sand, careful not to spill his drink.

———

JC JOGGED BACK to the idling engine and floored the V-8. He slowed as he rounded a tight turn, circling the wheel with his hand. Right over left, right over left, until a short straight away. This was a rural route that followed the old-time east-west Pony Express roads. The most frequent travelers were still rattlesnakes and outlaws. They slithered belly down across the border for decades.

JC drove from Tecate Road along the border and merged onto Route 94. They were making good time. He glanced at the Chevelle dashboard, "Hey, it's just after midnight, Carmen. Having fun?" And then thump. The Chevelle ran along on three tires and on one very deflated left front tire. The sound was like a bullet to his mood. Reflexively, he pulled over to the dusty shoulder of the road, wishing to preserve his beloved tire rims. The load came first but he was in love with the Chevelle. He parked her and jumped out. "She's OK," he said, wanting to cry and scream. "What's wrong?" Carmen asked.

Through clenched teeth, JC observed. "We have got a flat. I will ruin the rims if I drive anymore," he explained. "You stay here, roll up the windows and don't let anybody in here." He bent down and tied his shoelaces with double knots. Not pausing to think, he took action. "Look, I am going to make some phone calls. They must have one at that gas station we passed." He jogged around to the passenger side, he pulled open the gold door and placed his hands around her shoulders. "You don't know about the cocaine, right? I told Ramon, you know nothing of the cocaine," JC said. She was pinioned by the taut seat belt. JC thrust his hand into her tight bra and took possession of her breast and squeezed. "I'll be back soon. Stay here, do not leave the car." Carmen did not flinch. He slammed the passenger door.

He started walking quickly, south towards the gas station. He began to run at a steady jog through the warm, dusty night. He needed to get out of here quick even if it meant breaking a sweat. He glanced back at the dark undulating road. That product had to be protected no matter what. He stopped and turned all the way around. He did an about-face, so he could see the outline of Carmen, thirty feet up the road. He ran back a few feet and saw her in the car. With large circular movements, he indicated to her to roll the Chevelle's window up further. Lifting his right arm, he slammed his hand down, intending her to lock the door.

He waved and then turned forward again, running for five minutes at a time to traverse the two miles or so back to the station right after the intersection of the two rural routes. The road was dark and he panted with the exertion. He breathed in mustard flowers and cactus apples dusted with road grime. Whenever possible, he ran on the hard-packed dirt of the shoulder to avoid the teenagers high on weed and 151 rum, drag racing without lights.

4

DANGEROUS CURVES

JC SAW THE FORM OF A MAN IN A BASEBALL CAP AS HE JOGGED alongside the curving blacktop. Muttering to himself in exasperation, he ran southeast towards the gas station sign when he heard a voice call from the illuminated area. In the dim light, JC could just distinguish a thick man with stringy dark hair spilling from an Angels baseball cap. The melon head emerged from the sagebrush and called again, "Ay—Flaco!"

JC who stood five foot, eleven inches high and weighed in at 155 pounds was accustomed to this nickname, "Flaco." He turned and then stopped to size up the challenge. Breathless and sweating, JC pivoted to his left as the man with the over-sized head and Angels cap barreled towards him. Trying to look unsurprised, JC answered, "Si?"

The conversation continued in Spanish. Melon-head closed the distance between them and touched JC on the shoulder. In a drawling accent, he inquired, "Mira, Flaco, did Don Miguel give you the instructions?"

JC was familiar with all types of smuggling. He was well aware that this long, open border was filled with all kinds of crime. Smugglers who guided large groups of Mexican immigrants had used these same roads for years. JC had relatives, they were called "coyotes," who arranged for groups of 50 people to simply walk north through the wild hillsides that separated Mexico from San Diego County. Drivers would then pick these illegal immigrants up in trucks and cars, and drive them up to Los Angeles for jobs. "Just my luck," JC mumbled under his breath. "Alien smugglers."

The man looked up and down the road, "Where did you park anyway?" he smiled appreciatively. "Yes, they said you were experienced. Good not to park too close." He then extended his hand, "I'm Kiki."

Kiki confided, "La migra will not see our cars as they are always looking for tandem cars and convoys." Kiki grimaced, flashing his uneven, tobacco stained teeth. Kiki carried a black, foot-long, police-issued flashlight which doubled as a blackjack when needed. He could light up the night or crack skulls with this single indispensable tool. JC had seen, that like his own enterprise, alien smugglers controlled their business through violence. JC just wanted to keep himself and his cocaine safe, until he could return to his product.

"Keep your flock together," Kiki advised. "Don't let your chickens wander off, or you will be screwed." He gestured with his left hand, moving across his neck. Kiki did not smile with that comment.

Kiki handed JC a key. "This is for the truck." JC held the single key in his palm and reviewed this situation. JC knew that alien smugglers, just like drug dealers, used all kinds of cars and trucks to transport their loads of illegal aliens north. There were service trucks, ambulances, food trucks and furniture trucks to hide the fact that they were hauling people, illegal aliens. He glanced up at the furniture truck parked up on the narrow shoulder of the road, 20 feet ahead. No. This was not his plan for the evening. He was the wrong Flaco in another man's scheme. JC had gone over the plans many times with Ramon. This was not in the plan.

JC shut his eyes to make sense of this mix-up. Kiki mistook JC for the missing Flaco. Apparently, Flaco had been hired to move a load of illegal aliens, what the alien smugglers called "pollos," farther away from the border. This south-eastern part of San Diego near the border was deserted. Few people lived out here. Late at night it could become crowded with all sorts. Pollos and smugglers at times collided with cops as they all shirked their way north.

There was no benefit in telling Kiki that he was running back to a payphone to repair a flat tire. JC smelled trouble in the rotund form of Kiki and knew from his own experience that this was not the time or place to set the facts straight.

The shine of the Ruger Security Six revolver tucked in between Kiki's tumbling belly and the Los Angeles T-shirt caught JC's eye. This heavy and reliable .357 commanded the respect Kiki knew he deserved. "OK, Bueno," JC agreed as evenly as possible. "How much gas is in the rig?" asked JC.

"I filled it, topped it off myself. You have 20 gallons, more than enough to take you to the stash house," said Kiki. "I'll be following right behind, to make sure you get there safe."

JC's chest hurt as he wheezed for air. He glanced behind into the dark already missing his beloved. That Chevelle was gorgeous and irreplaceable. He had spent hours restoring her gleaming beauty. Ramon expected the cocaine. As for Carmen, she would just have to wait and keep her mouth shut and her legs crossed.

JC HEARD the crunch of a heavy man walking on the rock-strewn dirt shoulder. Kiki grabbed JC's forearm and hissed, "Flaco, there's a map and a flashlight on the seat. You'll be the only one in the passenger compartment but I will be right behind you. I'll make sure you don't lose your way. Follow the map." Kiki handed JC a business card. "Call this number when you get there or if there's trouble. When we count the pollos in LA, you'll get paid. In dollars. Cash." JC stared silently. "I'll be driving behind you. Behind you the whole way."

Kiki removed his hat and combed his bushy hair. He returned his hat firmly to his head, patted his belt. "No stopping. Follow the map, Flaco." Kiki caressed the Ruger in his waistband.

JC walked down the dark shoulder of the highway. In the dim light, he saw "San Diego Furniture" scripted along the side of the vehicle. Kiki followed closely to his rear and walked next to the trailer rapping it with his thick knuckles. "Hey, we're moving! Fasten your seatbelts!" he bellowed. As the man who loaded them into the truck, Kiki knew that no seat belts existed. The people were squeezed behind a false wall in the big box of the trailer truck. Despite this stern warning, chatter and coughs emanated from the cavernous interior.

"Shut up! Or la migra will ship you back! Shut up now! Ahorita!"

JC pulled the handle of the driver's door. It was unlocked. He recognized he was the only person in the cab of the truck. Kiki was standing outside the truck, watching him. Each illegal alien was paying $4,000 to $5,000 to the alien smuggling ring for the privilege of being packed and stacked into a furniture truck. The scores of people in the back were worth up to a $250,000 to Kiki's family business.

Just this one haul. This one one night. JC was well aware that like his own family's drug operation, this syndicate built its reputation on a reliable delivery service. Supply and demand. Southern Californians hired illegal aliens by the tens of thousands and Kiki kept the supply pipeline flowing smoothly. He ran a punctual delivery service for those who hired illegal labor.

On this empty highway JC had nowhere to go except where the man with the Ruger pointed. To refuse meant a face full of lead. JC chose to drive.

He jumped in the driver's seat and located a long metal flashlight and a map with a yellow highlighter trail delineating the route.

JC did as instructed and turned the ignition of the big rig. JC understood he had to get off the road and merge to Interstate 5 North as soon as possible. He must do this before the real Flaco showed up. JC had seconds to move out. He released the clutch and shifted into gear, flooring the gas pedal and hauling out on the highway. In the rearview mirror, he saw the lights of Kiki.

As he rounded the curve in the highway, he glimpsed a solitary silhouette emerge from the chaparral. Was that shadow the real Flaco or another pollo? JC mused. The challenging terrain forced him to focus on maneuvering the big rig as fast as possible up the road. He left his doubts behind him.

Boom, JC heard. Boom, the sound was made again. "Hey! Mira!" JC was momentarily startled. He looked around and then understood it was coming from the rear. He put his left hand on the rear wall.

"Hey! Driver!" JC heard a woman's voice call out. She continued, "Hey! I am thirsty, we are thirsty! Hey!"

JC who never worried about the needs of others, was

quick to respond. Reflexively, he answered, "Quiet! La migra! Sleep and you will wake up in LA! Just shut up!"

He punctuated the order with a slam of his fist to the back wall. JC rolled his eyes.

"Diablo!" He cursed. He shifted into higher gear and the truck lurched forward. He watched the speedometer arrow drift past 70 miles per hour. His nerves were on edge. This was his first time driving a truck this big. With a tight back, he deftly negotiated the twists of a road carved in the early part of the century, on this secondary remote roadway.

Each second ripped a mile further away from his precious load and Carmen. What was she doing now? Patiently waiting for his return to repair the flat tire? Was she hitching into town? Did he trust her?

He decided to picture her in a bra and tight satin panties, revealing the full curve of her butt sleeping on the newly upholstered seats of his lovingly restored 1966 Chevelle. Maybe she fell asleep and her sweating skin stuck to the gold upholstery. She was a patient girl. Carmen had to just wait, JC thought as he drove on, she just had to stay put and he would be back to get her.

5

CALL THE SAMARITAN JO

CARMEN LOOKED UP FROM THE BACK SEAT OF THE CHEVELLE, her nose pressed against the rear window. She blinked. She was disoriented to time and place. With resolve, she nodded her consciousness out of the fog of sleep. She did not have a watch but it seemed she had waited for a long time.

JC was always so selfish and easily distracted by other girls or errands or opportunities to make money. He knew how to hustle when it paid. Still he told her all the time how beautiful she was, that he loved her body and he loved taking her to the beach. Sometimes she believed him and believed in his love for her. Still this had been a long time even for JC.

She admitted to herself that he was at the least, competent but most of all she thought his family was more than competent and would certainly expect that this loaded car would be delivered.

She sat up and looked back down the road and saw nothing. Morning was coming and no JC. She was afraid. She had been afraid the night before. She was afraid of this North. She did not like drugs. Her mother did not like JC's family or their big house next to the mayor of Tecate. When she slept over at JC's, she was astonished to see they had a bidet. She had never seen one nor been to France or Spain for that matter. Monthly trips to San Diego was as cosmopolitan as she got. She soon learned, it was not for your hands.

JC had told Carmen he cared for her, that he wanted her. There was eagerness and urgency in his kisses but Carmen was afraid he did not love her. She was afraid she was a contrivance for the trip. Dozing in the Chevelle, Carmen realized that JC had not planned for a flat tire. He discharged his every desire. Accustomed to the power of charm, he told her "you cannot plan for passion." She knew better. For her overnights with him, she did anticipate and placed prophylactics in her purse.

No doubt, he ran south. She shook her head, accepting the inevitable answer. The border was far closer than the point of delivery. She had worn red stilettos for dancing and then what would come later. She could run nowhere. She did not want her mother to be right, that men had every advantage.

Tonight, alone in the car, she feared not just her solitude and the desolation of Tecate. She feared being the only person left holding the bag for what she knew was a big load of drugs. It was not her profit. It was not her responsibility. She feared the load in the trunk of the Chevelle.

Carmen was also concerned about the phone call JC had made before the flat tire. They knew. His uncle knew that they had crossed la linea. The drugs had to be delivered on schedule or there would be consequences. She had seen the dead bodies behind her family's shop. This was no threat. This was life or a barbaric end. For now, she was simply afraid to be alone on a deserted highway just outside of

Tecate, California with probably a fortune's worth of cocaine.

Earlier in the evening she did not fear she would get into trouble, as she was just coming along for the ride with JC. He promised her she was just the passenger and he would take all the risk. He told her that she was just riding along as window dressing.

Carmen sat up and looked out. In the dim light, she saw the bare outline of a two-lane twisting highway. She saw nothing. She heard very little except for an occasional bird of prey.

In her little girl mind she pictured the scuttle of scorpions and snakes through the rocky hills on both sides of the highway. Born in San Diego, she spent most of her life in comfortable interiors of the hard scrabble city of Tijuana. It was a big small town. She knew very little about this place over the border. In her big girl mind she pictured the tin-roofed hideouts of meth cookers burrowed in the hills.

She felt the heat of the macadam penetrate the car. It permeated the vinyl seat and then her skin. She stayed in the car as he had told her. Like always she obeyed. She rebelled in her heart.

Where was he? He knew they were both looking forward to delivering the car. She was along for what would follow afterward. Late at night on the beach in Coronado, afterwards in a stunning seaside hotel and then room service wrapped in his lean, strong body, and hungry kisses. She focused on igniting her passion to burn away her fear. JC had said, "We'll cross at Tecate. Drive the Chevelle to the pier. Grab some food, some wine and hang out in Coronado."

But now after the excitement of crossing, she was sitting alone on a dark desert road, waiting. It was so hard to know how much time had passed without a watch. She pulled out the keys.

On the key ring were three keys: the key to the Chevelle, the key to his parents' house in Tijuana where he lived and a key to the garage in San Diego where they were going.

She had no idea what was on that key chain until he had left. He had jogged back only to toss the keys to her. He had shown her the Chevelle's gleaming ignition key. In the dark, Carmen fiddled with the keys. She caressed their jagged ends and she soon distinguished the ignition key. She rose up, pushed the driver's seat forward and opened up the front door of the two-door coupe and stepped on the road.

As she stood, she saw a tractor-trailer rig as it barreled down the road. It was followed close behind by a passenger car. She paused and watched them go by and then slid into the front seat.

She saw the analog clock showed 2:00 a.m.

Where was he? Why hadn't he come back? I am not going to worry. I am fine! Carmen tried to convince herself. Fortunately, Carmen's most impressive talent was sleeping.

"I am not going to drive myself nuts wondering where he is," mumbled Carmen as she curled up on the front bench seat. She leaned up to lock the car doors.

She placed her red leather purse under her head as she shifted her legs under the large black steering wheel. She closed her eyes, and in a few minutes, she dozed off.

VISUALIZING A FUTURE FAR AHEAD, Carmen dreamed the vivid technicolor of her youth. She saw herself riding a train through a winding chaparral covered land.

She admired the cattle grazing and the pink hues of the

colored sky. She smelled the tangy chaparral, evocative of the rough and new country of Northern Mexico. The smell of campfires, running horses, carne asada, and the promise of surprise. Like a morning dew, cordiality glistened across the landscape. She found herself talking to an American, a blonde woman in her twenties.

In the dream, Carmen didn't notice the other woman's facial features, but she did see one quality: that the American's eyes were blue. Blue like the sky. Blue like the crayons she drew with in her coloring book, along with a yellow sun, there was always that light blue, happy sky. A happy day. The crayon box called it cornflower blue. She had never seen a cornflower in that shade. She remembered, it was blue like the American actor Paul Newman's eyes. That blue, that inviting, that well and foreign.

She looked into the American's eyes and she saw a steadiness that she never saw in her boyfriend's. She looked away, and then stared back, and shivered as an unknown electric tingle coursed through her, and Carmen smiled.

Hello?" Carmen opened her left eye. She exhaled, and licked her lips. "Hmm?" Carmen said out loud. For a moment, she wanted to stay in that other place, staring into those blue eyes. She kept her eyes closed, clinging to a safe place. She remained foggy, unfocused, and bleary, preferring a dream world to the abandonment in the Chevelle. Carmen heard a tap on the car window. The tapping and the greeting continued, and though unwilling and disoriented, Carmen opened her eyes. She looked around and squinted. Where was she? Was the dream over? Reluctantly, she opened both her eyes and recognized the vinyl seat and the black dashboard of JC's Chevelle. The dim light promised a desert dawn as she could see the California classic highway at sunrise. Carmen turned her fluttering eyes towards the tapping and the voice. On the dirt shoulder, directly outside the locked front driver's window, she saw a young, nattily dressed woman, leaning down and tapping on the window.

Startled at first Carmen jolted back at the sight. And then Carmen glimpsed the familiar eyes. The eyes of her dream. Carmen was not afraid.

––––––––

"HELLO? ARE YOU OK?" The strange woman slowly said, in English, with the even tones.

Carmen pulled herself upright and squinted at the rising sun. She then focused on the form leaning towards her through the window, the tanned face of an attractive woman, short brown hair, and remarkable azure eyes, the color of the cornflower blue crayons. Though steel-willed Carmen was easily startled, as she had been in a deep sleep. "What, who," Carmen began in Spanish, but quickly switched to English. Carmen had been content to wait for JC to return. JC had to come back. She knew the cocaine was above the price of rubies and that he loved that Chevelle.

"What?" Carmen asked apprehensively, tossing back her long hair.

The strange woman outside the car smiled softly: "Hey, I just wanted to make sure you are OK?" The tall woman gazed, paused and stepped back a few inches from the window of the car.

"This is a remote stretch of road and I saw your flat tire." The voice was a pleasant alto, with precise diction.

Carmen thought she sounded like a DJ, but she looked like some sort of serious athlete, tall, thin, and obviously muscular, for a girl.

Carmen sat up and rolled down the front window so she could hear every word, and get a better look at those eyes. What Carmen saw was both intriguing and scary. Her breath quickened as she stared at this intense young American. The blue-eyed woman was about 28 to 30, 5'9"or more and stood looking at Carmen. The woman was dressed in a light-blue man tailored collared blouse. She had tight fitting double-knit blue pin-striped trousers down her long legs and soft brown loafers. This stranger had no discernible makeup. She wore as her only jewelry plain gold-stud earrings with two earrings in her right ear.

Carmen cleared her throat and asked, tentatively:

"Do you know where I can get this flat tire repaired?"

"I don't think there is a gas station or anything for miles. I came from San Diego." The tall woman said and extended a hand. "So, I am Jo, and I am not from this area at all. I am just driving out for my job. I am happy to give you a lift or to help you with the tire."

Carmen was aware there was no spare tire in the trunk, but a spare load of something more costly. Carmen paused to consider if she should get rid of this unwanted approach. "Oh Jo, that's nice of you," Carmen replied, evaluating this stranger.

"It must be creepy to sit here waiting for someone. Were you here overnight?" Jo stared up both ends of the road. "There's no phones, no houses, just dry rocky hills and no call boxes."

Carmen pulled open the lock, slipped her manicured red toes into her high heels and opened the car door. This short-haired woman did not seem dangerous. She appeared to be authentically concerned for her safety. She smiled, "Thank you Jo, that would be great. My name is Carmen. It's nice to meet you." Carmen extended her right hand adorned with the same vibrant red nail polish as her toes. They looked into each other's eyes and lightly shook hands. Jo was surprised by the soft strength in Carmen's handshake.

Jo knew better than to offer a ride to this gorgeous stranger. Her gut told her there was something off about this young woman's story of a flat tire. Jo shrugged her shoulders, as she turned back towards her own car. No matter what unpopulated stretch of earth she travelled to, she had a crazy knack for meeting sensuous young women. She was a chick magnet of sorts. She could not decide if this new find was good or bad in the scheme of things. Jo was well aware that this road from San Diego to Tecate was a smuggling corridor. Jo simply could not believe that this particular young woman was the heavy in a criminal enterprise. Her own life experience had taught her, men commit almost all the crimes, solved or unsolved.

"I better grab my purse," Carmen said "and lock up the car since we are going to leave everything here."

"Do you want me to just fix the flat?" Jo asked.

"Thank you but no. We used the spare last month. We got a nail driving by some construction and we just never got around to replacing it."

Jo shook her head sympathetically and said to her new acquaintance - "Yeah, Murphy's Law". She strode ahead along the shoulder of the road where her convertible was parked. With her back turned, Jo rolled her eyes. Too convenient, to have no spare tire. While no boy scout, Jo's ex-girlfriends could confirm she was always prepared.

Jo opened the passenger door two steps ahead of Carmen. Carmen could not sit down, as there was a shoulder bag with a manila file spilling out on the car seat.

Jo said, "Oh, my brief case. Just throw that in the back."

On top of the briefcase, Carmen glimpsed a picture I.D., a photograph of Jo.

"Are you thirsty?" Jo asked. "Because I know how hot it can get out here." She dug into the back seat, retrieved a warm bottle of Coca-Cola, bottled in Mexico. Carmen swallowed her inside thought which was, "Yes, I too have some sun-warmed coke, but not the kind you drink. Ha, surely the pause that refreshes."

Out loud Carmen merely said, "Yes, that sounds good." Jo handed her the glass bottle, tinted green, and their fingers touched briefly during the exchange. Jo sensed the faint fragrance across the car seat of Carmen's dissipated perfume. What else did she recognize - aftershave? Was it that missing boyfriend who owned the 1960s-muscle car? Is that the boyfriend's Chevelle? Jo let the thought drift out to the dry highway where the sagebrush met the sky. Another fanciful question not asked and therefore not answered.

Carmen looked at Jo's fingers. They were long, tan and sinewy like the rest of Jo. With short, unadorned nails, Jo looked practical and all business. Her car looked like fun. JC would understand. He left her stranded in a desert in July. After all, she had waited the entire night until sunrise and he had not returned.

She hoped he was safe, wherever he was. But by this point she had no choice. Carmen could not sit in the desert without food or water for long. She could take this ride with this safe looking businesswoman. Jo seemed like a good bet for a fun ride, and to help her get to a mechanic.

She had to get that car off the road and then get that flat tire repaired. Carmen figured she could make sense of it all after some coffee and breakfast in Tecate, U.S.A. She would sort it all out and call her mother. She needed to get somewhere and talk to some family. She needed good advice. In all events she had to protect JC, the family - her own as well as his. Her family would not be pleased that JC left their beloved Carmen alone on a desolate highway with a carload of narcotics.

Jo had wondered if she should stop in the first place. It was summer in the middle of nowhere. She had read stories of both illegal aliens and unfortunate motorists dying in this desert. Sure, it was also a favorite stretch of road for all types of smugglers. Still, Jo refused to pass by if someone needed her help. Ten years of parochial school had not been entirely wasted on her. This morning, she remembered her catechism and the parable of the Good Samaritan.

Jo remembered those lessons well and stopped. She tapped on the Chevelle window. And then, she laid her eyes on Carmen. After taking on look at her splendid chassis, Jo was eager to take Carmen for a test drive.

"So," Jo interrupted Carmen's daydream as they drove back towards Tecate and the border crossing. Jo saw a gas station up ahead. "Do you want to stop here and see if they have a tire for the Chevelle or go to town to grab some breakfast first?"

Carmen felt her rumbling tummy. She was distracted by her rough night. She decided it might be a good idea to grab some breakfast as Jo had put it and collect her thoughts.

Carmen ached to just wash her face and brush her hair. It was a problem. There was no JC. She had no contacts in the U.S. Instead, she was faced with a broken down car and a trunk full of drugs. She was left alone with JC's sins. Her mother had warned her about him. The ride to town was the best alternative. Raised on faith, Carmen prayed Jo would drive her to a better place.

6

FRIED TORTILLAS

THE DIRT PARKING LOT WAS FILLED WITH TRUCKS OF EVERY make and model, with the occasional Border Patrol emblazoned in a deep green across the side. Near the entrance a gun metal grey bike rack was bolted to the ground with a number of rusted bicycles secured with heavy chains and thick padlocks.

For breakfast in Tecate Papas Y Tacos was the place to go for huevos ranchueros and chilaquiles. Jo pulled her convertible into the dirt parking lot, between two large government trucks, speckling the car's impeccable white-wall tires with dirt. Flashing in the window, patrons were welcomed by two pink neon signs announcing "open" and "abierto."

Jo led the way into the restaurant. A chubby woman with greying feathered brown hair and make-up applied with a trowel, greeted the two women at the hostess stand. "Buenos Dias, Ladies," she said and led them to a booth. Without comment, the waitress plopped two large plastic menus on the table with an audible thud.

"They have the best food and salsa," Jo said. "Have you had them?" asked Jo. Carmen shook her head no.

Carmen looked at the page breakfast listing but her thoughts were far from salsa and tortillas. Instead she was focused on the trunk of the Chevelle. JC had more than hinted there was a lot of cocaine. But she had experienced time and again that he was a liar. Better question still, where was JC? Why hadn't he come back last night, Carmen wondered silently. Carmen looked at her breakfast mate, who was staring at the entrance to the diner. Around her Carmen heard most of the patrons chatting rapidly in the accents of Baja California. Jo heard "blah, blah, blah, "dinero" blah blah" "cerveza," blah, blah "mota." Respectively money, beer, marijuana. Really, thought Jo, is that all I have to show for completing my language requirement at Stanford?

Carmen returned to her more pressing challenge. She was stuck in a diner with no JC. This was so avoidable, but he never planned for anything, and never learned from his mistakes. Charm and money smoothed the bumps in the road for him until now. This hot July morning Carmen had a carload of problems to unload.

Jo turned to face Carmen. She looked at Carmen's long fingers with a deep red nail-polish. She admired a bracelet depicting assorted saints and Carmen's deep brown, thoughtful eyes. Jo knew she liked what she felt and saw about this stranded girl. Quite a literal pick-up. In this weird border town, somehow, the scrumptious Carmen squeezed through.

Not yet thirty, Jo was plotting out life after seven years of higher education. She lived her life in grand themes to make the world more secure. In the icy winters of Chicago, Jo had daydreamed in high school, of heat, sand and sun.

This town of Tecate could not be more different than Chicago.

Carmen was thankful for the silence. She was a woman of few words in either Spanish or English. When she did speak, it was with deliberation, with a known objective. From an early age, she had seen the consequences of wasted words and actions. She used her skills to sidestep misfortune. She was a quick learner. She also considered herself unusually lucky. Her mother always said, luck always visits those with skill and persistence. Carmen was patient, hardworking and now grateful, to be so distracting to this new American convenience, Jo. She needed time to think. She hoped for a visit from luck.

Jo was content to sit and wait. Not many rushed in this town. There were few jobs to be had as there were essentially two career choices. Choice one was to smuggle and choice two was to arrest the smugglers. In the blaze of summer, she noticed the diners kept their sunglasses on even inside. The silence was filled by the sound of ice cubes clinking against the tall water pitchers. Education and reading was not a priority here. If the sentence was longer than a billboard the words weren't spoken. Jo kept her sentences short when she spoke in this town.

Carmen clearly came from somewhere else. Jo glanced at Carmen, thirsty for another look of what looked to be a lithe and lively young woman who was innocently up to no good. She wanted to learn more about Carmen. Jo knew she had to move slowly, or she would get burned.

The pudgy waitress rolled to their table. "Hi, Ladies!" the smiling talkative waitress offered. "How about some java gals?"

Jo slid her thick off-white mug forward and received a steaming hot stream deftly guided to the brim. Carmen let the waitress ask again, to which Carmen nodded "yes" and the waitress grabbed her cup.

"How about breakfast- how about some - chilaquiles, eggs?" Jo ordered:"Chilaquiles please." This brought the first smile Jo had seen emanate from Carmen. More of a wry smile in reaction to Jo's imperfect pronunciation, her gringo accent. "Y señorita?" "The same," Carmen answered in clear English.

"Sounds like you don't do Spanish," laughed Carmen, once the waitress had bounced away to fill their orders. "Well, actually, I took five semesters of Spanish at Stanford, but my accent could use some work and practice. It's hard to get rid of my Chicago accent." Jo stared directly into Carmen's eyes, though it made her very uneasy, feeling that tingle again. Jo shifted in the booth, pulling her perspiring thigh from the sticky plastic. This is verification, mused Jo, she was intrigued.

Jo, practical as ever, did not share her thoughts but spoke of the matter at hand, "What do you want to do about that car. I am planning on staying here in Tecate for a couple of hours and then I am driving back to San Diego probably around three or four."

"Oh," replied Carmen almost flirtatiously, tilting her head and lowering her voice, "Is that an offer to drive me up to San Diego?" "Oh yes," said Jo, attempting to match the same tone.

"I have nothing to do in Tecate, here. Can I hang with you until you drive up to San Diego?" asked Carmen, adding sugar to her black coffee.

"Well, Carmen," said Jo, pausing between the syllables of the new name, new acquaintance, new woman was she hoping into her life? "It's fine with me. It might be a bit boring. Let me see what my investigator says..."

As Jo was speaking, a muscled man in his mid-thirties swaggered up to the booth. Carmen noted each impressive detail of this man as he closed the distance from the diner's entrance to their breakfast table. He wore a pristine white tight fitting thin shirt, an authentic guayabera, with three open buttons. The shirt exposed a thick gold chain with an inch and half Conquistador Style cross resting against a soft lawn of thick dark chest hair. Before she inspected more, Carmen inhaled the strong tones of his cologne and self-confidence.

The man carried a thin black notebook in his left hand, while his right thumb was webbed inside a thick brown leather belt with the word "Chevy" etched in block letters on the face of the buckle. His short sleeves exposed his etched biceps and obviously muscled midsection. Carmen mentally undressed him as he approached their table in cowboy boots.

Jo, noting the other woman's gaze deployed rank, her sole unfair advantage, "Well, Carmen, let's see what my investigator says." "Hey, Jacobo, over here," Jo called to the tall man in jeans.

Jacobo Sanchez, from his 6'2" height, gazed down on the two young attractive women. This was not going to be a bad breakfast, independent of the food, mused Jacobo. He flashed his winning grin, nodded to Jo and held his hand out to Carmen, "Nice to meet you. I'm Jacobo Sanchez. Are you also with the U.S. Attorney's Office?"

Swallowing her surprise, along with diner coffee, Carmen replied with a simple straightforward "No." Carmen looked at Jo and Jacobo. They seemed decent enough. But she read in the papers the punishments they pursued against her countrymen. Ten, twenty years, life in prison. Not for murder but simply for crossing drugs.

They were trying to flirt with her. She flirted back to distract them from her own situation. Laughing and teasing she turned to other subjects. Explanations about the Chevelle's breakdown were pushed forward to another time.

Jacobo paused to appreciate Jo's appetite and aptitude for acquiring attractive and unlikely lovers. He thought perhaps post-trial Jo might share a few savory details, but now was not the time. Jacobo turned to Jo, "So Jo, how about an introduction."

Jo laughed quietly and shrugged," Well, Jacobo, we can both get that information at the same time." Jo extended her hand and said with a warm smile, "Carmen, it is nice to meet you, I'm Josephine Gemma, and you are?"

Carmen knew she could not give her real name in this company. Great. The Feds, of all people, the Feds had to save her after JC's flat tire. Well, she was not going to federal prison for 40 years for JC and his family's greed, corruption and stupidity. This was exactly why her mother had forbidden her from hanging out with him. "Carmen Cortez," was the even response as a millennium of savvy forbears had produced a steely core in this luscious progeny.

Jacobo, quick to the draw, quipped "It's very nice to meet you Señorita Cortez, any relation to the Conquistadora?"

"Sure," Carmen parried adept at verbal dueling in two languages "we both like all the same things."

"And that would be?" inquired Jo.

"Why gold, art and adventure," countered Carmen careful to use euphemisms for greed, lust and gore.

Her English was no match for the passion and description of her Spanish, and in these circumstances, this was fortunate for Carmen.

Jacobo and Jo laughed at what they took to be a quick

retort all in fun. In years to come, there would be time to reflect on the uncanny revelation in a simple sentence.

The hefty waitress set down plates of plentiful chilaquiles smothered in sour cream and salsa fresca, before the two women. Jacobo asked for the same dish from the waitress. In Spanish, he asked the waitress to add hot salsa, and spooning out a double entendre, he commented- "I like everything in my life to be spicy, fresh and hot." Carmen arched an eyebrow.

Jacobo took a swig of the coffee, hot and black and the two young women tore into their pile of corn tortillas fried with eggs, onions, and green chiles. Intrigued by this new conquistadora, Jo kept the conversation rolling, "Carmen do you have any place you have to go this morning? We have a vehicle viewing this morning at the impound lot here in town and then you can head back and get your car fixed." "That's fine with me," agreed Carmen.

"How long had you been there on the side of the road before I came along?" Jo inquired.

"I don't know," answered Carmen, "I figured I'd get help when the sun came up. And you know that is exactly what happened, my prayers were answered, thank you Jo," and as an afterthought "and Ja-COBO?" she added, emphasizing the first syllable of his name. Carmen continued, "You work at the U.S. Attorney's office? That must be really interesting."

Jo's answer was an exaggerated roll of her eyes. Her humorous reaction overplayed the opposite feeling. She chose this job the way she chose a lover, or a sport- it called her. Justice, for Jo, was a serious subject. At twenty-nine years old the United States Department of Justice was a serious job. She felt pride every time she stood up in the paneled, somber expanse of the federal courtroom in downtown San Diego and declared "Josephine Gemma for the United States." She believed she represented both the might and right of the legal system. Her defendants in the cases she prosecuted were getting paid $1,000 to $5,000 to cross drugs at the ports of entry that separated Mexico from San Diego County. Defense lawyers, prosecutors and cops called these criminals "mules." These mules were not more than pack animals because they received a tiny portion of the enormous profits earned by the drug trade.

From her studies in college and experience, Jo had learned that Northern Mexico was in fact a stew of cultures: Spaniards, Mayans, Americans, Germans, Chinese who produced a culture at times explosive, thrilling and tragic. Each condiment of culture added its unique piquancy to the Mexican mestizo over five centuries. Jo had been raised on her own family's immigrant saga of traveling to America for a better life. She empathized with the allure of America.

For Mexico thousands of miles of arid open, neglected border meant revenue—exporting people, raw goods, followed by a U-turn back south with the prized American exports. Dollars came to Mexico - from narcotics sales, from wages, cars stolen from suburban driveways. Prized American exports entered Mexico as well in the form of guns, cigarettes, and whiskey.

All of this, swirled in her conscious mind, but Jo's only words were "Yes, interesting."

Three years earlier, when she finished her federal clerkship, Jo had told the meat-faced United States Attorney for San Diego that it would be "fascinating" to work as a federal prosecutor.

At the time Jo believed it to be the ultimate feather in her cap. She swam competitively at Stanford, did well at University of Chicago Law School, and it was then her love of swimming and surfing that pulled her to the beaches of San Diego. She figured crime was crime. Boy was she wrong.

"Make a difference," that is what Jo mumbled to her bathroom mirror. After all her academic honors and access to the fast-track, she wanted to believe that somehow a few more bad guys were off the streets, and the innocents-the average decent person had a safer and better life because of her toil, dedication, long drives into desiccated towns, and long nights of culling through documents, phone logs, and interview notes.

Later, and forgoing the big dollars of a swanky New York, L.A. Or Chicago law firm, Jo looked down into her chilaquiles and felt doubt about this choice of dust versus dollars. Swallowing a mouthful of chorizo and egg, she nodded, and smiled.

After some small talk and a spicy breakfast, Jo said, "Carmen, ready to roll? Jacobo and I want to get this car viewing knocked out before the afternoon sun gets too scorching." Carmen stood up and collected her purse, saying nothing.

Jacobo glanced at the tab for breakfast, put it in his pocket, slapped a five dollar bill on the marbled wood patterned vinyl diner table and resolved the bill with the cashier while Jo savored the last drops of coffee. Carmen followed Jacobo to the cashier. Jo stood, stretched, and met up with her breakfast mates.

Jacobo held the metal door open as the two women transitioned from the cool of the air-conditioned diner to the glaring sun of summer in Tecate.

7

SHOW YOUR ID

"Want to ride in my El Camino," Jacobo said "It's got room enough for three in the front seat for you ladies." He pronounced these words flatly, trying to hide all of his lascivious fantasies. Jo rolled her eyes and Carmen twisted her lips in a wry smile. And yet they slid right into the front bench seat, seat-belted and sticky in the dry, building heat. The dust particles in the diner's dirt parking lot glistened, and beads of sweat collected on Jacobo's sideburns, pausing for the ready signal to roll down to his chiseled jaw.

Jacobo turned the engine on the powerful V-8, surely one of life's essential and reliable pleasures, the macho certainty of American muscle cars. He drove through downtown Tecate passing a cluster of one and two-story buildings from the 1940's.

Jacobo Sanchez then made a right turn down a dirty, dusty road. The road meandered through a flat stretch of chaparral, barely wide enough for the truck and for one way traffic.

The three soon came upon a two-acre flat expanse

contained by a low barbwire fence on four sides with the far border being a railroad track.

They were soon met by a grizzled man in dirty jeans and an undershirt flecked with the memory of cigarette ash. In a baritone voice reminiscent of Marlene Dietrich, he called out to Jacobo and his recognizable El Camino: "Hey Jacobo!" After parking the truck, Jacobo greeted the impound lot guard, "Hola, Diego. Can we take a look at the tractor trailer rig?"

Diego stared with no emotion for a moment. "The big one, that was the 2000 kilos of cocaine in March?" Diego whistled and swiped his left hand through his surviving silver strands of hair.

Still in Spanish, Agent Sanchez whispered "and keep your eyes off my two fine girls."

Diego cackled and ambled into a squat tan stucco building, almost a hut with a swamp cooler. Just large enough to accommodate a desk and a corroding commode. He soon retrieved a numbered key from a phalanx of brass hooks on the "office" wall.

He grabbed a legal sized clipboard with a sign in sheet. "Tu firma, por favor." In accented English, Diego rasped, "Agent Sanchez we need your identification, your ID, and those of these two girls if they are going to see the rig. We need them to sign here too, and the ID." Jacobo motioned to the two women.

Carmen watched as Jo quickly reached into the back pocket of her slacks and whipped out a gold embossed billfold. Jo opened the billfold exposing a photo of a serious, suited Josephine I. Gemma, Assistant United States Attorney. It was part mugshot and part glam shot.

Carmen walked right up to Diego and in softly Spanish

explained: "I had a fight with my boyfriend, we got a flat tire, and then I just forgot my Id."

Diego shrugged. Diego looked at Agent Sanchez and in Spanish said, "You take charge of her then. You make sure she behaves."

Diego handed Agent Sanchez the keys. He ambled into the stucco office and gazed at the mesmerizing rear view of Carmen.

Jacobo and the two women passed rows of cars of every size, make, color and year. Jacobo stared at the bounty of seizure vehicles that filled a two-acre lot.

Finders keepers was the law of the land and Jacobo knew this gave federal agents the added incentive to arrest so the U.S.A. could keep for itself the illegally gotten gains of the narcos. Regulations made cataloguing, and securing the storage of such seizures an integral part of his duties, He thought confiscating personal property by force could be called robbery.

The impound lot resembled a junk yard in the wide variety of vehicles represented. Arranged across the wide lot were pick-up trucks, speedboats, motorcycles, motor-homes and jet-skis. Anything with a motor, and even the engine itself was a potential hiding place for drugs.

After walking to the edge of the lot, Jacobo stooped before a tractor trailer rig. He called out to the prosecutor: "Hey Jo, let's see what's in the cab." Jacobo walked out front and opened up the driver's door effortlessly.

Jacobo hauled himself with his brawny arms and then calmly looked inside the cab. Jo called up to the searching agent-"Find a log?"

Jo shouted up to the cab. "Hey, of course you are going to follow protocol, but before you remove anything, take a photo."

Jacobo paused, and snapped a dozen photographs before gathering the assorted objects and stacking them on the driver's seat.

Jacobo then jumped out of the cab onto the grey gravel. He walked to the rear of the long trailer. He opened the trailer door to the refrigerated truck. On the floor of the trailer were a few rotting cabbage leaves, remnants of the decoy harvest. Towards the rear of the trailer, were dismantled plywood boards.

Jo stepped up and into the trailer. She kneeled down and touched the board that was affixed to the entire rear length of the trailer. "This was the false wall then, Jacobo? What do you think?"

"The cocaine was loaded in that false space between the real end of the trailer and this plywood fake wall, according to our reports. 2000 kilograms of cocaine, hidden behind cabbage. Cool," Jacobo deadpanned, expressionless behind his aviator sun glasses.

"Sort of a Trojan Horse?" retorted Jo. "We are going to go through the evidence for trial. Hey Carmen, we can take you back to the restaurant while we work here. Just say the word," Jo added.

Carmen, who had been standing many feet away, walked up to the trailer's edge. "Jo, that's fine. I can stay here. There were drugs in this commercial load of cabbage? Why would anybody put that much cocaine in a cold cabbage truck?"

Jacobo beat Jo to the answer "Just like Jo said, it was hidden in a very innocent seeming place. This company crosses the border every day from Tecate. They come in the same time, in the same truck."

Carmen looked at Jacobo and tried to look confused. Confusion was seldom an emotion she experienced. Working in her family's elegant café since her quinceañara, she had dated exciting men who dressed well, flashed cash and knew how to entice a sassy beauty. Those eight years had taught her much about flirtation as well teaching her the finer points of the cross-border drug trade. Working the cash register and waiting tables she acquired the ability to calculate the total bill and tip in her head. She had a talent for numbers and fast mental calculations. Her mother worried that this mental acumen for math did not transfer to judging appropriate boyfriends. When dating café patrons, her mother cautioned Carmen to never over-estimate character. Remembering her mother's stern warning gave her a shudder even in the heat of the impound lot: "A mistake in love, is made in blood, and is not easily erased."

Jacobo continued, "The driver is the defendant, a real truck driver." Carmen continued to stare vacantly. "His defense is that he was tricked, and did not know. All we have to prove is that he knew because there is no question that the white stuff we found is cocaine, and that he was driving," Jacobo said.

"I can't believe that this is a trial," Carmen said.

"Believe it and even better come watch the trial next week," Jo said. Jo wanted to get to know Carmen better. This was her foot in the door to ask Carmen out.

"Why did they use this truck and trailer?" asked Carmen

"Why? They want to make sure their product gets to market. Think about the time and expense to make cocaine. To grow it in Columbia. To transport it to northern Mexico. They get their profit only when that cocaine sells in America," Jo said.

"For drugs, anything is possible," said Jacobo. "Some have called America 'insatiable' when it comes to hunger for drugs, but I don't know if that word even begins to explain the extent that these cartels will go to smuggle drugs across the border," Jacobo said.

"Can you give me an example?" Carmen asked. She understood that timing was everything. She knew to play her advantages. This was a once in a life time opportunity.

"Yeah, they hide drugs everywhere," Jacobo said.

"What do you mean by that?" Carmen asked.

"I have found drugs hidden in car wheels, in tires, in trunks, engines, side panels, bumpers, dashboards, seats. Then there is the canned food category, mole´, chiles and frijoles. I have found drugs in baby diapers, luggage, and of course strapped to a body, inside underwear and shoved inside where the sun does not shine."

"The smugglers put a lot of thought into this, so they don't have to work. That's the easy answer," said Jo.

Carmen looked at Jo and said, "Have you arrested anybody?"

"Oh yeah, when he first came in," Jo said.

"He is in jail?" Carmen continued.

"The driver is, yeah," Jo confirmed.

"Always seems it comes down to money, doesn't it?" Jacobo said. He continued, "My parents' Mexico needed a release valve for a population explosion. This happened in my own grandparents' life. Mexico was a quiet rural country at the start of the twentieth century with 13 million people. Today, the late 80's, Mexico has about 84 million people, and growing. Now, that's motivation, feeding a growing family. And to escape corruption. Why not walk north for a shot at the American Dream? Ain't we living it?"

"We can't catch them all, we just wave everybody through our border. We have every single day on that border just in our district in California about 38,000 cars coming north, and 19,000 people walking in," Jo said.

"Now that's what I call a golden opportunity," Jacobo joked. "And especially for those aching to hire some cheap labor."

"More like an incessant game of hide and go seek," Jo said.

"Yeah, Jo, just an endless, mind-numbing game of hide and go seek," Jacobo replied.

"Anybody looked at rig before us?" Jacobo asked Diego slowly in Spanish.

Diego answered in English "Agent, you can look at the clipboard, everybody who comes in the lot, signs the sheet."

"Looks like Heidi Vandeweghe has been here," Jacobo said.

"Ayer," Diego agreed nodding with his head.

"That is interesting news. Usually defense lawyers call to help with the red tape to see the seizures. I guess they didn't need any help from us for this one," Jo said.

"Why does that matter?" Carmen asked. "The jury wants us, the prosecution to re-enact everything for them to check everything for them, just like on television, only this isn't television. We have 1000s cases and just a few weeks to put together a case," Jo said.

"A jigsaw puzzle, with no picture, and lots of missing pieces. Sure, we can put those puzzle pieces back. But look around here, they are sure hard to find," Jacobo said with a smile. "We can only investigate here in the United States but the defense sends their investigators all over Mexico.

"Well, my work is done," Jacobo said. "No deals here?"

"No way," Jo said.

Jacobo tapped the steering wheel and gazed out into the impound lot, watching the seized cars sizzle in the July sun.

"Looks like the cartel hired Heidi Vandeweghe to make sure our bad boy keeps his mouth shut," Jo said.

"My game is baseball. But this game, has rules too.

I never go on that other side though I have a lot of family. Not after Kiki Camerana," Jacobo said.

"How long are we going to fight this war, is what I want to know," Jo said.

"I can retire at 50, but I might go another twenty years. That gives me until 2008 to win this War on Drugs and then I will retire with pride," Jacobo said.

8

A CRAFTSMAN HOME

"I'M GETTING SUNBURNED," JO SAID. "I THINK IT'S TIME TO pack up this trailer and head back to the ocean breezes of San Diego. Carmen, can I give you a ride back to your Chevelle?" Jo volunteered.

"Thanks Jo," Carmen said.

"Jacobo, will finish the inventory and photos of the evidence. I am going to need those reports as soon as possible. Heidi is going to wig out when she finds out we took photos, we are going to have to get copies for her," said Jo.

"Well, it may be awhile until I get that report approved by my supervisor, but as soon as that happens, I will drive you out a copy. The photographs will be ready tomorrow," answered Jacobo.

"I will call you tomorrow with a witness list and we will fax the subpoenas for the trial," Jo said as the three of them walked back to Jacobo's car for the drive back to the diner.

"You know Jo, my car still has a flat tire," Carmen told the young federal prosecutor.

"Pretty and demanding," mumbled Jo under her breath.

"What, you say something?" said Jacobo, not taking his

eyes off of the road. "You know Carmen, you might be a bit optimistic. Do you know this area, and the people who live around here? You'll be lucky if any of your tires are still on that car," Jacobo said. The only miscreants they passed was a herd of ambling cattle, confined behind a wire fence.

"Nice to meet you Carmen, hope we meet up again soon," Jacobo said as he parked the El Camino. The two women slid out to the dust of the hot parking lot. "

Thank you, Agent Sanchez," was all Carmen said in reply. "He was joking about the tires," Jo said.

Jo opened up the door to her convertible and walked around the hood and waved goodbye to Agent Sanchez. "I'll call you," Jo mouthed, pantomiming the receiver with her extended thumb and pinky. She revved the engine, and put the AC on high. "Carmen, we'll be back to your car in 10 minutes. She reached over with her left hand and patted Carmen right above the knee, before releasing the clutch.

She pulled her sunglasses down from the bridge of her nose to reveal blue eyes and said softly "It will be OK." Carmen sat bolt upright in the front passenger seat, showing no emotion but feeling an uncomfortable and unfamiliar tingle emanating from Jo's hand. The slacks, the gesture, made Carmen think. The touch made her uncomfortable. She swallowed the thought, and turned to look at the radio.

"I will make sure that your car is OK, Carmen, I am not going to leave you in the middle of the desert, even if we just met. I believe in the Good Samaritan and all that stuff," said Jo. She continued to drive, glancing every few moments at Carmen. Was this going to be goodbye?

"Let's stop at the gas station, it will be up ahead in a few minutes," said Jo.

The two women stopped at the small gas station,

manned by a bald man in a blue work shirt embroidered with the name "Mike" partially hidden by a pack of Marlboro cigarettes.

"Can you follow us Mike? We had a flat tire a few miles up the road?" Carmen asked as she pointed. "We don't have spare, so I guess I will have to buy one..." she continued. Mike took a step towards her.

"I can get that tire. You got cash? I'll be needing that Andrew Jackson up front, like I said," Mike explained.

Carmen stared back blankly. Jo stepped forward and pulled out her billfold. She unfolded a $20 bill. Mike pocketed the cash. He grabbed a thick wad of keys and hustled over in his scuffed boots, to a turquoise Ford pickup. Mike lit a cigarette and spoke to both women, using the singular form of address, "Hey Missy, don't your daddy teach you to keep a spare and tools in the trunk?" Jo and Carmen said nothing at first.

"We don't have a spare," Jo finally answered.

"How far is the car from here?" Mike asked.

"Oh, it's just about two miles," Jo said.

"How much will that be to just put on your loaner tire, and then take me back to the station to buy a new one?" Carmen said. "$200" was the answer.

"That's pretty stiff, can't you help a lady out?" Jo said. "That is the price lady." Mike added, questioning the last word.

The two women jumped back in Jo's convertible. Mike followed close behind in the pick-up. Jo made sure that she did not brake suddenly in the short ride as Mike drove fast and turned without warning.

Mike pulled behind the stranded Chevelle, replaced the flat with a used tire. "Here's a receipt, Miss," Mike said handing Jo the change and pink customer copy. "Will this tire get me back to San Diego?" Carmen asked.

"Sure will." With the transaction completed, Mike drove east back to the station.

Jo and Carmen stood alone after the morning breakfast and impound lot investigation. They shared the silence and the peace of two women together on a desert road. Jo spoke first "Do you have any plans for dinner tonight?" "No," Carmen said.

"It's not much more than an hour and change back to my house in Hillcrest, why don't you follow me there. You could use some fun. My roommate is a professional chef, and we are having a bunch of ladies coming over. It will be delicious." She ripped the tire receipt in half and wrote:

Josephine Gemma, Esq., 1321 Rigoberto Place, San Diego. "Just follow me up the highway, we will hit the interstate, and then I will take you straight to my house."

The two cars drove in tandem into central San Diego. They turned down a quiet cul de sac by the early evening. Carmen drove slowly on the street and looked around to see a neighborhood full of well-maintained Craftsmen houses from the early 1900s. Quaint and well-maintained homes, with flowers, and trimmed bushes lined both sides of the street. She saw two blond girls skipping rope on the sidewalk. Not like Tijuana or Tecate. Clean, quiet, orderly. Jo pulled up to a gray Craftsman style house with a small driveway and a one-car detached garage. Carmen parked alongside Jo, on the small driveway.

Jo jumped out of her convertible and grabbed her briefcase and suit jacket, and was alongside Carmen's driver's door as Carmen was gathering her purse. Jo glimpsed the caramel of Carmen's supple neck as she scooped her belongings from the floor of the car and her pulse quickened. Jo smiled as she enjoyed the sweet smell of Jasmine from the garden together with a new tangy scent, Carmen.

Jo paused to clear a moment of calm. She opened the driver's door and said with genuine joy, "Welcome to our home. You are going to love my roommate Rosie!"

9

MEXICAN COKE

JO SKIPPED UP THE SLATE FLAGSTONE PAVERS TO THE RED front door. The walkway was flanked on both sides by golden California poppies. Jo gently tried the front door knob with her left hand, finding it unlocked. She flung open the front door revealing a small living room adorned with honey-colored oak.

"Nice," Carmen said aloud and noting to herself that it looked comfortable. Adjacent to the living room, was a dining room that overlooked a fenced backyard. Carmen saw a formal dinner setting laid out complete with candle sticks, white linen, and ten chairs. Jo placed her brief case on a wing-backed chair in the living room. "And you will make eleven, for our dinner party. I will go tell Rosie that I am going to squeeze you next to her." Jo dashed out of the room and returned with a swivel chair on wheels. "Filled to capacity," Jo said, as she squeezed the armless swivel on the right-hand side of the head chair.

Off the dining room was a long narrow, ship's galley-like kitchen and a number of pots boiling. Carmen spied the broad shoulders of a person cooking with a pink dishtowel strewn around a pale and thick neck. "Hey Rosie," Jo called from the dining room. The large shoulders performed a surprisingly supple pirouette, and the ruddy face of a beefy woman in her late twenties was presented. The roommate sported short tousled peroxide-blonde hair that was Marine Corps short. Her size and breadth rendered her an ideal candidate for either the roller derby or the Iditarod.

"Hi, I'm Rosie, and I do all the work around here," the large woman said, extending a hand. Carmen took the wide red hand, and withdrew her hand fast.

"Jo, can I have a tour?" Carmen said. She did not like Rosie's style at all. The men's clothes, the military hair. Carmen liked being a woman, the high heels, the dresses, the perfume, the doors opened, the man paying the bills, the protection. She liked what she had with JC. She missed his muscles and dominance.

It had been twenty-four hours since they crossed the Chevelle, and here she was in another universe with these women. She searched for the taboo words. American lesbians? The Chevelle was parked in a driveway in Hillcrest of all places, in front of an American Federal prosecutor's house.

She had no idea why JC had not come back last night. She knew he loved her. Or at least, wanted her and wanted to have sex with her. The physical reality could not be denied. He aroused her. She enjoyed his whining, panting, demanding desire. When they were together, it was with hunger. She liked what they cooked together.

Jo touched Carmen's shoulder, "Hey Carmen, let me show you around. First, here's the restroom, if you need to wash up." Carmen pushed the wobbly brass knob of what looked like the original hardware, and stepped into an old timey bathroom, complete with old fashioned faucets and a claw foot bathtub. She turned on the faucet labelled 'C' for cold, "not for caliente" she mumbled to herself. "Everything is opposite."

She splashed cold water on her face and gazed into the reflection. Different place, same face. She smiled at the beautiful woman in the bathroom mirror. The problem was Carmen's family. They did not like her running with JC who was a "junior" in the drug business. Carmen's family believed in education, hard work, and following the laws of God and man.

The family wanted her to marry into a nice Mexican, middle-class life, to include a husband, children, and house in a good colonia. Of course, her husband would cheat, that's what all Mexican men did, but as long he was loving to her, gave her money, maybe they would also buy a holiday home in Coronado on the beach. Perhaps, her family together could enjoy the sights of San Diego.

"I have to make a phone call, "Carmen told her reflection, knowing that she had to make telephone call. Her mother must know that she was alive and that JC had run off.

Carmen had no idea what to do with the cocaine or the Chevelle. She did not forget about that, not with all her smiles, the breakfast this morning, the federal agent, the ride back to San Diego. The home of an Assistant United States Attorney for now seemed like a good place to hide from the cartel goons.

A knock was made on the bathroom door. Carmen turned off the faucet, "Yes?" she said.

"Carmen, are you in the bathroom?" came a high voice. Carmen opened the door slowly to see the blonde woman looming in front her. That high voice, so incongruous and the demeanor so disconnected. A Chihuahua voice on a Rottweiler body.

Carmen squeezed by Rosie into the living room where Jo was lounging in a chair. "So, Carmen, Rosie - she's a chef downtown-but she's our chef tonight," Jo said.

"Is that your van parked out front," Carmen said.

"It is, my pride and joy," Rosie said, pleased by the compliments of this new cutie.

"It looks fun," Carmen said. "Not as fun as I am," Rosie squeaked. She walked back to the small kitchen, seemingly occupying all available space. She stirred a sauce, while humming softly to herself.

"I need to buy some cigarettes, is there a market near-by?" asked Carmen hoping to find a moment alone so she could make an untraceable phone call.

"Yeah, about half a mile south of here, down Reynard Way" said Jo pointing, we call it PLO Market, but I think it is called Farmer's Freshest -You can't miss it."

"What time is the party starting?" Carmen asked

"Whatever time our guests arrive. We told them 6:00 but you just never know with them," Jo said.

Rosie stepped out of the kitchen "So come back by 6:00 honey," she winked.

Carmen did not want Rosie so interested in her return. Perhaps there she could exploit this interest to her own benefit. Without delay Carmen turned on her high heel, and then twisted back with a smile. "Is that your garage Rosie?" Carmen asked.

"It is. My name is on the lease and that no account federal prosecutor is just subleasing from me," Rosie volunteered.

"I noticed the garage was empty and I have a classic

Chevelle. I just wondered if I can park it in the garage if you are not using it."

"Sure thing-the door is spring loaded, the padlock is open, just pull open the door and the spring will catch. You can drive in. I may have some tools in a tool box. Just put it aside, and pull in," said Rosie.

Carmen left with the "Yes" still lingering in the air, and called back "I'll see you in a few." She needed to get away from these women and have a few minutes alone. With a break of fifteen minutes, could think, make a phone call, and finally have a cigarette.

At the convenience store "PLO Deli" they had called it, she had made change and dialed the telephone numbers from memory. She approached the phone, her heart racing, her breath constricted. She lit a cigarette and weighed the choices. Why had he abandoned her? She just had to tell them what happened, otherwise she was as good as dead. No matter where she was, whether in Tijuana or L.A., they would find her and her mother would find her dead body. End of story, another nobody murdered over drugs. Carmen stomped out her cigarette after just a few puffs. She didn't want to be snuffed out by El Chiño. She very much wanted to live.

Carmen picked up the scratched black receiver and read the graffiti etched into the metal coin plate on the pay phone. "Cunt!" it read in large letters. The familiar ring of a Mexican telephone, and then the most familiar of voices. She lit another cigarette.

"Mama, it's me!" Carmen said immediately in Spanish.

"Oh, Carmen, I was so worried," came the answer.

"Mom I am fine. We had a flat tire on the other side. Yes, I am fine. I am staying here, on this side. I found a place to stay. Yes, Mom." Carmen paused to take a drag on the cigarette.

Her mother asked, with real concern and a choked tear, "My little one, are you safe? Where is JC, they want to know."

Carmen took hit from the cigarette, fortifying her resolve with the nicotine rush. She could not tell her mom about this now. "Mama, I will be smart, I will find JC, I will stay safe, I love you and I will see you soon. I have done nothing wrong except go on a date." She hung up, knowing she had told three lies.

Carmen pushed on the silver cradle that held the receiver. From the thick black telephone came the insistent demand "Please deposit $1.50. Please deposit $1.50." Carmen hung up the receiver. She had ended the conversation before she could lose her nerve. They were looking for JC. They knew she was just JC's latest piece of ass, no more. It was JC they wanted. The cartel thought she was just another dumb chica who was in the dark about the cocaine. And it was up to her, to use their underestimation of her know-how against them.

She walked back into the store and asked first in Spanish if they had Mexican Coca-Cola.

The middle-eastern cashier stared at her with a confused looked. She laughed, and repeated in English, "Do you have Mexican Coke?" "Mexican Coke?" the cashier repeated, spreading his arms. "What is that?" "It is like American Coke only sweeter, and authentic," she said.

The cashier walked her to the long row of shimmering glass refrigerator cases displaying the cold soft drinks and swiftly Carmen pulled in front of him, bending down and retrieving the familiar green glass, "hecho in Mexico," imprinted on the bottle.

She darted to the counter by the cash register and paid for the cigarettes and soda.

"Keep the change," Carmen called over her shoulder as she carried her Mexican Coke and cigarettes back to the Chevelle.

Carmen slowed down the car as she approached Jo's house. There was a clear path to the detached garage and she drove up the short concrete driveway. Letting the car idle in park, Carmen examined the garage. She touched the open padlock on the manual garage door. She removed the lock and then lifted the mechanized spring up.

In the twilight of the evening, Carmen peered into the garage. It was big enough for the Chevelle. She saw an old work bench, some saws hanging against the wall. She flicked up the light switch to get a better look.

She needed the car off the street. She needed the contents of that trunk out of sight. How long could she keep the Chevelle, and its load of cocaine, hidden? That was the answer she did not have. Carmen glanced around the garage, and found a large metal tool case. She opened it up and took out a large screw driver. Kicking off her high heels, she knelt down on her knees. She stopped, listened for a second, glancing back to see only a trimmed lawn, an avocado tree heavy with its ripe offspring.

On the floor of the cement garage floor were a series of wooden slats across a five-foot-long oil change pit. Carmen scanned the greying timber covering the opening to the oil pit. Carmen felt the old timber and saw that it was loose. She pried it up with the big screwdriver, and took the board out of the slot. She looked down and saw the deep hole into the ground. The pit appeared to be at least six feet deep.

"An oil pit," she observed.

She stared at the cobwebs and the dirt, and thought. It

was an oil pit from the old days, when oil was just oil, not toxic waste. In those old days, it was convenient to pour the waste out in a pit in the garage. A person would take the Model T and just change the oil out in an oil pit. Her great grandfather had once laughed about this at a family gathering. A large smile spread across Carmen's face, and her large eyes sparkled.

This pit could be used for more than storing oil, Carmen surmised. It looked like it had not been used in the seventy-five years since it was first constructed.

Carmen had stumbled into a place she could keep the cocaine for now-and then ditch the Chevelle when the time came.

She would make those arrangements when she had time. She would have to come back to the garage later to strip the Chevelle and store the cocaine. She had to use her assets wisely and like all things in life timing was everything. Carmen took a moment and looked at her trembling hands. She said a prayer to the only power that could help in her in this place, in this time, with one thousand kilos of cocaine. Jesus Malverde, the patron saint of drugs smugglers. She unclasped the gold chain around her neck and pulled the medallion of Jesus Malverde, the talisman JC had given her. With no time left and in need of some holy help, the decision came easy.

She kissed his gold lips and dropped the medallion down between the cracks. She thought she heard a faint plop on the soft dirt. She squeezed her eyes shut and prayed intently for a miracle while on her knees in the garage.

Carmen put the grey boards back in their slot, wobbling it over the oil pit. She returned the screwdriver to the tool box. She carefully carried her high heels back to the Chevelle on the driveway. With a tender turn of the steering wheel, she eased JC's pride into the ancient garage.

She put on her high heels and closed the garage. She pulled down the clasp and bolt on the outside of the garage door.

Carmen was back to the party in fifteen minutes with a single bottle of Mexican Coca-Cola.

Carmen closed her eyes for a moment and opened them with a smile. She tossed back her hair and unbuttoned her blouse. She brushed off her dress with her right palm. She stepped towards the house and her new friends, inhaling the fragrance of the night blooming jasmine, suffocating the summer breeze outside the old garage.

Carmen walked in the open door to find Jo talking to a slender blonde woman in pink canvas shorts. They were standing in the small living room, sipping white wine from long-stemmed glasses. Carmen looked to Jo, her face flushing uncontrollably. She had been gone for only a brief time. Out of sight, out of mind. Carmen knew she had just the antidote for that. She was a virtuoso when it came to playing libidos. Oblivious to Carmen's mood, Jo was focusing on introducing the two attractive women and making a good impression on each.

"Carmen," Jo said, gesturing to the blonde, "This is Lana Del Rey," and this is Carmen—ah Cortez," pausing as she remembered the last name.

"Can we get you some wine or sangria? Rosie is whipping up some of her Spanish favorites, including paella."

Sangria sounded good for Carmen, and she helped herself to a glass as Jo poured.

"How do you know Jo," Carmen asked in her lightly accented English.

"I live down the street, and surf at Tourmaline," Lana said.

Carmen glanced at Jo with her short tidy dark hair and fair skin. "Girls, surfing?" Carmen continued.

"Yeah, that's why we go in a large pack," Lana said. "Sometimes the locals can be real assholes. Cutting us off from the good rides. Saying stupid things about girls."

Jo nodded her head in agreement and she smiled at the two women absorbing their good looks more than the conversation.

"We go five at a time and surf long boards and over the years most of the time the dudes tolerate us, Lana said.

"Why don't you get some guy friends to go along with you?" Carmen asked.

"It's a girl thing, we do it because," Lana flipped her sun-bleached blonde hair, put her hands on her tight pink shorts and looked into Carmen's eyes "we don't want to be with guys," she stated slowly pausing between each word.

"Yucky container, that's what they are. You should come surfing with us and check it out," Lana added.

Jo's living room was filled with women. The conversation rang with laughter and talk of surfing Tourmaline, and then the pleasures of straight girls. With the last subject, Jo turned to see Carmen talking with Lana, and feeling uneasy.

Rosie emerged from the galley-like kitchen to herd the surf-pack and Carmen down to the meal, and into the dining room.

Rosie declined offers of all help from her seated friends. She deftly carried in a heavy plate of paella, the steam rising up. Carmen inhaled the enticing smell of the garlic shrimp, sweet paprika and ripe tomatoes. Seated next to her, their bare elbows occasionally touching, Jo smelled the same dish. She imagined that Carmen's aroma would be very much like paella, spicy, aromatic, shrimp.

Over pitchers of Sangria and plates of paella, the dinner party of women filled the house with giggles and banter. Carmen learned she was the only woman had never gone surfing.

"We will remedy that," Jo said. "That's all settled! We will take you out. You will you stand on a board."

"We are so taking this party to DeFcon 2," said Rosie. "What does that mean?" said Carmen.

"It's just a gay bar down in the warehouse area near the old train tracks."

Carmen said nothing.

"The first Friday of the month, they have a drag king and drag queen show. I have it on good authority somebody from this dinner party could be crowned royalty tonight," Lana explained.

Stomping to the door with VW keys swinging about, Rosie shouted: "Women, I'm driving, I can get nine in my van." Rosie led the way to her van. Rosie called back to Jo behind her. "Jo, you can take Carmen in your car, let's go."

10

BEHIND THE ORANGE CURTAIN

Friday, July 15, 1988
2:00 a.m.
Interstate 5 North
Orange County, California

ONLY NINETY MINUTES HAD PASSED SINCE JC HAD LAST KISSED Carmen good bye on a desolate road in Tecate but J.C had no time to think, connect the dots, plan. From the time he began jogging towards a pay phone, he was in reaction mode. He was just trying to find time to breathe, to stay alive, to grab some quarters and call his uncle in Tecate and explain how he and the 1,000 kilos had been separated.

Instead of sipping Patron in San Diego he was in the driver's seat of a furniture truck, moving pollos north, with a fat man with a fatter following him. They made it easily enough past the Border Patrol check point at San Onofre. Those nuclear power plants were large and round, with a red lighted dot on top. JC turned to the left at the plant, lighted in the dark, glowing with the radiation of two large illuminated breasts. He daydreamed of the preposterous concept to form a nuclear power plant to look like giant breasts, to distract him from the present pressures.

JC drove on for another twenty minutes when there was a pounding noise on the dividing wall behind the driver's cab and the cargo area. Shouts of "Necessito! Baño!" followed by a series of pounding. JC listened to those pleas and pulled to the side. Kiki immediately stopped behind the truck driven by JC.

"Flaco, what's up with you, hombre?" Kiki said. "This is not it Dreamland. Dreamland is on Katella. This is not it." JC nodded. Kiki put a foot on the side rail of the truck and leaned his head down, so that his jowls were inches from JC's face. "No stopping, you understand we are almost there." "Necessito, Baño!" the cries erupted.

Kiki shrugged. "We are stopped already, this one time, next exit though, farther away from la migra, outside of L.A. County. Only the U.S. Attorney in San Diego prosecutes alien smugglers, Los Angeles does not care. We need to get over the county line. Follow me, we'll get off in San Juan Capistrano, like the swallows. I know a side road by the orchards. There will be nobody there."

The convoy turned right back on the interstate, without answering the call of nature. Up the highway, three men and a pregnant woman hopped out of the back of the furniture truck, and disappeared into the dark dirt agricultural road. Minutes later, they returned to the crowded truck. The rest of the people, seventy-nine in all, remained crouched and dozing, packed in like fruit, on the hard metal floor of the furniture truck. They waited for the trip to end, and the road to riches to begin. Kiki closed the doors and locked rear door.

"Flaco, first get off at Katella, yes, the Disneyland exit. You will make a left. It's the Dreamland Motel. I will give you the address." Kiki pulled a pencil from his jeans, and scribbled an address. "You will get paid when we get up to Anaheim. After the pollos unload." JC stared at Kiki and said nothing.

"Look for Dreamland Motel, it's got a fluorescent sign in pink." Kiki got out and walked down the dirt agricultural road.

JC headed back onto the highway and followed the signs for Disneyland. He pulled onto to Katella, found the Dreamland Motel. There was a flashing pink and blue custom neon sign which illuminated each of the letters in sequence. D-R-E-A-M-L-A-N-D in pink with a white cumulus cloud flickering on and off. Emphasizing the contrast also in neon lights M-O-T-E-L. Continuing the explosion of light was a sketch of a castle in white, and in flashing red "no vacancy."

JC decided to follow the instructions he was given, for a change and drove to the parking space assigned to room number 117. He parked the truck and left the engine running. He turned on the dome light, and checked his Rolex 3:55 a.m.

"Flaco!" JC opened up his eyes. A large man in a snug T-shirt slurped coffee from a large take-out cup. The stout man waved at JC. The man pointed and said - "Go underneath the lamps."

"I'm Arturo, I will pay you once I count the pollos." Arturo unlocked the rear of the truck. In the light JC read a large flat cardboard box at the front labelled "Dinette table and four chairs," Arturo pulled himself up to the truck floor, hitting waist high for JC, but clearly lower than that for Arturo. Once a top the truck platform, Arturo unfolded a collapsing ramp and attached to the rear of the truck. He rolled and then pushed the large box down the ramp.

Arturo ordered "Hey, we are here. Quick walk down the

ramp and we will wait for your family together. Come with me, we have good food and Coca Cola."

Under his breath JC heard Arturo counting. Kiki smiled, "Oh, we love our furniture trucks. All here," Arturo said. He jumped down and tossed JC a key. "Flaco, I am taking the first group to 10, you and Kiki go to 301, come get me." Together, with JC following Kiki, the smuggled people straggled behind to room 301.

JC waved leaving the room key with Kiki. He descended the cement stairway back to the first floor and knocked gently. A woman who looked like she had lived six hard decades, stood in the threshold staring at JC.

"I was told to come here by Arturo," JC said pronouncing each word slowly and clearly in Spanish for the woman. The woman gestured to enter and JC stepped into the shabby Dreamland interior. The room was dark except for a light from the adjoining bathroom. He saw the silhouette of a large man. As JC hesitated, Arturo walked towards the increasing light streaming in from the motel hallway.

Arturo pulled a wad of cash from his front jeans pocket. "Flaco, here," said Arturo handing JC a wad of cash. JC took the money and put it in his pocket. "I'll give you the rest of the money, the full $500, after we get paid from their relatives." JC nodded in agreement.

JC walked quickly out the open door. He should have a lot more money coming. He felt the smooth, cloth-like texture of the money in his pocket. This was nothing, nothing compared with that fortune of cocaine waiting in the Chevelle's trunk. The load in the Chevelle meant millions on the street here in Los Angeles.

Money aside, it was good to be out of that truck. The point was to get as far away from Arturo as fast as possible.

JC walked slowly down the motel stairs, his hands shoved into his pockets. When he got some place alone he would count those dollars. Hopefully, it would be enough to get him back to San Diego.

JC walked onto to Katella Avenue. It was still dancing with activity, even at this hour. He walked down Katella for five minutes by his wrist watch. He scanned the motels that dotted the street. Ubiquitous like cactus in Tecate. He saw another neon side and this time, he turned towards it to read the promise. Green Mansions the sign read. JC yawned and walked down the circular drive to the glass motel door entrance. A bell tinkled, a fairy-chime, as he entered the faded green carpet that led to the night desk.

A gray-haired man with a short-sleeve collared shirt looked up. He approached JC, fighting to keep his lids from slamming closed. In clear English JC said, "I like to have a room, one night for one."

"It's late. Park closed at midnight," the night clerk said, glancing at the large wall clock which was slipping close to 4:00 a.m.

"Yeah I know. I was waiting to meet up again with my girlfriend, but she must have just gone home." JC tried to look disappointed. He didn't have to act.

The night clerk, never a hit with the ladies, nodded in sympathy. "Tease," is all he said. He conveyed a lifetime of shattered romance. "We've got ground floor, two twins, no smoking. Room 120 Mr.?" JC thought and the name filled the void, Guillermo Romero. "Ok. -"Gil can I see your driver's license?"

JC fumbled in his rear pocket and pulled out a social security card he had lifted from the stack of documents he had found in the furniture truck he had driven early that evening. "I have my social but I left my license with my stuff in my girlfriend's car." That was easy to say, because it was a modification of the truth. Everything was in that Chevelle.

"I have $50." "Let me see your card." Milt glimpsed at the apparently valid social security card, returned it, and picked up the cash JC had subtly placed on the front desk counter top.

"We can take the cash. Do you need a receipt?" JC shook his head no. The night clerk placed the key on the desk, the keys displacing the same volume as the cash.

"Mr. Romero turn to the right and room 120 will be five doors down. Check out time is 11 a.m. or you will be charged for another day."

Only four or five hours had passed. He had not made the drop in San Diego. Was Eduardo pissed? Furious? Should he call Eduardo or Uncle Ramon? He was tired, so tired he could not think clearly. He needed sleep. If he called Eduardo now, what could he tell him? Or would he just say, "I am alive, I am in Los Angeles. But I got separated from the load, I have no idea where it is, or I do, but I am just not there." He could stand here frozen in regret or he could act.

As with all important, unchangeable decisions, JC pulled out his lucky John F. Kennedy half dollar, that one that his father had given him for his first molar at 9 years old. In the light of the motel hallway, he flipped it high letting it land on the soiled and frayed carpeting. He said aloud, pledging to himself, tails I don't call, heads I do call. Tails it was. JC turned the key in the room and opened the motel door to room 120.

He flipped on the light switch to see two twin beds with a mustard yellow bedspread, and large posters of Disneyland and Mickey Mouse decorating the motel room. JC kicked off his shoes and pulled his clothes off down to his underwear. The motel room was icy in contrast to the heat of the July night. He pulled back the thin bedspread and then walked over to the window, near the pressed door, and closed the curtains all the way. He turned the deadbolt on the door, and padded back in his black socks to the twin furthest away from the door.

He flopped on the bed, belly first, superman again if only for a second. He rolled to his side, facing the wall. Exhaustion defeated apprehension and his snores replaced his hurried prayers in the dark.

11

A FULL TANK OF GAS

THE LOUD METAL CLANK, CLANK, CLANK OF THE CLEANING cart caused JC to start up in bed. Disoriented in the dark, he had no bearings, no familiar landmark. He was tired. He knew that this was not his bed, this was not a bed for two. He saw no other person. He licked his lips. He was thirsty and hungry, and the dark room was hot.

Reacting to the noise, JC listened, this time with intent. He remembered. He had no gun, he had left that at home. It was a Smith and Wesson Combat Magnum that was his 17th birthday present. But only the truly weak of mind would ever cross drugs and guns into the United States. Mexico didn't make guns. America made the best guns. "Better and easier to just buy a gun in San Diego if a man needed to," Uncle Ramon had said. JC knew that was one piece of advice he always followed: do not take a gun from Mexico into the United States.

JC peeled his weighted eyelids apart by rubbing his knuckles softly into his eye sockets. He opened his eyes leaving his head on the lumpy, synthetic pillow.

First the right eye opened and this was not his mama's

house, this was not his room in Tijuana. This was not Carmen's house.

He opened up his other eye and looked around at the darkened room, with a slice of light pouring in from a sliver of an opening between the blackout curtains. He inhaled and listened to the rustling, and again some voices in Spanish. JC sat up rubbed his hair, and pulled himself out of bed switching on the light switch.

He looked around and noticed this room was not in Mexico. As his eyes focused the blur into recognition, he observed the garish posters of the Magic Kingdom. JC walked over to the telephone, looked at the number on the receiver, it had an unfamiliar prefix.

He shook his head accepting that he must be somewhere in L.A. or Orange County. He was behind the Orange Curtain. He then opened the drawer next to the bedside table. He pulled out the big book of yellow pages. On the cover was a large picture of the iconic Disney Castle, and in large cursive letters, all capitals and a vibrant blue the name: "D-I-S-N-E-Y-L-A-N-D. THE MAGIC KINGDOM. The respite of forgetting was over. JC remembered the hellish night, each unpredictable event, that he was forced to confront alone.

He had caught a dozen hardballs thrown at him last night, and he had landed here, in Anaheim. The time flashing in red lights from the plastic wood grain clock radio read 6:20. JC scrambled to the window, glanced out the drapes, exposing the penetrating sun. He felt like rolling back into the soft mattress.

So far, it was just, listening to all his relatives direct him. He generally conformed to their orders, but never with one hundred percent faithfulness. Last night, alone on the highway in Tecate, he was forced to choose. It felt unfamiliar and terrifying. In this dismal motel room he had a few moments, probably no more, to plan.

JC had confidence he could find a way to travel one hundred miles back to his car and complete the delivery. He feared that the hours of delay were costly.

He needed to unscramble his thoughts. In careful letters, he wrote four roman numerals and next to each number, a title:

I Carmen | II JC | III Competitor | IV Forget

In Category I, was Carmen, abandoned by the side of the road. She would be fine as she was locked in that car, and she would hitch a ride back to town and be fine. JC understood that going back to Carmen and the Chevelle meant going back to the Family. It meant completing the job he had started.

Category II, presented the concept that he could retrieve that abandoned car and pursue what he had always dreamed of, but the opportunity had just never presented itself until now: smuggle for himself. He could distribute that load, and just fade into another part of the U.S., young, rich, and anonymous. Category III meant working for the competition. This option had always been alluring to him, because his family was so overbearing. His uncle, his father always underrated him, devalued him, and emasculated him. He was a man, not a boy, he could be more than a courier. If someone would give him half a chance, he could show his true skills.

The Competition might protect him from this mishap, but it was far from certain.

The final, and least appealing choice, would be to Forget and then abandon everything. To walk out of this motel and walk away: from the drugs, from Carmen, from his family, from the competition, from the money, and from the cartel. He could reboot his entire life and disappear into the United States.

His mind was numb with too much thinking. It was just too early. He need more sleep and he did not like sleeping alone. He always slept better touching a naked breast. It was hard to spend a night without Carmen. He missed her body last night as she was always a good lay.

He looked into the small medicine cabinet mirror in the bathroom. He stared at his exhausted reflection and reviewed his options. He realized that any of the four choices could be a dead end. The cartel would find him here and his death would be certain if he lingered in the motel bed. He could not head back to Mexico after last night. It was Russian Roulette. He had to spin the cylinder and pray.

Reluctantly, JC glanced at his gold Rolex. He was fortunate that Kiki and the other alien smugglers had not seen it in the dim light of the rendezvous. It was now 6:33 a.m. It was also the same time 100 miles south, just north of the international boundary between the United States and the Republic of Mexico, where that Chevelle was parked alongside the road in Tecate. It seemed like a century ago that he left his home.

He had to check out of that motel. He had to call Uncle Ramon and get back to Tecate, get the car, get the cocaine and deliver the load. Carmen would be fine, she was a cat. She was flexible with her body and her mind. She would land on her feet. It was his life on the line. It was his future that was in jeopardy.

JC again, looked at his unshaved face. He was proud of his heavy stubble, pure Spanish that was for sure. His eyes were set off by the red streaks. He stroked his chin and his prominent cheek bones. He turned on the bathroom light and checked his right front pocket and found the wad of money from his cash payment for driving the pollos.

He grabbed the motel key dangling on the edge of the bed table and tossed it on the imperfectly bleached off-white and spotted bedspread. He pulled on his designer jeans and slipped on his running shoes.

With his grooming imperfect but complete, JC left the "Do Not Disturb" placard on the door knob of the room and softly closed the door. He walked forward without looking and careened directly in a large, chunky woman with a cleaning service uniform and a cleaning cart.

"Lo siento, I'm sorry," JC reflexively uttered in both languages.

The woman, accustomed to collisions, messes, and mishaps of all sorts said only "No problema."

"Yes," JC said, and to himself, "if only."

For a reason he would never answer, JC dropped off the motel key at the front desk and headed up Katella Boulevard, joining the pedestrian stream heading towards the Happiest Place on Earth.

JC was not happy nor headed towards the amusement park, at least not until he recovered the mammoth load of cocaine that had disappeared on his watch. Death could come easily now and at any time. He walked down the sidewalk, scanning the businesses. He looked for a pay phone with a booth to make a private telephone call. He had reviewed the options and made the first choice, to return to Carmen, the cocaine, the Chevelle, and hopefully to the good graces of his family.

As terrible as it would be to make that call, he knew he had to pull up his big boy pants and face the situation like a man.

He pulled his aviator sunglasses from the breast pocket of his shirt, as the sun rose in the morning sky. He looked at his Rolex a second time. He squinted at the bright sunshine. The sun in Anaheim was not as brilliant as the same sun in Tijuana. In the bright sunshine, he watched families walking towards the theme park. The roadway was choked with cars, and JC coughed on the carbon-monoxide as he walked quickly on the pavement. He was quietly terrified. His entire life, he had meticulously calculated value, price, and image. The price of the Rolex, designer jeans, stunning Carmen, and ultimately the price of cocaine.

He had to tell Ramon some version of the truth. JC had always delivered until now. His own work had made the cartel millions. JC had been chosen to make the crossing. This past history was the reason Ramon made the commitment to the gang in L.A. Now that past record must buy him time.

JC knew Ramon had contacts everywhere. Ramon was old. He was rich and ruthless when it came to money. The longer he walked down the crowded sidewalk, the more JC realized he had no choice but to call Ramon. He could not escape the long reach of the lawless. Ramon would find him. When Ramon found him, the retribution would be slow and would end with a closed casket funeral.

After walking a few blocks with these thoughts careening through his psyche, JC remembered he had missed dinner and breakfast. Walking past diners and taco shops, JC smelled the familiar aroma of coffee at the Pancake House. The smiling teenage hostess helped him change a five-dollar bill for a pocketful of quarters. JC then sat himself down at the counter without removing his sunglasses. He chose a seat near the door and ordered coffee and a large stack of Iowa corn pancakes. He left his jacket at the counter seat, mouthing the words "pay phone." The weary waitress pointed around the counter to the right.

JC waltzed around a corner into a narrow hallway, and saw the empty phone booth. He picked up the receiver, and as an afterthought pulled the accordion door shut for privacy. He dialed "0-1-1" the country code for Mexico, the same time zone, but really a separate reality. Click, click, click. The mechanical saccharine voice, distant, yet authoritative demanded payment upfront. Caught in the clutches of a ruthless monopoly, JC paid this ransom in quarters.

Each coin was acknowledged with a 'ding' and the payoff was the ringtone of Mexico, followed by "Bueno?" the voice answered in Spanish.

JC said in Spanish, "Uncle?"

The conversation continued in Spanish. "Who is this?" "It's JC," he said.

After a pause, came the response, "It's about time," Ramon said, in an eerily even tone. "Tell me, are you with the product?" JC leaned down, put his right hand to his face and said, "Uncle, wait, it's complicated. I just need some time to make it right."

Ramon said, "JC, we have a delivery schedule. Where are you calling from?"

JC said, "A pay phone in L.A. Look, Carmen is with the car. We had a flat, she does not know about the load."

Ramon said, "Bueno, look, El Chiño wants the product yesterday. It's not just me, it's everything and everyone. You understand. I do not want to hear from you until you tell me El Chiño has delivery. There is no time. El Chiño will find you. You do not want that, Juan Carlos."

JC said, "Yes, uncle."

Uncle Ramon in the same even tone continued, "Call me later today, when El Chiño has the delivery. Go with God."

JC hung up the black receiver of the pay phone, and opened the glass accordion door of the telephone booth. The phone rang and the demanding mechanical voice ordered additional payment. JC dug into the pockets of his designer jeans and gave Ma Bell every last cent but still came up short. What Ramon did not say, clarified JC's confusion. He had to find that Chevelle, before El Chiño found him. There was no alternative.

Still in the phone booth, he opened his wallet, and counted all the bills, and found that he had $17.00. This was enough money for a bus ticket to Camp Pendleton that would get him at least back to San Diego County but still far away from Tecate. He exited the phone booth and walked back to his seat at the counter. He saturated his waiting pile of corn pancakes with the sticky contents labeled "syrup" that the pale waitress had set before him. He ate every last bite and licked the dark, sweet, dripping mess on the fork, just as he had done last week with Carmen.

JC knew that he did his best thinking at meals, usually over conversation. Well he had a conversation of sorts with Uncle Ramon. He pulled out the Dreamland Motel Pen he had snagged and scribbled on the napkin a rough plan. It was a "to do" list for the day. He wrote: * steal a car * drive to Tecate * find Chevelle * Call tio. JC was now a man with a plan and he had direction. He folded the napkin carefully and placed it in the rear pocket. He drained the mug of generously sweetened black coffee. Cognizant of all he could not guess, JC placed a $10 and a $5 bill on the counter, and caught the eye of the pale waitress, who mouthed a "Thank you." He knew if he had more time, he could have gotten more than lip service. JC then exited through the rear doors of the restaurant leading to the parking lot.

He sauntered through the parking lot, hunting for a car

with an open window. He located a gold AMC Spirit with an open window near the rear of the lot. He looked around and observed the lot had no people, just cars.

He approached the little gold car and pulled open the vertical door lock on the passenger door. He found wires under the ignition. He cut those wires with his folding Buck knife and soon the engine was humming. The gas needle showed close to a full tank of gas. "That should be enough," JC said in prayer. He peeled out of the parking lot directly onto Katella, and then straight south on the interstate towards home.

12

A SAILOR IN A CAGE

Jo opened the door of her convertible and then ran around the long hood to open the door for Carmen. Drama or oversight? Carmen voted for drama. It was an easy race because Carmen was in no hurry. She never was. She took life as it came. The pleasures and the vicious violence punctuated daily life with trouble.

Carmen counted every blessing. This made the good times and the passion more potent because she knew men and women could die for a footfall or trespass. Or on a whim. In Tijuana, it was a daily affair. She saw bodies shot down intentionally and more terribly at random. Early in the day as she set out the pastries at her family bakery, she saw the dead bodies hauled away with the morning trash.

Carmen did not care for chance so she made sure to summon an inviting smile when the murderers stopped by for a sweet cup of Mexican hot chocolate. She knew a smile could make a difference. Carmen understood that the federal prosecutor could provide an entry to other opportunities as well. The first thing she permitted Jo to open tonight was the passenger door.

With deliberate moves Carmen slid across the bench seat and smiled her perfected grin up at Jo. Jo returned the same electric look she saw in the diner that morning. The prosecutor's light blue eyes penetrated even in the limited light of the car. Carmen reached up and flicked on the vanity light in the car to apply a deeper coat of blood red lipstick. Jo was soon beside her absorbing the reality of the exquisite stranger riding next to her. Jo quivered inside wanting to smear that newly applied lipstick in places unseen. She gunned the engine, and directed her desire to the night's amusements. Jo hoped to be painted in red tonight. Carmen refused to ease the tension and remained perfectly silent.

Always following the rules, Jo did not turn her head and kept her eyes on the road. She looked straight ahead but her mind was very much on Carmen. Jo spoke to the road ahead and not her sole passenger. "It is just a few miles away, the club. They have great dance music. It's usually a lot of fun."

"I like fun," Carmen said with emphasis on the first word. Jo opened her mouth to take the bait. Oh yeah, she was hooked.

"That's our first shared interest. I like fun too," said Jo.

The two women drove on, Jo thrilling to the throb of the car's power and Carmen's coolness. The power of the engine vibrated through the car as Jo pulled up to a dark and crowded parking lot amidst a row of World War II era two story grey metal warehouses.

"It's a warehouse on the outside, but it's Sodom and Gomorrah inside." Carmen just stared, not understanding the biblical allusion. "It's a place in the Bible," Jo said.

"I go to church, but I never read it. That's what priests are for."

"Exactly," said Jo, as she opened Carmen's car door,

extending a hand to help her out of the low seat in her scarlet stilettos.

Carmen stared at Jo, "I've got way too much experience to get help," Carmen said.

"I'm amazed that you can manage to dance in them but I guess I must pay the cover first to see that thrill," Jo said. Carmen did not respond but answered with her actions, rising slowly from the car, careful not to take Jo's hand or touch her in any way. Jo perspired in the cool night. She led the way to the club.

Rosie and the other women were waiting at the entrance. Flashing in red neon, were the words, of both warning and temptation, DEFCON 2.

"Good news, Jo the big lawyer is paying the cover for all of us," said Rosie, who continued, "Right, Jo?"

In response, with Carmen looking on, Jo whipped her slim wallet from the front jean pocket, and lightly removed three twenty dollar bills, the cover for all of her friends.

The door check, a husky fortyish woman with a smoker's cough and dark circles under her eyes said flatly "Sometimes, it's good to know a lawyer."

Rosie elbowed by Carmen to be the first to enter the club. Jo and Carmen followed into the thud of booming bass electronic house dance music.

Jo quickly weaved through the ground floor and reached for Carmen with a strong grip and onto a dance floor filled with fit, slim, shirtless men dancing together. She did not pause to move to the driving rhythm but pulled Carmen towards a winding metal staircase that led to an industrial looking second floor.

Carmen allowed Jo to pull her up the winding staircase. The new American acquaintance had a physical strength she had first overlooked. Jo kept a tight hold on the gorgeous

Carmen, knowing that even in this crowded club, the lovely Latina stood out. Jo did not let up until they reached the destination at a table near a railing that overlooked the dance floor. Jo motioned with her hand that she was retrieving drinks and returned with two Mexican beers.

"To new friends," Jo toasted, and swallowed a heart full of effervescence.

The blaring music made conversation possible only through shouting. The visual symphony of writhing homosexual couples mesmerized Carmen. She stared in horror. At the same time, she was amused to see men as sex objects, for once. To communicate this thought, Carmen shouted, "There are some really cute men here!"

Jo replied "Yes, but the women are even hotter," and she looked straight at Carmen. Carmen felt heat spread across her face. Carmen did not know if it was shame, arousal, terror or the packed club. Carmen went to church every Sunday. She liked dating JC, until he abandoned on the side of the road.

When Carmen first met Jo, she seemed to be "all business."

A few hours later, Carmen did not really know what to think about Jo, and her group of surfing friends. She could not think straight, not with that Chevelle, packed with God knew how much cocaine, and Jo the Assistant United States Attorney breathing down her neck.

Carmen looked around the club and her eyes fell on two men shirtless and perspiring, pierced through the nipples, writhing and groaning and deeply French kissing in a not sufficiently dark corner. Carmen tried to look away, disgusted. But she looked again at them from her second-story perch, and was weirdly fascinated. Carmen took another sip of beer and she turned back again, to observe the pierced men, going at in the corner. Her eyes widened as she a man grinding himself down on another man's leg.

Moments later, Carmen's eyes trailed a large chunky woman in baggy pants, and an oversized baseball T-shirt swaying with a woman on the dance floor. She followed the couple with her eyes and witnessed the woman in the hat palming and squeezing the other woman's breasts on the dance floor. Carmen shuddered and tried to shut down her arousal.

Jo looked directly at Carmen and said: "Never been to a gay bar before, Carmen?"

Carmen shook her head no; it was the truth. A bit too earnestly, Carmen volunteered "I am a good Catholic girl, this is a sin." Jo stared at her beer bottle and took a cue from her pounding heart.

Jo walked around the table, until she was less than inch away. Carmen could smell the mixture of Jo, botanical soap and good perfume.

Jo touched Carmen's left hand, without a ring, and softly said, "I'm Catholic too. Love is a good thing, Carmen. Love, as we have been taught is always the answer."

Before either woman could say a thing, a waiter approached them in tight jean shorts, displaying tanned and muscular legs, work boots and snowy socks. He asked, "Some drinks ladies?"

Jo said without hesitation, "Two tequilas, for a start," gesturing two with her left index and middle finger.

"How do you know I like tequila, how do you know I am even old enough to drink," Carmen said.

Jo said immediately, "Your name gives away the answer to the first question. And I checked your driver's license at the impound lot today, when you showed it to Diego."

Carmen said, "Good one Jo, but I never showed him any I.D."

Jo took a breath, and playfully said," So, are you old enough to drink tequila, little girl?"

"Count the tree rings. One thing I did learn at Our Lady of Perpetual Suffering in Chula Vista was a young lady never reveals her real age after you been served alcohol and actually," Carmen pointed to the empty beer bottle, "finished an alcoholic beverage."

"But Carmen, I see you do have some beer still left in your bottle." Jo said.

With faultless timing, the blonde waiter deftly placed two gold double shots of tequila on the table.

This time, it was Carmen who proposed the toasts "To new experiences." Carmen downed the flaming golden liquid, bit into the lime and gave Jo a steely stare, with a barely perceptible smile.

Jo drank the shot, and exhaled with an audible breath and shaking her head. Jo answered Carmen's toast but stepping closer and whispering directly into Carmen's ear, "Is this how Mexico tastes?" Carmen looked back down onto the gyrations of the dancers one floor below. Jo, encouraged by the tequila, took hold of Carmen's arm and said, "Let's dance."

The two women unable to talk because of the incessant pounding of the loud music, descended. The dance floor was sticky with the moisture of bodies and beverages spilling down. Carmen glanced around at a closer level through the subdued lighting. One gnawing annoyance repeated itself with alarming regularity not a single one of the many attractive men she saw, acknowledged her in any manner. She was invisible, or so it seemed to them. This experience, was new for her. "Gay," she now understood.

Jo led Carmen to the center of the floor, adjacent to a small elevated metal cage where a blonde, small man, about 5'6" or so was dancing rhythmically and trance-like. He was dressed as an homage to some sinister military allegiance, tight black synthetic shorts cutting into his muscled thigh, gleaming black combat boots, a sailor tie decorating a shaved, developed chest, a spiked dog collar, and his buzzed hair crowned with a snowy white sailor cap.

Carmen was simultaneously fascinated and horrified by the dancing sailor. He was caged like an animal that had been brought up from the interior jungles of Mexico and displayed in the city, for amusement. Amidst this exotica, Jo and Carmen moved to the music and danced.

Jo closed the distance, as Carmen began to move away. Carmen focused on the music and her arms and hips followed the demands of the pounding base, lithe and graceful, no setting could disguise her intrinsic grace and powerful femininity. With the curtains of Carmen's eyes closed, Carmen smiled to the simple pure fun of dancing. It felt good, and she looked damn good doing it. Jo broke one of her sacred oaths and stared at this newest woman in her life. It was safe to do so as Carmen's eyes were closed. Jo stared, but she did not touch, not quite yet. She felt Carmen's soft lips, and knew the taste would be sweet, and piquant with a sad after taste or was it tragic? Too bad she did take more Spanish in school. That would have been just too convenient. After a few songs, the beat slowed down for a slow dance. Jo moved in and grabbed Carmen's waist.

In sports, in water polo, Jo had learned that difference between winning and losing was not luck or even talent, but just taking the shot. So, she took the shot and Carmen said nothing. They danced and danced, both heady with their unstated connection. The men peeled away from the floor, too stoned or drunk to stay on their feet so late into the night.

Nudged by propriety, Jo glanced at her watch. "its 1:45 a.m. Carmen, let's get out of here."

Carmen looked at Jo and felt an unexpected tingle and Jo registered the response. To deflect the sparkle of attraction, Jo turned to Carmen and they neared the exit "We are going surfing tomorrow," said Jo. Frozen by fatigue, Carmen followed.

Jo was quick again to open the car door for Carmen. For the first time, Carmen caught Jo red-handed staring at her body. As she entered the car, with the door held by Jo, their arms brushed and Carmen slid into the bench seat of the car. She kicked out of her pumps.

Jo opened up the driver's door, got in, and brought the engine to a roar. That was only her first magic trick of the night. With the car still in park, she retrieved a chocolate coated peppermint patty from the pocket of her jeans.

"Can I offer you dessert?" Jo said.

"I'd love some," came Carmen's surprising answer. Jo slowly unwrapped the candy and popped it into Carmen's open mouth. Just as slowly Jo moved close to Carmen and thrust their hips together as she gifted the peppermint candy. Jo moved in for the kiss.

"Yum" Carmen said. "That was wonderful."

Jo slid back and accelerated from "park" to "drive."

13

SINK OR SWIM

July 16, 1988
Saturday
8:00 a.m.
Tourmaline Beach

FOR SATURDAY MORNING, JO DRESSED CAREFULLY IN A SURF shop tank top, men's swim trunks and yellow flip-flops. She then jumped up on the bed, picked Carmen up and carried her to the bathroom. "You're learning to surf today and I'm going to teach you. I can surf as good as I dance." The two women had shared the night on Jo's double bed. Jo held Carmen's naked body in her arms. "Carmen you are beautiful." Jo knelt down and placed her gently on the cold tile floor of the bathroom. She stared into the other woman's glowing eyes and softly stroked her long dark hair with her left hand. With her right palm, Jo moved down the naked woman's body and stroked Carmen's exposed ample breast. Carmen shuddered and sighed. "God you're beautiful," Jo repeated breathless with renewed desire.

"Jo get up. I don't want to make you late. I can't go swimming in my birthday suit."

Carmen pushed Jo out of the bathroom. Alone before the round beveled mirror, Carmen admired her reflection. Her thick hair was tousled. Her cheeks were flushed from a night in Jo's bed. Her brown eyes burned with joy and excitement. This was her first time with a woman.

As Jo undid her bra last night, she told herself it was an act of necessity to make sure she could stay safe until she reunited with JC. He would never consider a girl to be a rival. It was not cheating. It was fun to be with Jo. To have Jo attend to her every desire. Jo made her the main attraction. With JC, her needs were his afterthoughts. Carmen was sore everywhere in a good way. She had never come so many times in one night. And now she had to learn to surf.

Carmen changed into the surf shorts and T-shirt provided by her hostess. She tied and knotted the shirt above her navel to expose a trim waist.

"The boards are on the bus, Rosie's behind the wheel and the pumpkin is ready to take you to the ball princess," Jo sang. Carmen answered as if she didn't hear what Jo had said, "Where are we going?"

Jo said "Tourmaline."

"Where? I've never heard of that. I've never been north of Coronado before," Carmen said.

In fifteen minutes, they were parking in a large empty beach parking lot.

"Step one is to put on a wet suit," Rosie said, after turning off the engine.

"Here? Put on the wet suits here?" Carmen said.

Rosie answered, "Yeah, listen. That's what happens. We are here to catch waves and have a great time, just like the surfer dudes.

Carmen stared back, and just shook her head.

Rosie said "Look Carmen. If you're going to surf you have to change your clothes. You want the thrills, you have to take the risk that some clown is going to get a glimpse of your tits." Carmen did not budge.

"I will make this easy for you. Change in the van while we change outside," said Jo. Carmen stood in the van and squirmed her body into the short-sleeved wetsuit. Both Rosie and Jo slipped on their wet suits outside. Carmen emerged from the van, glistening in the tight wet suit.

Jo was excited by the sight of curvaceous Carmen. Her assets were accentuated by a skin tight synthetic rubber wetsuit. Carmen could not look better. Jo wanted to kiss her on the lips. Instead, handed Carmen an eight-foot yellow surfboard.

"Here you go, lady. The waves are gentle today. They are perfect for learning. Let's eat the beach. You do swim, don't you?"

"Yes," Carmen said. The three women walked quickly in their bare feet through the thick mist of an early summer morning on the San Diego coast.

Many of the women from Rosie's dinner the previous night was sprawled out on the beach.

"Hi guys" they chimed in as Jo, Carmen and Rosie joined their encampment.

"Grab your board Carmen, we are diving in headfirst." "Sink or swim," screamed Rosie, running towards the waves.

Carmen stood on the surfboard by the end of the morning. She felt the exhilaration and absolute liberation of riding a wave to the beach. She was washed over with the baptismal cleansing of the ocean.

For the first time, she also knew freedom. "Woohoo,"

Carmen shouted in a full-throated joy, picking up her yellow longboard, "that was – incredible."

The women returned to the beach, after an hour of chasing waves like a harem of seals. "Missy, you earned your breakfast," Rosie told Carmen.

"Carmen," Jo called as she toweled the ocean water from her damp hair and face.

Carmen came beside her and whispered in Jo's ear, "I am here."

In the moment, Jo pulled Carmen towards her and kissed her. Jo wanted more. "God, you turn me on," Jo said with her lips against Carmen's ear.

Wet from head to toe, Carmen kissed back.

14

CASH ON DELIVERY

July 15, 1988
Friday
7:45 a.m.
Interstate 5 South

AFTER SUCCESSFULLY HOT-WIRING THE AMC SPIRIT, JC headed out of the Pancake House parking lot. He stepped on the gas pedal and shot onto the jammed street filled with tourists streaming towards the Disneyland entrance gates.

Step one: he was not going to rush any of this. He would not permit himself to think about the alternatives. He had already seen too much in his life. He did not have to guess about the inevitable retribution from the drug cartel, his own Uncle Ramon, if he did not deliver on his promise. It was forward or oblivion.

With sleep, coffee, and a heavy breakfast, he was a new man. He had beaten the odds his whole life, and today was no different. The most difficult part of his day was done; he had woken up, and gotten out of that damned parking lot.

He was half way to success. Just go with the flow of the interstate South, and he would find the Chevelle. He arched his eyebrow for a moment to consider the fate of Carmen.

JC was thrilled to be moving south. He forgot Carmen and focused on this car trip. "Yes!" JC pumped his fist for the first victory towards the day's goal. This was his first lucky break after a night of very bad news. He had, in his life, benefited greatly from a car full of lucky breaks.

After graduating high school, JC had made many trips to Los Angeles, sometimes with loads, cash, or guns. And definitely, what Carmen so loved about him, he was a man who could mix business with pleasure. Carmen teased him with that phrase "business and pleasure." That thought made him hard with desire. He loved coming to Disneyland on dates, and staying in the Disneyland Hotel. He and Carmen loved swimming in that sparkling pool. They would check in at the front desk of the hotel as Mr. and Mrs. Raul Rodriguez. That was the alias he used, both with Carmen and with the half a dozen other pretty girls he brought north for celebrating indulgent dates. They were decoys for the drugs as he crossed through the various ports of entry: Tecate, San Ysidro, Otay Mesa, Calexico. So yes, for him, there was business, and then so many pleasures.

JC breathed easier with each mile South. He was putting distance between himself and the alien smugglers. The pain in his chest eased. Less than twelve hours earlier, in Mexico, he had forgotten to grab the inhaler for his asthma from his bathroom drawer. In the tension of the night that followed, this was the least of his painful problems.

This car would do the trick, JC prayed, to get to that place just north of the border. He planned to abandon the little AMC Spirit after wiping her down and erasing his prints. He could sell it to someone headed south where the car would disappear forever into the abandoned grave yard of dismantled and cannibalized car parts. He had seen worse. He had seen the same thing done to people. He believed what he was told. This was not a crime, this was a business.

JC lived without ambiguity, where his desire, or need was followed by action. This made him an excellent management trainee for the cartel. Uncle Ramon had told him that in the United States, the most terrible events were not the work of a single leader. Instead, the most evil acts were carried out by a faceless and uniformed enforcement squad. Ramon had told JC, this was a brilliant strategy as victims had no one to blame. The killers claimed ignorance, when in truth it was a team effort. "The best defense time tested by history," Ramon called this the American legal system.

These thoughts fueled his trip down the Interstate 5 South. He had a plan for the day. JC believed he was safely away from the alien smugglers at least for now. With a tank full of gas, he could make it all the way to Tecate. All the way to the Chevelle. All the way, back to the good graces of his Uncle. Then he would dump this crap AMC Spirit. The car, like a girl, was easy enough to hot wire, but not to keep.

For a moment, JC equivocated. It was so strange to be alone in the car, without a friend, or even Carmen. He was coming to a crossroads on the freeway. It was an important decision: Tecate or San Diego. He had to find the car, and yet he knew he could not keep the enforcer, El Chiño waiting. He knew he had to find that load before he contacted El Chiño. He would tell El Chiño what happened. The flat tire was not his fault, there was a collision of strange events that he had never before encountered. Most importantly, whom could he trust?

Once he found the load, he would find El Chiño. The emphasis was on the after. The cocaine was everything. This was all business. Cocaine and the profit meant life. Even so, JC had learned to navigate between blame and responsibility. He had a different set of ethics for his romantic affairs.

The founding principle of the narcotic delivery business, JC had been taught, was one hundred per cent accountability. In this profession, there were no half measures and no excuses. The expectation could not be clearer.

JC was told that he delivers the load or dies. He could avoid the gringo cops, but he did not doubt Uncle Ramon would not accept a rain check or I.O.U. In this business, it was Cash on Delivery (C.O.D.) or Dead on Arrival (D.O.A.)

JC continued to drive South without stopping. His thoughts swung between cautious optimism and terror. Under no circumstances did he wish to be stranded again on the side of the road. He did not want to take the risk of the engine stopping. Such thoughts and the increasing smoggy heat of an Orange County July day caused sweat to sting JC's eyes. The salty tension dropped down into his eyes. There were no tears, yet.

He chose at the last minute to go East to Tecate. It was hard to know, what was the right choice in any situation. He chose with his heart. The heart never lied, his favorite rock ballads promised. That's how he urged his dates to jump in his Chevelle.

Yes, it was viernes, Friday, afternoon already. Maybe his luck had turned. He knew what happened to the unlucky.

JC had seen too many tortured bodies beaten to death like piñatas, and then dissolved in acid, and poured down the drain. A life, a dream, a destiny, a soul, flushed into the sewer. Not a reverent death. Worse, there was nobody that would be called to answer for such death, not ever.

His mother raised JC to believe. Today, JC chose faith. Faith in the fidelity of Carmen, and her very real love for him. He touched his chest for the gold medallion of Jesus Malverde, Patron Saint of Drug Smugglers. It was not there. He remembered, he had given it to Carmen last night, along with the keys to the Chevelle.

The pendant would protect her as well. He kept telling Ramon, she knew nothing of the load. He would not marry her but he did not wish her death. He could never smile again at Carmen's still very attractive mother, if anything happened.

Closing the miles between him and his gorgeous car, he applied Ramon's schooling. He didn't want to get too close to the load car, because there was still the possibility the cops, the gringo cops had found the cocaine. If they did, there would be surveillance on that Chevelle. Arrest by the Americans would be the least of the two dangers. With them and their imbecile legal system and judges, he had more than a fighting chance. With Uncle Ramon, not so much.

He was driving East fast, and the scenery changed from chain restaurants and stores, to junk yards and sand pits. He squinted at the rock formations and ramshackle homes. He stared in his rearview mirror. No traffic. JC slowed to three miles under the speed limit. He scanned the opposite side of the road, hoping to see his beloved. Where could she be? Oh Jesus, he needed a miracle. "Jesus my Savior, Blessed Virgin Mary, let my car, let that Chevelle be there," he prayed. He closed his eyes for a moment.

The curve of the road and his desire for self-preservation forced JC to open his eyes. Still no miracles. Nothing. Nada. In the privacy of the car, he shouted "Where the hell is she!

(the Chevelle)!" He pulled over to the side of the road. He knew it was somewhere.

He reviewed the events of the previous night. He was certain it was on this road. Sure, this place looked different in the day. Hell, he felt so different than he had the night before. He thought it was just a short run to get help.

An empty glass Fresca bottle gleamed green in the sun. This iridescent glass caught his eye. It had been a hot four-hour drive from Disneyland. He knew his promised delivery was getting later, as it was now a few minutes past noon on Friday.

With the reflexes of the adroit striker that he was on the soccer field, he bent down and grabbed the bottle by its narrow neck. JC smashed it into imperceptible jagged pieces of green glass in the middle of the road. He knew that now some stranger could also suffer a flat tire in the near future. Neither his terror nor anger were pacified by the act.

JC jumped back into the idling AMC spirit. The gas station had to be close. Where the hell was Carmen? "Chinga, "he said. He did not see his gold Chevelle where he had left it twelve hours earlier. JC could not fathom that the puta Carmen moved the Chevelle. He was in disbelief. Did Carmen get the car repaired? Somebody must know.

JC drove the AMC spirit a few more miles down the road. Like an iridescent mirage, he saw the neon of the now open Discount Gas Station sign. This pink and turquoise sign contrasted with the dull colors of the desert in the summer. It was visible on the left-hand side of the road. He had to ditch the stolen AMC, or run the risk of an auto theft arrest by the local Sherriff. He turned on Jim Road, really just a dirt lane. Out of sight from the gas station, this road would be a good place to park the car.

JC shifted the AMC into park behind a large live oak

tree. He stared into the rearview mirror, smoothing his brown hair with his ever-present black comb. He could not help but smile at his handsome reflection that won admiration from young women daily. He was tired, but he was always ready with a provocative word for the right girl.

JC walked slowly towards the grimy gas station office. As he kicked the rocks, he reviewed his credible lies. At the entrance to the gas station office, JC saw the sunburned potbellied Gringo look up from his Soldier of Fortune Magazine.

"Hi," JC said when he stood ten feet away. The older man spit, and did not look up. "I left my Chevelle on the road. She's perfection, 1966, classic and five-slot rally wheels. I left her maybe a mile from here. Have you seen her?"

The Gringo looked up with blood shot blue eyes. He took a good close red look at his visitor.

He looked to be a young man, somewhere about twenty-five or twenty-six Mexican but light-skinned, and stylish. The visitor was dark-haired and light eyed. He wore tight fitting designer jeans, a fine collared shirt and running shoes. The older man hoisted his loose blue work pants up to his waist. He extended a grimy right hand. JC took it, and shook. JC noticed some of the mechanic's grease had been transferred to his own palm in the exchange.

Mike pointed to his uniform shirt with the name "Mike" embroidered over his left chest. "I am Carlos," JC said as a half-truth. "Have you seen that classic Chevelle? I had a fight with my girlfriend. Maybe you saw her-Carmen? Pretty, you know," JC paused, and drew an "S" with his left index finger. Mike appreciated the pantomime but did not respond. "She drove away in my Chevelle, after we had a fight on our way back to San Diego." Mike said, "Hmm."

The mechanic stared, not comprehending this strange

idiom nor its context. JC rambled on, hoping to prod the old man to help him recover the car. "I was driving, and we started fighting. I just pulled over, and walked out into the sage brush, to cool off and I walked back, and the car was gone," JC explained.

Mike took a drag on his unfiltered cigarette, and took a swig from a dark iced beverage in a coffee cup. It was Coca-Cola and small batch Bourbon. Mike showed no response in his watery blue eyes. Who was this kid fooling? Tecate might be in the middle of nowhere, but it was and had always been a vital location in this century's northbound smuggling game. He reached into his breast pocket and retrieved a fresh cigarette. Mike took another puff of the cigarette, a futile effort to ignite the lapsed synapses of his undertaxed mind.

Naw, he did not give a damn. Whether this sharp dressed, and lying smuggler found his load or not, that was between him and unknown third parties. Not his business. Not his concern. His loves were few: engines, firearms, cigs, and a quiet lady who knew how to keep the beer cold, and the meat rare.

With an impassive flick of his cigarette, Mike drawled with the echo of his Oklahoma roots, "Yeah. Two girls came by, on..." Mike paused, to take an impossibly long drag on his cigarette. JC tensed ever muscle, and said nothing, not knowing how to read this redneck geezer. "Yeah, they came by. I didn't get their names. One had really short hair. Your lady?" "No," said JC. "My girlfriend, she has very long straight dark brown hair." Mike looked up, and shook his head, in the affirmative. "Oh yeah, there was another, younger girl, who had long hair, and very high, spiked heels." Mike chuckled, not respectfully. He was going to make this little shit pay for anything he gave up. Mike liked those girls alright, they respected him, and said please and thank you, as a young lady should. They sure appreciated his help, he was damn sure about that.

"Yeah, they bought two tires. Funny, no spare, they said. They had no tools, that's what she said. The long-haired girl stood and watched the whole time. So that's your girl-friend?" "Was," JC said in an uncharacteristic moment of truth. "Funny thing was, I drove them back, oh a mile or so, to where the Chevelle was parked, and they were real polite, sweet really. And then we get out there, and the long-haired one, Carmen you said her name was?" Mike said. J.C shook his head, "Yes." "Carmen said they had no tools, and she could not open the trunk. Or wouldn't. She stared at me the whole time. Just stared as I put on the new tires. She just would not open the trunk." Mike took another long inhale of the cigarette, and stared into JC's sunglasses. "She said she was sure there was no spare tire in there?" Mike probed, knowing how strange it was to have a tricked out classic Chevelle with no spare. "Did she tell you where she was heading?" JC asked.

"I heard her talking to the other girl, the one in pants. I heard the tall one give your girl directions to San Diego. I think the tall one said she lives in a certain neighborhood, Hillcrest." Mike glared at JC, seeing if he could make this punk flinch. "Do. You know where in Hillcrest? What street," JC said.

JC pulled out an extra set of keys on a Chevy key chain. "I have the keys, I always keep an extra, just in case..." JC said. JC kept the rest of the sentence to himself, which ran, 'just in case he needed to deliver the car, and store it, and then retrieve the drugs at a later time.'

Instead, JC continued with his cover story, "I miss her,

and I need to find my car. I still have a loan on it, and I miss that sound of the V-8."

"I know what you mean," Mike said. "I love, I mean I love my cars. That'll be why I stay here, it is a great place to drive, and fix cars," Mike hitched up his loose pants. Mike shuffled through the piles of inventory lists, and yellow receipts on the nicked metal desk. "Oh yeah, here we go," Mike said. He read, "Josephine Gemma." "Yeah, they had to get two tires. So, they put their money together. Your girl, she didn't have enough, so the tall one lent her some money. She said, "You can pay me back later."

"Where can I find my Chevelle?" JC asked.

Mike uncrossed his arms, and pointed a greasy, calloused index finger west. With his Oklahoma drawl, he said "San Diego."

JC coughed. He would not concede to defeat. The minutes were ticking down, and this was a match he could not lose. He had to find Carmen and the Chevelle. He fished into his designer jeans pocket. He pulled out 85 cents. He had one good meal today, and that would have to sustain him for now.

He put one dime and one quarter in the Coca Cola machine outside Mike's grimy office. With the reassuring "clink," the machine dispensed the reliable refreshment. He retrieved the green tinted bottle, and put its frosty glass to his temple, cooling in the July heat. He tried to ice his fear, and take the pause to plan.

JC snapped off the cap with the built-in bottle opener on the Coke machine. He drank down hope. As the cold beverage washed down, he reflected that the long arm of the law was nothing compared to the violent and certain retribution of the cartel. He had to find that Chevelle because he could not pay cash for the lost load. His business experience taught him that money was more important than blood.

JC sat down on the curb outside of Mike's office. He combed his hair and finished the last sweet drops of soda. He could delay no longer. It seemed like an eternity. He stood to look at the large clock tin the mechanics bay of the gas station that displayed a time of 1:35 p.m. He squeezed his eyes, and realized that it was still only Friday afternoon.

15

BREATHE EASY

July 15, 1988
Friday
Noon
Tecate, California

WHERE COULD HE FIND UNCLE RAMON? AT NINA'S, A topless restaurant where all the jefes (bosses) gathered? He opened up a folded business card for an auto repair shop in Mexicali. He dialed the number at the pay phone.

The waitress, JC knew as Norma, answered. "Norma, it's me JC. I need please, to speak with Don Ramon, he is expecting this call." JC said in Spanish.

Nina answered unimpressed," He is eating and does not like to be disturbed."

"I understand," JC Countered, "But please, please tell him it is me, and this is an emergencia."

Norma said, "Ay" and then the line was silent and JC heard the click, click, of a woman scampering down a tiled hall in high heels.

There was a sneeze and then a tongue limbered by a few

shots of tequila. "Juan Carlos, I have asked if made the delivery. He said No. Where are you?"

"I made it, I just had some, um, car problems," JC said

"Juan Carlos, you are family. This is why you are not dead already. Only because you are my cousin's son, I will give you five days. That is all." Ramon firmly replaced the black receiver and went back to his lunch, and the young strippers.

For a family member, JC understood a sober warning could be just as potent as a death threat. JC's stomach tightened.

He knew that Carmen took his car west, to San Diego, and very likely, to a certain neighborhood, with this short-haired lady in business clothes. Who was this other girl, and how did Carmen know her, JC wondered. Was that just a stranger lending a hand, or was this Carmen stealing his load?

He was going to find that car, and get it. He had the key. He just needed the car. Carmen was not capable of stealing that car. He would soon learn what had happened.

He dialed another number scrawled on the business card, a San Diego number, not a Mexican number this time.

He spoke in English, careful to flatten out his accent to the flat tones of So-Cal.

"Hi, it's JC" was all he was able to get out when the response poured out angry, and insistent "Where the Hell are you? We got the whole crew together. Looking for you, asshole. I am being squeezed, man. Shit is coming down." JC glanced over at Mike, shuffling paperwork at his desk. Mike was out of ear shot, so JC did the unmentionable. "Look Eduardo-" but JC Was cut off. "Asshole, don't you ever say that name again on the fuckin' phone Eduardo whispered, "I have five days to get the load. I just spoke to

Ramon. No worries. Carmen has the car, she is in San Diego. Everything is safe, intact. I will meet up with Carmen, and then meet with you for the close," JC said.

He heard some voices in the background, and then Eduardo coughed, loudly into the receiver. JC dropped the payphone handle. He heard loud laughter. Eduardo said, "I will meet you at the end of the Ocean Beach Pier at 8:00 p.m. tonight,"

JC said, "Got it."

"They will pick you up."

JC reviewed if he should give Eduardo his precise location. He had very few options. They would find him, better to find the Chevelle with Eduardo, than to have Eduardo find the Chevelle without him. He had to get ahead of this situation. Eduardo then abruptly ended with "Stay put, he's leaving now." Eduardo summoned Jose´ and tossed him a set of keys attached to a silver pistol key chain, grim homage to the profession.

"Where are you?" Eduardo Chin, unaffectionately dubbed "El Chiño "by the Feds, asked. "I am at Discount Gas, just north of la linea."

"Uh Huh, don't move," El Chiño ordered and slammed the phone. El Chiño picked at the string of pork fat wedged in his incisors with an ivory tooth pick. He would see that idiot kid soon enough.

JC sat down in the sliver of shade offered in the shadow of the gas station business office. He was a man who liked to move. He had to stay and wait. He had nowhere to go, and no way to leave. He sated his growing hunger with a peanut candy bar and tortilla chips from the gas station vending machine. Even so, his stomach was in knots.

Periodically, he dusted off his designer jeans, rubbed his now dusty running shoes, and jogged out to the highway, to peer up the road for his ride. It was a relief to get away, for a moment from Mike's openly curious stare. Did he know, that JC was connected?

Without a muffler, the grinding engine noise, cut through the electrified guitar music emanating from Mike's grimy office. A faded blue Impala attacked the gas station lot, and a beefy bearded giant of a man emerged, unfolding himself from the low seat with obvious energy and strength. The large man's dark eyes joyfully anticipated a confrontation.

The bearded man looked about, peering in the hot son for his designated passenger. A thin clean-shaven man, in a pressed sky blue collared shirt remained inside the car, with air conditioning blasting on high, and the engine still running.

JC walked quickly to the car. He did not say a word.

Mike, got up from his chair with a creek, and said flatly "You are welcome kid."

JC did not turn.

The bearded man opened the rear door of the Impala. He nodded to JC. Don Ignancio spoke to JC in Spanish, in a dialect and tones which reflected his university training in Ciudad, Mexico.

"Get in Juan Carlos."

JC responded in Spanish, "Yes, sir."

Without turning around from his position in the front passenger seat, the slim man laughed, "1000 kilograms and Carmen, that's a lot to lose." JC failed to see the humor.

Sweating stinging his eyes, he struggled to keep his tone even: "Don Ignancio, there is a difference between lost and just misplaced."

Ignacio was known by his nickname of "Nacho" to his friends, enemies and surveilling law enforcement on both sides of the International Border. Nacho, spun around mongoose-like at the comment and slapped JC hard across his right cheek. A violet bruise rose from JC's cheek, marking the disrespect.

"Next time, Juan Carlos," Nacho said softly "it will not just be my hands." Nacho emphasized the final word. "You should listen to what I tell you until we both visit El Chiño." Nacho continued, "Juan Carlos, let me introduce you. It gives me such pleasure to introduce the large and enigmatic Jose´ Contreras." JC nodded at the large bearded man who had showed him the back seat of the car. Jose´ lifted up his carefully pressed white shirt to show a Sigsauer P226 9mm semiautomatic pistol, big, black, and as JC knew effectively deadly. It was snug in its discreet concealed carry holster attached to his dark trousers.

Nacho glanced at the heavy gold watch on his wrist- "It's 6:05 p.m. We will be at El Chiño's for drinks at the Seaside Bar and Grill. We can watch the sunset." Squeezed behind the wheel, Contreras floored the Impala, and chased the sun west.

Mike wiped the grease from his hands with a clean, red oil rag. He took out his USMC zippo, lit another cig, and he spat onto the dust outside his office door. "Narcos," he said, grinding his teeth. He stared at the Impala heading out Route 188.

As instructed, JC uncharacteristically sat silent. Nacho unleashed his tension, this was the biggest delivery by car, if the load was not recovered, JC could not live. There were rules that could not be broken, Nacho reflected. There was the overhead. Not just the product, but the payrolls, and the payoffs, the Federales, the occasional American Customs officer, and the campaign funds to the District Attorney. Nacho just shook his head, in anger and in disbelief. "How,

how do you lose 1,000 kilos," Nacho said, expecting no answer. JC squeezed his fists. He did not want to ignite the highly flammable emotions of Ignacio.

Nacho turned around the seat, fixing his deep brown eyes on the now hang-dog countenance of JC. "You are going to find that car, that Chevelle and our cocaine. There is no other way imaginable." JC listened.

Nacho turned back around and tapped his right hand on the car door, keeping tune to a narcocorrido song playing on a cassette tape on the Impala's tape deck. He removed a pack from the glove compartment, and quickly lit up a cigarette.

"Cigarillos Jose´?" Nacho asked the driver, who gladly accepted the offer.

Soon the two men were puffing away in the closed car. JC felt every breath of the sixty-minute ride from Tecate to Ocean Beach. JC fought to find the explanation expected by El Chiño.

JC interrupted Nacho's conversation with his staccato coughs.

Choking out a broken syllable, JC said, "I have —asth-ama."

In a silent response, Nacho blew rings of smoke up to the roof of the car.

16

DON'T MAKE IT A FEDERAL CASE

Monday
July 16, 1988
5:00 a.m.
U.S. Federal Court House

CARMEN OPENED HER EYES TO LOCATE THE DIGITAL SCREECH. The culprit was five feet away from Jo's bed, on the other side of the room. Through heavy lids, she saw the ascetic time of 5:00 a.m. She was no saint. And this was too early to get up for such a pretty girl. To her knowledge, she had never been awakened at such a ridiculously early hour. She loved the night and all that it brought. It was July, and yet, fog in this neighborhood masked the sun. She could have slept for hours, if not for the screaming of the electronic alarm. Crazy, loco Americans twisting technology to lower the quality of life.

The events of the last few days smashed into Carmen's frontal lobes. The pageant of events began with JC, the breakdown, the breakfast, Jo, muscular Jacobo, Club DeFcon 2, and surfing with all the crazy Lesbians. A few days ago, she was in her own bed in their Rancho in Tecate, Mexico. It was better having fewer alternatives.

Now fully awake, Carmen sprang from the soft bed, to silence the alarm. She was relieved she was alone, and sober. She could sort out her next move. She was in a place, and with a person, off-limits to JC and his family. It was deliciously bad luck. Jo Gemma, Josephine I. Gemma, officially was an Assistant United States Attorney, an American Federal Prosecutor.

While Mexican police, prosecutors and judges were routinely disciplined and murdered by the cartel, they had yet to touch the Americans. JC had been explained in very explicit terms: "That border means money, by crossing that border from our country into the Los Estados Unidos, our money, our profit doubles, triples and more as the product gains value - as soon as we cross that line. We kill their officials, and the border closes. They put the Marines, and every FBI on our border, which means our product does not move. No, we will not touch them in their country, but they better stay on their side. After Camerena, they get the idea," JC had instructed her.

Carmen looked around the cozy room, into the misty summer morning. She saw a tidy lawn, a small vegetable garden, and a cascading fountain.

Like Tecate, San Diego was almost desert, but the Americans stole water, like they stole everything else. They filled their reservoirs, swimming pools, and saturated their green decorative lawns. The time had come to get something for herself. With a house full of snoozing women, came opportunity. Carmen's time was now.

Carmen quickly pulled on Jo's surf shop t-shirt and men's polka dot boxers, and found rubber sandals. She slipped out the kitchen back door that led to the garden.

Gingerly, Carmen turned the knob handle of the back door, and glanced over her shoulder, to see that nothing had stirred. Her chest tightened. She closed her eyes, and prayed to Jesus and Mary. Jesus would help her hide that cocaine.

Better yet, she prayed to Jesus Malverde. She had placed that medallion, a hand-off from JC on Thursday night, down in the oil pit. The gold pendant was good luck and if her luck ran out, it was still 24 carat gold. She stepped outside to the wooden deck leading to the garden. The deck was spongy from age and termites. Silently, she closed the door. Carmen was adept and gentle. She navigated a rock path through the grass to the clapboard detached garage.

She entered through the side door to the garage. It offered a quicker alternate access. She checked the varnished brass knob, rickety after seventy-five years of use and pushed. The door moved, and Carmen let out a breath.

Carmen opened the door into a dark garage. Her heart slammed against her chest and reflexively she pushed her right hand over it to slow it down. "Chinga! Gracias" Carmen exclaimed. The Chevelle was still there. It was JC's car. But possession is ninety-nine percent of the law, and now it was hers. He had abandoned her, the car, and the load. Was he dead, drunk or distracted? She didn't know and at this point, she didn't care.

Carmen unclenched her balled left fist and stared at the key she had brought with her. In the dark garage, she stepped carefully to the rear of the Chevelle.

She opened the trunk. Breathless, she pulled up the immaculate trunk upholstery and saw brick upon brick of densely packed white powder, wrapped tightly with silver electric tape. Carmen paused, listening to the stillness, to confirm there was nobody else around. She leaned down and pulled out a brick. "My parent's house." She said to herself, realizing the potency of this load. This one brick could pay for their house.

Carmen looked at the floor boards over the oil pit she had observed on Friday evening. Loose boards covering the old oil pit could provide a cache for the trunk's kilos. The Jesus Malverde medallion would watch over it and keep it safe. She put the brick back with its fellows. With great precision, Carmen replaced the factory trunk upholstery. She quietly but firmly closed the trunk. She shook he head and said "Gringo flojo." She could only hope. And pray.

Taking care not to flip-flop too loudly, Carmen paused on her return trip through the garden now dappled with the July morning lingering in fog.

In a corner near the orange California poppies, Carmen spied the mint and basil planted no doubt by Chef Rosie. She carefully twisted off a few sprigs of both, and put one and then the other to her nose. The smell of an unforeseen and unpredictable fortune.

Carmen moved into the kitchen through the back door. She looked around, perspiring. Still quiet, still dark. Carmen placed the herbs on the kitchen counter. She then bustled about the well-ordered kitchen to prepare a traditional Mexican breakfast for her hostesses.

At 7:00 a.m., Carmen rolled Rosie and a snoring Jo from slumber. After a few forceful tugs, Jo looked up, and emitted guttural sounds. It was the smells of the kitchen that motivated her to rise from the living room couch. "Mm, smells amazing," Jo said with her eyes still shut.

With some fresh gel applied to her pink flat-top, Rosie entered her kitchen. With surprise, Rosie saw that breakfast had been made by Carmen, eggs, tortillas, cheese, and fresh coffee. Jo joined them in the small dining room off the kitchen where Rosie was busy taking a large bite of eggs. Jo poured coffee into a large mug with 'Stanford Swim' emblazoned on one side and redwood tree on the other. "Ugh"- Jo exhaled and stared out into the garden. In her imagination, it appeared momentarily as a primeval forest. In the early mornings with the green ferns hanging and the manicured palms trees in the back, she half-expected small dinosaurs to be hopping about sharing sustenance with the local Jack rabbits and possums.

Jo turned back to the dining room as the fog of fatigue began to lift from her consciousness with each sip of strong coffee. She blinked bleary eyed from sleep and myopia. Jo squinted without her contacts, trying to bring Carmen's face into focus. As she remembered, it was a sight that was worth seeing with clarity.

Carmen caught the sleepy prosecutor's eyes and flashed a white, penetrating smile.

"You are dressed up. Not going surfing this morning?"

"I will be trying to surf through the waves of Justice," Jo said. "Today, my wetsuit is a business suit. It is a humorless hobby and the judges just don't take you seriously if you don't wear the proper attire and have the right equipment."

"Oh, Jo, you know you have the right equipment," Carmen said, not missing a beat.

Swallowing hard, Rosie chimed in "And remember Jo, Carmen went surfing with us, and she's inspected that equipment very closely." Rosie laughed, her pink crew cut bobbing with her head as she convulsed in laughter to the point of tears.

"Nothing like enjoying your own joke, huh Rosie," Jo remarked.

Jo sighed with dread. "I hate Monday mornings in federal court, and I really hate today! Judge Mack! He hates me because I won't flirt with him. He is such a bully, he goes on these long insulting tirades." Lowering the register of her voice, Jo mocked "Next time you have this typo, I will sanction you counsel. It will be a $500 fine!" Returning to her normal voice, Jo said "Give me a break Mack."

Carmen asked "You are in court, this morning? With a Judge Mack? What time?"

"9:00 a.m. answered Jo, sighing again.

"What kind of court do you have?" Carmen asked. "Do you mean what kind of case, or hearing?"

Jo said. "And it's a trial, a drug trial like pretty much all of my cases and trials. It is the only thing, I guess, my bosses see as crime. You know the War on Drugs, that Reagan declared and all that," said Jo.

"I haven't mentioned the trial, because I really don't like to think about it unless I absolutely have to." She looked at her watch, thinking of her Dad, Giacomo Gemma, who had presented it to her for her college graduation. He was a cop, actually a detective, in Chicago. "Actually, it's because of today's trial that I was out in Tecate on Friday and ran into you and your flat tire," Jo said.

"This trial will go very fast. Judge Mack is a Jackpot for the Defense. He is out to set a new land speed record for fastest federal trial of all time. He does not care whether Justice is done as long as it is fast, all the evidence is marked, and all the witnesses are subpoenaed and sitting on the hard benches in the court hallway," Jo explained.

"Aren't judges all the same, old, rich and conservative?" Carmen asked.

"Ah Judge Mack," Jo continued, "with his insults, threats and sanctions, maybe a job as a bus girl or dishwasher is looking better and better. There would certainly be less verbal abuse, but I just could not match this lifestyle to which I have become accustomed, "Jo laughed, gesturing to the small, sparsely furnished bungalow she shared as Rosie's roommate.

Jo slammed down her mug, now empty and stood up. "That's it!" She said and theatrically unbuttoned her collared blouse. "Quick, give me a black t-shirt," Jo said as she pumped a fist into the air. I am trading in my loafers for sandals, I am becoming a full time lesbian surfer." Rosie just stared. Carmen did not know what to say.

After polishing off a tall pile of eggs and tortillas, Rosie said," Carmen, you known imitation is the highest form of flattery, so you got to lead me through this step by step."

"Chilaquiles are simple, tomorrow I will teach you, Rosie," Carmen replied.

"Eat your breakfast Jo, you need your food for your trial," Rosie said.

Jo grabbed her pinstriped jacket and briefcase with United States Department of Justice gaudily embossed in gold on the front. Jo looked around, frantically "I need my Creds. I can't get into the Courthouse without my Creds."

Carmen questioned back, "Creds?"

"My United States Attorney Credentials. To prove I am the good guy, it's in like a leather wallet with my picture in it."

Rosie said dryly, "Try looking in your briefcase, zipper compartment on the inside."

Jo followed directions, "Oh yeah, here it is, thanks Rosie." "It's already 7:30 a.m. I have to split. Just ask the courthouse guard where to find Judge Mack's Courtroom. We should be picking a jury most of the morning. Trial starts at 8:30. He will seat twelve bodies as jurors, preferably they will be deaf, blind, and without a pulse. Ignorance of English is a big plus, they just need to reach a unanimous verdict either way, so he can log another completed trial and beat out his courthouse competition. He bet Judge Flynn he can get the record of the most jury trials presided over by a Federal judge in United States History!" Rosie shoved Jo to the red front door of their bungalow.

Jo turned, and looked right at Carmen, catching a peek of Carmen's cleavage. For a moment, Jo lost her train of thought, distracted by the young woman's stunning body. Jo recovered her composure and said, "The opening statements will probably start at 1:30 p.m. today, so see you then."

Jo stepped out the front door, but before the door was closed, Carmen caught the opportunity to softly touch Jo's neck and kiss her on the mouth. She whispered in Spanish, meeting Jo's ear with her wet lips, "Buena suerte, Cariño." Jo did not want to leave. She managed to shut the front door, breathing heavily. She jumped in her car and drove the two miles downhill to the U.S. Courthouse to prosecute yet another border crime.

17

LOOKING FOR A GIRL

IT HAD ONLY TAKEN A FEW DAYS, BUT JC WAS FINALLY WHERE he wanted to be. He was in San Diego. But he still had not made it to the beach. On Thursday night, he expected to be at the beach in San Diego by 1:00 a.m. Friday morning. Instead, he was in San Diego, twenty hours later, but without the car, cocaine or Carmen.

Thanks to Mike at Discount Gas, he now had the name of the girl who moved the Chevelle with Carmen. He reviewed her name, it was Italian, Josephine Gemma. JC lived in a world of nicknames brimming with El Flacos, El Gordos, El Chiños, El Negros, El Blancos, El Vaqueros, and they all shared the commitment that they would go to their deaths before they would speak their true identity to the Americans. The continuity and sanctity of the family, of their wives, children, and cousins, counted more than this one human life. The money they made in the cartel would sustain the family until the final sunset.

Josephine Gemma was a name in San Diego. He had a full name and network and he had motivation.

He would trade everything for that car. He did not want anything to happen to Carmen. Not that he loved her. She was not wife material. She was no virgin, which is why she was so amazing in bed. After his meeting with El Chiño, it was obvious she had to be discarded. Perhaps, he would just let the cartel handle it for him, and he could feign ignorance and go to confession, along with all his other many sins. He didn't owe her an explanation. Not that she would let him explain. Why couldn't people just take things as they were? How come she never believed him about anything?

Explanations. Gringos wanted drugs. Mexico had nothing. Produced nothing. Nothing worked there, not the sanitation system, not food safety. Not the politicians, the police, nor Los Federales, the national police. Sure thing there were laws, but a crisp $20 bill in American dollars of course, was a hall pass that could make a lot happen, the best table in a restaurant, a speeding ticket forgotten, an underage prostitute procured, a counterfeit visa stamped.

JC smiled. His first one of the day. And then he wheezed in the closed Impala. If the system actually went through the bother of arresting you with a Mexican warrant, then release could be bought at a cost of about $5,000 depending on the family relationship and particularized greed of the officials. Prosecutors and judges were actually for sale.

JC sighed with satisfaction. Mayors could be persuaded. He had read in the American newspapers that it was actually the Mexican Attorney General that ordered the execution of the American Drug Enforcement Agency Special Agent Enrique Camerena. And that was the top law enforcement official in his country, it trickled down and became more insidious at the very local level. As he knew through practice, all politics were local, and in his experience, corrupt.

Laws were enforced only on those who did not already possess the key to their own escape: money and connections. As the nephew to the jefe in the organization, JC had taken a risk by crossing such a large load himself. That was one of two ways to move up in this business. The other way was less desirable. He was not blood thirsty, just as he was not risk adverse. He did not wish to make a career of killing, no judgement, just not his personal taste. He ran loads, instead.

He scraped by unprepared school, and never read anything, except Esquire Magazine, in English, so he could learn the important things, like what watch and shoes to buy and how to impress girls. He had a good natural ability with numbers and organization. Most importantly, he had a great memory and no imagination.

These gifts manifested early, when as a seven-year-old he would welcome his grandpa picking him up at school in Chula Vista and driving him to the Greyhound Racetrack at Caliente.

"You are my luck, Juan Carlos," his grandfather would tell him. He had a full name then, as opposed to the initials that the Cartel bestowed in place of his Christian name. With some guidance from his grandfather, young Juan Carlos would choose the winning greyhounds and whippets.

The Impala came to a stop and Jose´ firmly escorted JC out of the backseat and onto a dark parking lot. A blood orange sunset dipped over the long pier to the West. As JC's eyes adjusted to the light, he spent a half a second in a sense memory, enveloped with his grandfather, and his weekly training for manhood.

For his fourteenth birthday, he learned the truths about the family business. He learned how each advantage had been in fact, planned by a series of family, marital, and geographic connections. JC at last, understood why his parents had made meticulous arrangements to make sure he was born in the United States. Now, knee deep in recovering his lost cocaine load, it all started to make sense.

His mother, born and raised in Tecate, Mexico, made sure to hire an American doctor so that all of her children were born in a San Diego hospital. She learned early in her marriage, the precepts of the 14th Amendment to the U.S. Constitution, which bestowed "all persons born in the United States...citizenship." This was his family's most unfair advantage, easy access to market. JC's family had no intention that they would live in the United States, pay taxes there, or indeed abide by any one of their ridiculous laws.

For JC, America was a vacation destination, and of course, a business hub. By blood, allegiance, passion, and language, JC was one hundred per cent Mexican.

JC was bilingual, having paid attention to his schooling in San Diego, at least to the playground, and soccer field conversation. In his family, had work was rewarded abundantly. JC craved status more even than pleasure.

Riding in the smoke-filled car with Nacho, he knew that reputation in this business as in all things on this earth, was everything. In San Diego he was a criminal. In Tecate, accessorized with voluptuous girlfriends, and a wallet thick with a stack of twenty dollar bills, he was respected. And so, he was a modern-day Robin Hood, in song if not in truth. Mexican radio stations blasted the narcocorrido songs celebrating the heroics of his very own family business.

As a U.S. Citizen, he could pass back and forth across the border. With $100 in Tecate, JC was somebody. In San Diego, he was just another young Mexican, exploitable and expendable. JC did not like that. He didn't like the way

Nacho treated him either. Once he found that Chevelle, Nacho would have to stop smoking when he was around, or he would face the payback. For now, JC gasped for oxygen.

As an American citizen with roots in Mexico, he straddled two countries, two languages, two cultures, two consciences. JC did not feel like a citizen of America. When he was in San Diego, it was almost always business. He had never been farther North than South Central Los Angeles, in the city of Compton. He had gone there for a delivery.

———

CONTRERAS AND NACHO led the way into the loud, smoky, and crowded bar and grill.

Glancing behind, Nacho motioned that they were going up the steep wooden stairs in the rear of the restaurant. At a table with his back to the wall, facing a large window which framed the entire expanse of the Ocean Beach pier, JC caught site of the unmistakable bulk of Eduardo Chin. He was seated, but at 6'3" and 290 pounds, he was a presence that could not be mistaken nor ignored.

Eduardo preferred the name given him by his mentors in the organization, El Chiño.

With a Mexican mother and a Chinese father, he was a U.S. citizen officially, as he was born in the El Centro, California community hospital. He was fluent also in three languages, Spanish, English, and Cantonese. He was polite to a fault, and he immediately acknowledged the entrance of Nacho, Jose´, and JC. He did not stand.

"You made good time," El Chiño said in Spanish. "Good, we have a lot to accomplish before the sun sets." Four other men were seated at the table, also very large, bearded, and all Chinese. They sat facing the staircase, their backs to the expansive view of the ocean.

The largest of these men kicked any empty chair out and gestured to it. He stared at JC, and JC sat down.

El Chiño spoke again, "You have until Tuesday. Find it." He then handed JC a business card that read "Judy's Big Kitchen-The Best Breakfast in San Diego" and on the back in small neat handwriting was a San Diego phone number.

El Chiño then reached down to a bowl full of whole cooked shrimp and plopped one into his large mustachioed mouth, whole. While still crunching the shrimp tail, El Chiño said, "Call the number." Punctuated by a long, annoying squeal of metal chair legs on a linoleum floor, El Chiño rose more quickly than JC could have expected.

Beneath El Chiño's shiny black leather jacket, JC saw the glint of the Big Man's Colt Commander, nickel plated, and immaculate. The four enforcers rose from the table, filing behind El Chiño.

The largest of the men, sighed in genuine regret as he bid a glance of farewell to a full beer bottle and an entire platter of fresh shrimp. Jose´ Contreras turned away from JC and towards the empty table. He sat at the table and poured a glass of beer from a full, untouched bottle. He grabbed a clean plate and eagerly served himself a large plateful of shrimp, rice, and corn tortillas.

JC's stomach soured although he had nothing but candy and Coca Cola since breakfast. Five days. He had a name. He had a neighborhood. This was not impossible.

Finishing the last of his beer, and seafood, Jose´ turned to the silent JC and asked, "Do you need a ride to San Diego. I am going downtown." This was not a question, but an order. Even so, JC appreciated the bigger man's subtlety.

JC looked at the driver, and hesitated. Jose´, not waiting

for a response, said "Nacho went with El Chiño, if you did not notice."

He smiled at the very irreverent dangerous Freudian slip, amused by his own daring.

"They are figuring out how to deal with the gap in you know the delivery to L.A. that you created, temporarily? You know, shit just doesn't run uphill. Except, for the New River."

"Yeah?" JC asked.

Jose´ saw an opportunity to display his erudition to a new victim, "You know the New River in El Centro and the Nile are the only rivers in the World that run from north to south. The point is shit does really run upstream from Mexico into America. Up. With the New River, it's all the chemical crap the Mexicali maquiladoras dump in the river."

"Sure, that's not the only shit that runs uphill to America? "JC said "but no smoking, and I am rolling down the windows to air that car out." The bill had been paid for by El Chiño, and the two men went out alone. JC hopped into the seat left vacant by Nacho.

The night was warm and the car still reeked from the pack of cigarettes smoked on the inbound trip from Tecate. In under ten minutes, they were cruising on Broadway, the main street of the city, lined on both sides by tall office buildings and both the state and federal court houses. Facing the harbor, stood the Naval Headquarters. It was built to resemble a ship and was readily mistaken for such by many a drunken sailor returning from shore leave. Further down the harbor side, JC saw the Star of India, an old re-fitted sailing ship form the 1880s bouncing at anchor.

JC said, feeling the cool breeze, and seeing the smiling tourists, "Hey Jose´ , think of the slums of Tijuana, the dirt, the trash, and then this ten minutes by car, due north It's like a different planet." But JC knew better. Violence and greed knew no boundaries, or geographic limits. Neither the border nor conscience stopped los narcos from killing in San Diego, but economic interest did.

18

CHEAP AND CONVENIENT

Jose´ turned the Impala into a large downtown parking lot, and handed a folded $10.00 bill to the attendant. Overlooking the lot was an ancient six-story brick building with a faded cigarette advertisement from the 1930's. 'Smoke! For Health!' were the only legible words printed in two-foot-long lettering on the San Diego Downtown Hotel. This place had seen better days. Troubled faces looked down from the top floor, once a luxury hotel, now descended to a flop house. It was a place off the street for $20 a day, $100 a week.

"Cheap, and convenient," Jose´ said. The two men walked into the lobby. Jose´ said "One room, two twins, ground floor please, one week," he spoke in Spanish. The hotel clerk took the $200 dollars handed over in $20 bills and said nothing.

Jose´ looked at JC and said, "I am your new babysitter until we find that Chevelle. You will sleep in the bed next to the bathroom." The two men spent Friday, Saturday and Sunday night in the flophouse. Jose´ kept the younger man in his sights at all times.

JC was startled by a Jose´ on Monday morning, who handed him a paper cup of coffee and a cinnamon donut.

With a big foot to and a push to JC's rear, Jose´ pushed JC out into the dismal lobby. "Sorry honey, Jose´ joked, "our honeymoon is over."

The two men left the small room and walked out into the lobby of the time-worn hotel. "Reagan, you know, their President, let out all the crazy gringos from the mental wards," Jose´ said, pointing to the people loitering near the San Diego Hotel. Jose´ said "and some of these people, living like this, they use their government payouts, their social security to buy our product."

Jose´ glanced at his watch and finally shared with JC the purpose of this field trip to the downtown area. "We're going to the federal courthouse to make sure they shut up. You are coming as well, don't talk." The two men passed through the courthouse security quickly.

Jose´ and JC streamed through the panel of glass doors with the courthouse tide returning from lunch. JC was pushed by the swarm of office workers. Jose´ elbowed JC, as he recognized familiar probation officers, and I.R.S. Special Agents, along with the nameless, rude court clerks of prior dealings. Some federal workers carried take out with them, returning to the confined cubicles, regulated by time-clocks and rigid regulations. Jose´ explained to JC, that this was the sustenance of the federal bureaucracy. For Jose´, seeing this sorry lot just confirmed his career choice.

Jose´ led the way, parting the herds of people with his girth and muscle. As they navigated the courthouse hall-ways, JC realized, he was not just seeing the courthouse, as an afterthought, this was a communication from the organization to him. "No escape from the cartel. Ha-ha," was the message. JC swallowed. This was no errand, but his very own remedial lesson in loyalty.

This was a club he could join, but never quit. Not in Mexico, not in America. The cartel will find you anywhere and even watch your very public trial in a United States Federal Court House. The cartel will send enforcers to watch and write down everything said at trial. Everywhere, there will be eyes, ears, and the long arm of the lawless, with a slow, and lingering death for those who think that the cartel could forget that their family could die as well.

For the last ten years, JC had listened to his cartel bosses and babysitters. He overheard the conversations about the Americans, the Feds, the United States Attorney's Office, the law, and the prosecutor's agenda. JC had dared to ask Uncle Ramon this nagging question. "Uncle, are we working together with them, to keep the price of drugs so high?" He got a wry smile as his answer.

The footsteps of the two men echoed through the polished courthouse hallways. Jose´ walked quickly and with purpose. Not once did he stop to ask for directions.

It appeared to JC that Jose´ had clearly been in this courthouse before, perhaps, many times before. After a series of turns, they found a bank of elevators. To the right of the elevators, Jose´ scanned his finger on posted calendars for each courtroom. Jose´ paused at the schedule for Courtroom Ten. Jose´ motioned to JC and they rode the elevator up to the top floor. Jose´ whispered, "Courtroom 10."

Before the doors could close, a wiry man, in a well-worn dark blue Brook Brothers suit, scanned the two Mexican men slowly. He then gave them both a condescending smile. The three men rode together in silence.

The blonde man motioned with his hand to permit Jose

´ and JC to exit first. The blonde man then followed them, as the elevator door closed with a rickety vibration. Jose´ walked down the broad hallway, with floors waxed to a mirror-like gleam. He arrived at the destination, and read aloud the princely placard etched in six-inch-tall brass letters at the wide entrance to the courtroom:

"The Honorable McKinley L Mack, United States District Judge, Courtroom Ten."

With the blonde man trailing behind them, both Jose´ and JC seated themselves in the courtroom to the immediate right of the entrance doors, in the last row of the courtroom.

As they quietly filed in, they saw an old man in a black robe, with his entire face distorted by a broad sneer. Jose´ elbowed JC and nodded with his head at the attractive court reporter, a strawberry blonde in a tight sweater. She typed away in the work pit below the judge's bench. JC could hear the tap-tap-tap of the stenography machine recording every word emitted, like a slightly muffled wood-pecker. JC turned to see the source of another sound, high-pitched and loud coming from a young woman, expensively dressed, blonde and smiling.

"Oh, your honor, of course my client is inn-o-cent. That is why he has taken this matter to a jury trial. He has proclaimed he is innocent, from my very first meeting with him."

"Thank you Miss Vandeweghe, that will be enough!" Judge Mack interjected with a wave of his hand, and an amused look of disbelief. Sitting in front of the two men was a woman in the front row of the audience.

She had filed in minutes before them, and sat in the precise spot Jo had requested, front seat, directly behind the prosecutor's table.

Carmen did not turn around from her place to notice the entry of her wayward boyfriend, JC.

JC sat impassively on the hard courtroom bench. His uncle words at last made sense in this setting "The foundational myth of America," Uncle Ramon had said, "is that judges are more wise, knowledgeable and moral." Sitting in a courtroom for the first time, it occurred to him that he was supposed to pretend that somehow the angry old man on the bench should be respected like the purity of a priest and the erudition of a professor. JC knew better.

The judge directed a new tirade to the other young woman in the court room, standing near the jury box. JC deduced, by the laws of elimination, she must be the prosecutor.

"Ms. Gemma, I ass-ume the Government is prepared to proceed immediately," the old man said.

In a conservative blue pin-striped suit, and a man-tailored white shirt, the young woman looked anything but feminine. JC searched for the word, and released it from the tip of his tongue, "Androgino" in Spanish. Cool. The girl was so man-tailored she had all except for the tie, and well the dick. The pantsuit prosecutor said," Your honor, the motion hearing was last week. The defendant was arrested on Saint Patrick's Day, March 17. This is an extremely serious case, with a lot of investigation."

Judge Mack shook his head in agreement and then held up his hand. He had heard enough. He was the law. It was time to lay it down. "Ms. Gemma, I have heard the Government's position. The court is well acquainted with those border busts. Whether it is 50 pounds of marijuana in a car or 2000 kilograms of cocaine in a truck, the evidence, the investigation and the trial are same. I myself have brought a case to trial in 10 days," Judge Mack said.

JC saw the pantsuit slump in her chair. He then noticed the lady defense lawyer glide over in her high heels to her client, the prisoner. This was a man, both Jose´ and JC knew as a long-time commercial trucker and employee of their organization. The defense lawyer touched Garuda's back softly with her well-manicured hand, accentuated by long pink nails, which were visible to JC in the back row of the spectator seating.

Heidi in Spanish, combined with her Milwaukee accent whispered, "This is good." Garuda, deliberately did not use a Spanish language interpreter for the most intimate conversations with his lawyer, on her advice. Soon upon meeting, Heidi shared with him her favorite quote by Benjamin Franklin "Three may keep a secret, if two of them are dead. Despite her Midwest roots, Heidi was both discreetly bilingual and even more secretly, bisexual. The interpreter, her highly paid services unneeded, quietly reviewed the New York Times Cross Word Puzzle in ink. Heidi and Garuda exchanged words with no witnesses.

19

BORDER BUST

GARUDA GORDON CORDERO SHOOK HIS HEAD AS HEIDI talked, looking serious, as Heidi instructed. Both prisoner and judge looked pleased. Judge Mack enjoyed the tranquility of a courtroom moments before the commencement of trial. The crux of democracy, is what Judge Mack was proud to call his courtroom. Garuda Garrett Cordero was comforted to see the familiar faces of his compadres, JC and Jose´. He felt safe, knowing they were there, reassuring his lady lawyer, there was a $100,000 "acquittal" bonus at the end for a job well done.

Garuda liked ritual. He was familiar with the liturgy of the Catholic Church. "This courtroom," Heidi advised "was the Church of Justice, complete with the sacraments and splendor of vestments, holy relics, traditions, unassailable authority, recited in an archaic language." Heidi told him, "instead of the 10 Commandments, the Americans had the 10 Amendments to the U.S. Constitution. They even have a statue of Moses in the Congress." This made sense to Garuda. It made sense to put faith in a document, in a promise. Garuda enjoyed the services of the curvaceous certified court interpreter, so he could half-listen to the words of the angry old man.

Judge Mack continued "Counsel, this is a garden variety border bust. As such, there will be no attorney void dire. This is not an opportunity for you to argue your case." Judge Mack theatrically gestured with his bifocals, that he had momentarily removed from the bridge of his nose. "Ladies, the point of voir dire, or jury selection is to get a fair jury, not charm their pants off."

The two female attorneys exchanged smiles, at Judge Mack's comment." Heidi took the cue, "Your honor, Miss Gemma has provided I and the defense team with full discovery. Heidi understood any delay meant opportunity for further investigation by the Government. This would be bad as she also knew that Garuda was oh, so guilty.

Heidi understood the job well. It was to get Garuda off, without losing her law license. Starting trial today would mean an end to the investigation. Federal agents would not get more time to carefully collect circumstantial evidence against her client. This could be achieved through trash runs, mail covers, telephone record searches, and additional interviews with a busload of witnesses. In other trials she had lost, Heidi had cross-examined federal agents who picked through her client's garbage cans, taped together shredded notes, and intercepted mail deliveries.

Heidi, a proud graduate of Columbia Law School, had told her clients repeatedly "Don't throw anything away. If you want to be truly safe, burn it. And talk in person." Foolishly, many believed that in America nothing happened without a warrant.

But on the balance, of course, crime paid. Crime paid for her beach front house in La Jolla, her Cadillac, her designer clothes and her positions on charitable boards across San

Diego. In public, she voiced her ardor to protect each person's Constitutional Rights, but when she washed the artifice off her face every night, she was left with affluence and a dirty conscience.

"May I have a moment your honor, to confer with my client," Heidi said. Missing nothing, Judge Mack admired Heidi's trim, stylish figure and shapely, 33- year-old legs. Jo waited silently at the prosecutor's table, the one closet to the jury box. This was the federal court equivalent to the home team dugout in Major League Baseball. The prosecutor was the home team in federal court. They got the table and the side of the courtroom closest to the jury, so they could make eye contact. The prosecutor got the opening statement and the closing argument. The prosecutor got to ask the first questions of the jury. But the defense got Reasonable Doubt.

Out of the corner of her eye, Jo observed Garuda Gordon staring at her, unabashedly and unapologetically. Or so she thought. Instead, Garuda was looking beyond that table to his friends in the back. Jo followed his gaze, and stared at the blonde man in the Brooks Brothers suit. It was Special Agent Jason Teeter, scion of a rich San Francisco family. Teeter had been upfront about his ambition when they first met on this case. He was perfecting his Spanish, and his knowledge of tequila as a federal agent for a few years, with plans to go back to get his M.B.A. at the Ivy League. His fair complexion, and East Coast suit made him easy to spot in the courtroom.

With Heidi still speaking to the defendant, Jo approached Teeter. She bent down to speak softly to the special agent, "Jason, double back with all the witnesses on the list and make sure the first five are seated outside this courtroom by 11 a.m. Mack is hell-bent on breaking the land speed record for fastest Border Bust ever tried." Jo's sole consolation was her belief she would go to prison following the jury trial.

Special Agent Teeter looked at her with aquamarine eyes, and Jo did not melt. Jo said, "To be clear, here is a witness list. Make sure they are set tight and sitting here. Of course, Jacobo Sanchez." "I told them all to show up after lunch, but we can get them here ASAP and their butts will be sitting on those hard courtroom benches within the hour. They are probably on their second cup of coffee at the U.S. Ulysses Hotel across the street and are browsing the Sports Section of the newspaper," Teeter said. He had no intention of making this a career, so he spoke his mind. Jo dispatched Teeter to shepherd the witnesses. As Teeter pulled open the cumbersome oak door separating the courtroom from the hallway, Jo touched his muscled arm. She ordered," Tell Jacobo we need the cocaine, all 2000 kilos to put into evidence for the jury." Teeter sighed and under his breath, and said "Pain in the ass." "That's right this is dog n' pony, shown n' tell. Those jurors get to play with millions of dollars' worth of blow, but they must convict our Defendant," Jo said. "Let's put on the show," Jo said.

She turned back towards her counsel table and pushed through the swinging doors. She wrote on the yellow legal pad her goal. "GUILTY!" That was her prosecutor's affirmation. Jo scribbled away until she was disturbed by a strong tanned right hand touching her shoulder. She turned to see Special Agent Jacobo Sanchez in aviator sunglasses and a suit.

"Don't worry," Sanchez said touching the aviator shades "I'll lose these as soon as the jury files in." He flashed his most devastating smile- a complete dud- for Jo. "But listen Lady D.A.- I see you brought your personal chic along and his smile grew even bigger. "Where's Teeter, then?" "He's with all of our witnesses in front of Courtroom 9 up the hallway. Guarding them from predators."

"Good work, Jacobo. I didn't want them creeping out the jury panel." "No! Never," Jacobo answered. "Nobody can touch 'em. I put them down there because I wanted them safe from Vandeweghe, her Quasimodo defense investigator and those two crooks in the audience out there. Hey lady, don't you dare stare at them," Jacobo said.

"Which reminds me, Jacobo. Where is the cocaine, the 2000 kilos for this trial and did you get an I.D. on the crooks in our courtroom," Jo said making sure to look only at Jacobo and smile.

"It will be here bright and early on a dolly- all 200 packages."

"As far as I know, those two guys were probably sent here by their defense lawyer so they will know what a jury trial looks like. But I will get one of the court officers and stop and ID then on their way inside the courthouse. Or I will get a uniformed Border Patrol Officer do an immigration check," Jacobo said.

"All rise, in the presence of the flag, and the Constitution for which it stands, all rise for Honorable Federal District Court Judge, The Honorable McKinley L. Mack, presiding," declared the rotund and tightly girdled court clerk from her diaphragm.

Judge Mack, climbed the three steps to his perch on the federal bench. He was known by Assistant United States Attorneys and Defense Attorneys alike, as simply McJustice. Not a single human being ever speak that name to his face. But behind his back, it was widely whispered.

McJustice took a moment to absorb the grandeur of his position. After the Presidential nomination, and the rubber stamp by the Senate, he had gone back to the D.C. hotel. "Ah, lifetime tenure. Not a bad job. If you can get it. Reliability and connections were the essential prerequisites. Intelligence, equanimity and knowledge of the law were certainly added bonuses, but not always found in aspiring judicial candidates," he said to his then wife after a quick two glasses of champagne and jumbled nerves.

McJustice savored his domain as he called his courtroom. Mack, when he referred to himself in the third person, which was not infrequent, knew that this was a lofty landing for a law enforcement major with a C- average from San Diego State. He was a reluctant writer, and not much of a reader, but he had infinite confidence instilled in him by his Basque mother, and his tougher Basque grandmother who always advised "Vengeance like water is best served cold."

When he had nothing to say, he always pulled a wounding word from a well-stocked armory of insults. His deftness with demeaning slights at the perfect moment, catapulted him to his exalted position. His colleagues both loathed and feared him, for a one-two punch of a sharp tongue combined with a noteworthy work ethic.

Mack loved the fight. He was a trial lawyer in his prime, and he never let anybody forget this. These traits evolved from centuries of hard living in the Pyrenees, which is what he told the keepers of his legend.

His reverie ended as the jury panel, filed in. This is where he could really shine, lecturing these non-lawyer citizens. This morning, he told his new law clerk, Tom Urquidi "Pick a theme that encapsulates your theory on why your defendant is guilty. Not just facts. Themes. Not just reason. Emotion. Enthrall the jury from the first moment you step in the courtroom. Look at them directly in the eye. Rise when the jury enters and rise when they leave. Be a gentleman at all times. Display extraordinary courtesy towards the defense attorney, and of course, the presiding judge. To earn the letter of reference the law clerk was forced to gaze adoringly and listen. "The job of a prosecutor is older than the written word or the first ethical code etched in stone: the violator must be punished to keep our tribe safe. The only alternative is chaos and rule by those bestial violent few," Mack loved to repeat.

"Good Morning Ladies and gentleman. My name is McKinley L. Mack. I am the Federal Judge presiding. Seated to my right closet to you representing the United States of America is the Federal Prosecutor, Assistant United States Attorney, Miss Josephine Gemma. Next to her is the case agent, the United States Federal Agent, a Special Agent with United States Customs, whose primary mission is to examine all items coming into the United States, with special interest in that which is contraband, forbidden by law."

Jo started to rise up from her seat, but Judge Mack ordered her down with emphatic wave of his hand. Never one to miss an opportunity, Heidi sprang up before Mack could turn from the prosecutor greeting the dozens of citizens pressed into service for jury duty: "And good morning!" Heidi began with a sweet smile "Ladies and gentlemen, my name is Heidi Vandeweghe and I am the lawyer for my client," and she gently touched her client's shoulder, "Mr. Garuda Gordon Cordero, the owner of the Cordero trucking business. Judge Mack was left with "Why, thank you Miss Vandeweghe."

Judge Mack, turned back to the jury "I would like to tell you a bit about this case.

This is a criminal trial. The Defendant, Mr. Cordero, has

entered a plea of not guilty to all charges. He sits before you now an innocent man, unless and until the United States is able to meet its heavy burden of proof and prove the Defendant Guilty beyond a reasonable doubt.

This case involves the importation of controlled substances, commonly called illegal drugs, from Mexico into the United States. In a few moments, I will instruct the Assistant United States Attorney Miss Gemma to read to you the indictment. You are instructed that indictment is not evidence. Jo then read the indictment as Mack instructed.

Judge Mack continued, "I will now conduct a process called from the French voir dire.

It is a custom in our American jury system to ask the potential jurors questions. To make sure all who serve as jurors can do so fully, fairly and impartially. He then asked,

"You understand that you may be called upon to deliberate even after the trial has ended?" Mack asked, lowering his eyebrows to punctuate the solemnity of their answer.

"Does anybody have a felony conviction?" Judge Mack, with a smile and said, "I see no hands." Judge Mack talked on for over thirty minutes with a list of his standard questions.

20

LIFE ON THE INSTALLMENT PLAN

JO HUMMED TO HERSELF AS MCJUSTICE RAMBLED interminably on. "A Life sentence on the installment plan, boring," Jo whispered to Jacobo.

Agent Sanchez let his thin lips curl slightly, but he was too seasoned to talk in front of the Judge, so he wrote in big letters on her long, empty yellow pad: "You know that they say about jurors-12 people too stupid to get out of jury duty."

Jacobo had busted his tail for this case, personally subpoenaed all the witnesses, made the follow up telephone calls and organized the evidence. He never complained. He knew the score. He played his cards. He played to win. He listened to all the jail recordings, he made trash runs, and sifted through the suspect's trash. He gathered the key circumstantial evidence that would convict Garuda. Jacobo wrote back, "Rack twelve, and shut up."

Sanchez had seen this all before, about 1000 times. Typical for an experienced crook, Garuda proclaimed his innocence. Garuda owned the truck, but not the trailer where all the drugs were stored. Yeah, the defense would repeat the incantation "unknowing courier." Jacobo could not even say the words without spitting, "unknowing courier." Jacobo loved his job, because he hated what the cartels had done to his ancestral home. Teeter had asked questions about life in Mexico. Jacobo told his partner what he knew.

"It is just different. It is about family. And group gatherings, Catholic festivals, plentiful slow-cooked food, rhythmic music, lively dancing, and nurturing, loving women." Teeter listened. "Life is a struggle there for most, but the love and trust of my family made my boyhood stable, predictable and magical. We stood together through everything, "Jacobo said.

For this case, he had go to U.S. Customs HQ every day. He could not wait to get the evidence assembled for trial, and hear the jury say "guilty."

Just that morning, Jacobo had told Agent Teeter about his border town. "Even now in Tecate, Tijuana, Mexicali, in the cities of Northern Mexico that bumped up to the California border, the sprawling rundown cardboard dwellings, filled with children who begged, and went hungry. Meanwhile, the drug business boomed. If this was not contained, what would be left?" Jacobo had said to Teeter. It was an easy sell to Teeter. Jacobo's hardest opponent was apathy, in San Diego where relaxation was the number one priority.

Every Christmas Eve at family celebrations, Jacobo justified his job. "I am just trying to stop the bad guys from winning," he explained to his cousins. All that mattered was that his wife understood. Jacobo had been an Army Infantry Officer. He received high ratings for physical and moral courage on his officer evaluations. His wife Myra understood that underneath Jacobo's cologne and the swagger, was indeed a man who would brave danger to chase down the bad guy.

But this civilian work was different, Jacobo had learned.

He was not a man who had the stomach to focus on writing memos and kissing up to the bureaucrats. This behavior prevented him from acquiring the title "supervisor" to his badge and office name plate. He chose to forgo promotion and instead to focus on catching crooks, and kicking ass.

Finally, the old man in black said," Ladies, approach the bench." The attractive court reporter, Amber, scooped up her grey steno reporter machine and carted it over to a side of the high judge's bench.

In a stage whisper, Judge Mack told the lawyers: "I don't believe there are any grounds to challenge the jurors for cause, you agree?" Heidi Vandeweghe grinned from ear to ear, and squeezed a response in a soprano, "The Defense is satisfied." "Your honor," Jo, began "Your honor, further questions for juror number 8, who appears faltering in the English language but fluent in Tagalog, the major language of the Philippines."

"Denied!" Came the booming response, loud enough to startle the jurors. Without taking a breath, McJustice asked, "Preemptive strikes?" Unfazed, Jo ran through her checklist of judicial error and Judge Mack expediently denied each of Jo's objections.

McJustice had reached his goal of twelve jurors and one alternate selected for trial well before the noon lunch break. As the appointed ringmaster, Mack advised the impaneled jury, "You will now hear an opening statement by Miss Josephine Gemma, Assistant United States Attorney. "

Jo rose up quickly, and steadied herself with help from the podium. McJustice declared that she had to be within an arm's length of the podium. She decided that touching it was the safest place, like touching first base with her foot in softball, before trying to steal second.

Jo flipped the bangs out of her eyes, and earnestly, told

the Garuda's story of guilt, the man in the driver's seat. "When you review the evidence, the value, the methodical, professional nature of the packaging, you will come to the only conclusion consistent with the law and the evidence, that is that the Defendant is guilty of importing 2000 kilograms of cocaine," Jo concluded.

Garuda stared pleasantly at the muscular United States Marshall to his right in his peripheral vison. "Don't worry," Garuda wanted to tell those big men. He had no intention of going anywhere, but home.

JC had heard and seen enough. He motioned to his bulky babysitter, and the two men slipped out of the courtroom. "That's her, that's the girl who drove Carmen to the Chevelle. We got to tell El Chiño." The bigger man nodded. Together, they left Courtroom 10 to find a payphone. El Chiño would place his order now, before lunch.

21

DRESS LIKE A LADY

JUDGE MACK, GAVE THE JURORS A FIVE-MINUTE BREAK between opening statements.

When court was reassembled, Judge Mack gestured to Heidi, and she energetically accepted. "On behalf of my client, Garuda Gordon Cordero, I want to deeply thank you in advance for entering this courtroom with an open mind, so you can then render the only verdict consistent with the law and evidence and that is a verdict of not proven, not guilty. Let me explain the acts of this case, and then provide you with the road map to reach the only just decision in this case: Not Guilty."

Petite, pretty and flirty with every curve of her 33-year-old body, manicured, creamed, and scented, Heidi presented a fragrant case for the eight men and four women on the jury. They stared and stared at her smiles and gestures as did Mack. He was going to throw that puppy a bone. He liked Heidi, her deference, her unshakable good humor, her Columbia Law Degree, her penchant for flirtation and fun. She was a pleasure to see, she relieved the draining monotony of the endless Border Cases.

As soon as the last juror exited the courtroom, the judge dropped his veneer of common courtesy. "Ladies," Mac said, "I will see you both at 7:50 am. Sharp. I am instructing Ms. Littleton, my deputy clerk, to have the courtroom doors open at 7:50 a.m. All final motions and motions in limine or potential issues will be presented at that time, or shall not be raised. The court will not entertain any sidebars." Jo wrote in block letters, large enough for Jacobo to read, "McJustice has spoken."

"Is that clear Miss Gemma?" Judge Mack asked.

"Excuse me, your honor," Jo answered. Mack's thick neck whipped back from his gaze at the well-coiffed head of Heidi. He stared back at Jo. She was, and it took oh so little imagination to surmise, a h-o-m-o-s-e-x-u-a-l. She dressed so mannish. He was going to try this boring case fast.

Let the defense have a fighting chance. Tonight, as he dined with the President of the Point Loma Yacht Club, he would mention "Yes." to any opportunity to join the 9th Circus, and ascend to an even higher bench. After a few scotches, they would agree about the advantages of federal judges Mack to know the next step. Yes, a career politician would select the best judge to move his, and then appoint a judge for life. Mack knew he was in position. This pleasant path now interrupted by the cloddish AUSA.

Jo took a stab at freedom, and opened her mouth. "Your honor, we believe we cannot possibly anticipate every possible circumstance that may arise..."

"Denied," Mack said. His favorite, ubiquitous response, second only to "Bring in the jury."

McJustice continued, "Miss Gemma, this hearing is over. Time for your beauty sleep. You may consider wearing a dress, a traditional form of clothing for the female gender of homo sapiens. As you no doubt have observed, the Defense

Attorney shows her respect for these proceedings by being properly attired."

Mack rose from his opulent leather chair. Ms. Littleton trumpeted" All rise." Both the Defendant and Special Agent Jacobo Sanchez rose, as both lawyers had remained standing.

"If we had any other judge in San Diego, in the Southern District of California, we would have had at least another two months to investigate this case," Jo said to Jacobo as she packed up the case file and carefully loaded it in a large trial brief case.

Jacobo said "Wow, that is a big file case. I don't think I had a suitcase that big when I left home."

"Thanks for your sympathy, Agent Sanchez," Jo replied.

McJustice interrupted the conspiratorial whispering of the short-haired prosecutor, "Miss Gemma, tomorrow morning, with a dress." Under his breath, "Antidote to dykes, like garlic to a vampire- a dress," McJustice chuckled as he entered his spacious chambers.

When the door to McJustice's chambers was closed, Jo looked at the court clerk and the dapper, muscular U.S. Marshall staring at her. Jo now answered the empty bench "Well, I am off to buy a dress and prepare for my cross examination of the Defendant. I really can't decide what is the best use of my time."

Pulling a cigarette from a gold case and tapping the cigarette with her pink, painted nails, Heidi paused and in a genuinely sympathetic voice said, "Jo, you can swing by my office and I bet you could find a conservative skirt to borrow."

Jo grinned. She shook her head no. "Thanks for the gesture Van, but I don't think this would be right, to borrow clothes from opposing counsel, even if it's just for the day, and well, for this judge."

Heidi stared at Jo for a moment, asking her to reconsider with her look. "Thanks, really we're good. I admit it, I am a fashion felon in the eyes of Judge Mack. But I just have to say no."

"See you tomorrow, Jo," Heidi said, as she pushed open the swinging "attorney's bar" doors.

"Mrs. Littleton, can I leave my exhibits in the courtroom, at least until tomorrow. I have about ten really large exhibits."

Mrs. Littleton, who absorbed the authority and approach of Judge Mack, said simply and solidly: "No."

With the air of long-suffering forbearance, Jo turned to Jacobo Sanchez, "Can you help me carry these exhibits back to my office?"

Carmen, who had been sitting in the courtroom throughout the first day of court, stood up. "Hi Jo, don't ask me to carry anything more than my purse," Carmen said.

Agent Sanchez shrugged, and picked up the exhibits.

"You know Sanchez, it's all about the journey, not the destination. That's certainly true of these ridiculous charts."

The prosecutor and the agent stacked the ten large charts on an oblong rolling metal case basket, specifically constructed to carry the 100s of weighty in terms of poundage cases carted back and forth by the federal prosecutor to the courtroom.

"OK Gemma, forget the trial, let the jury just bring a scale, and whatever side's file weighs the most, they should win. Isn't that what they mean by scales of justice, the most evidence?" Jacobo said.

"Very funny. Is that what they taught you at Special Agent School, to slay the bad guy with your one-liners?"

Jo carried a three-ring binder, and various code books that looked as weighty as an armful of bricks. Together, they dragged their evidence back to the United States Attorney's Office.

After walking in silence for some minutes, Jo said," We have more evidence, and it weighs more, and they should give our evidence more weight. Because we are the good guys."

Carmen said, "Well it was a great first day, Jo I'll see you back tonight?"

Jo said, "Carmen, it's going to be a late night, but I will see you later."

Carmen waved goodbye to the prosecution team, and punched the elevator to the ground floor.

22

THE AUSA ALWAYS WINS

HEIDI VANDEWEGHE REMAINED IN THE QUIET COURTROOM with her client, watched silently by the United States Marshalls, and ignored completely by the court clerk Mrs. Littleton.

Heidi touched her client gently on the shoulder, and brought her rouge lips right up to his hairy, waxy ear and whispered her favorite phrase in the English language "Reasonable doubt."

Mr. Garuda Cordero smiled. She continued, in her quiet tones, her gently whispers, motherly and yet almost romantic, "no knowledge, Not Proven." Garuda Cordero nodded with serious understanding. It was their stupid system, and they were going to beat them at their own stupid game, playing their rules, with an American lawyer, accomplished with Mexican evidence and Mexican money.

Garuda Cordero inhaled Heidi's French perfume as she bade him goodbye: "Sleep well, we have a long day tomorrow."

A man of action, and chosen by the organization because he was a man of impressively few words. Garuda nodded, and held out his hands and legs to be shackled by his legs and hands and be led back to his cell, waiting for dawn, and the trial. The trial would determine if he would go back to his small town a rich hero, with a Cadillac, many children, a wife, a mistress, a boat. Or, if we spend decades in America, in the federal prison system, which was not too bad, but had no women. And was very boring, from what he could tell. With a shuffle, clink, and tug, the U.S. Marshalls were pushing Garuda out of the courtroom and into the long, fluorescent, cement hallway that led to a series of subterranean corridors underneath downtown San Diego, and led up into the Federal Metropolitan Correctional Facility where all prisoners were housed pre-trial.

Garuda did the custody shuffle in his brown plastic prisoner sandals, and his tan cover hails with twelve inch letters that read "M C C" printed on his back. Garuda smiled again to himself, his face unseen by his two-man escort. He had the loveliest lawyer, a biased judge, a flustered prosecutor, and fresh snort of cocaine purchased for him and smuggled in his jail lunch. He was in leg irons, but on this afternoon, his spirit soared.

All Heidi saw was her foul smelling, rumpled, unshaven client being led into the custody exit from the courtroom. She had a chance with this trial. A not guilty on a case this big would make her quite the commodity in town. It was hard to win at trial. Harder still to win in federal court. As a general rule, and knowing the Feds, the rules probably had a number, and a subsection a, b and c. But the general rule was that the Feds did not take case to trial unless they knew they were going to win it. In fact, it was well known among the defense bar that they would rather dismiss a case, than lose it. Even if the odds were 50-50. The Man did not bet.

The Man stacked the odds. That's why so many of the

Judges were ex-prosecutors, because the prosecutors needed the evidence and the forum stacked entirely in their favor.

If they couldn't have the home field advantage with a crooked ump, well they would forfeit the game. But Jo was a different kind of prosecutor, she was young, hungry to make a reputation, and she was a real competitor. Maybe because she was so obviously a dyke, she had something to prove, or maybe it was just in her DNA, or she got dealt just too much testosterone for a woman. Heidi liked men, she preferred men, but she had to admit, she liked flirting with Jo, and Jo definitely was not blind to her Vandeweghe blonde charm.

Heidi picked up a thin rose-colored leather folder, purchased specially in Manhattan, and pranced out of the courtroom.

Yes, if the verdict depended on the physical weight of the documents provided by the parties, it was clear the Defense was at a material disadvantage. Heidi swayed out on her high heels, exaggerating her femininity. Her rear end did not go unnoticed for the courtroom security officer who had remained behind to lock and secure the thick courtroom door to the courthouse hallway.

By this time, Special Agent Sanchez and Jo had crossed the covered elevated hallway bridge that connected the United States Attorney's Office to the Federal Court House.

"That's convenient Jo, to just walk back to your office with all this stuff."

"It would have been a whole lot more convenient if that wizened biddy Littleton would have just let us keep that stuff overnight. If it was frozen food, it would not even defrost. We will be back there before she knows it. I don't know what the big deal was."

"I think," said Sanchez "She's just following orders. They don't pay federal workers to think."

"Yeah," Jo said.

"You know Jo, the only place 'Success comes before work, is in the dictionary," Jacobo replied.

"Oh, Sanchez have you not learnt anything today?

The only place success comes before work is in the judiciary," Jo said.

"Sounds like a perfect fit for you," Special Agent Sanchez said.

Sanchez pushed the full cart of evidence, sealed plastic bags with large yellow tape prominently labeled "Evidence." He jammed the cart into a small office with a name plate outside the door that said AUSA Gemma

"Jo, it's 5:30 -let's grab a beer and a burrito," Sanchez offered.

"No," came Jo's immediate reply. "I have work to do."

Jo dropped her armload of books onto an already full wooden desk circa 1945. Agent Sanchez strode to the office doorway, one foot into the hallway.

Leaning back in, he called, "I'll see you mañana, then Josephina." Sanchez pulled down his tie, opened up the top button of his collared shirt, and removed his suit jacket, and flung it over his broad, muscular shoulder, and strolled towards the exit.

Jo stared outside, to the afternoon sky of mid-summer. A perfect San Diego evening, she could see the trees outside gliding with the breeze coming off the harbor, sailors, and tourists, enjoying the sun and warmth, and she was stuck inside with her terror. She opened the gate of her mind, so she could ramble through memories of a fun weekend, of Carmen's suggestive smile. She rubbed her eyes with her fists. There was work to be done. She took off her suit jacket, and hung it on the back of her decrepit chair.

"That Defendant is so guilty," Jo said aloud to the

impressive pile of evidence and reports gathered on his behalf, but actually to his detriment. "Why does Mack have to make a hard one out of an easy one?" Jo said again aloud, thinking that she was in an empty office space.

Jo plopped down on the old chair with an audible "squeak" and grabbed a long yellow legal notepad and wrote with her Skill craft government issued pen in a large, still girlish cursive handwriting:

Factors of Guilt
1) The Driver
2) Professional Driver
3) Value

Jo looked away from her legal pad and saw a vast body blocking the door. She saw the friendly face of Shawn Deaver casting a long shadow across the worn and stained blue industrial carpeting. His ample soft belly pushed against his tailored shirt and dark trousers, and was not lessened by his 6'4" frame.

"How's the trial going, Jo?" Deaver asked. "Shawn, if you blink, it will be over." Came the answer delivered with deliberate disinterest. "Are you kidding? Isn't this like 500 kilos of cocaine?" Deaver said. "But it is the world's most brilliant judge, McJustice and the man or should I say the Monarch-he detests me. It could be my boyish good looks, my political party, Stanford pedigree, or maybe it's just all of the above." "Listen Jo, he wants street justice, not case cites. Look at the bright side, it's another trial coin from the U.S. Attorney and with that lucre, you can cash in with the Big firms," He added. "Either way, you win. You got to take my approach, it will at least save you from a brain aneurysm. Listen, if you win the trial, well you get slaps on your back from everybody here in the office. You can tell your future civil litigation partner in L.A. what a big shot Assistant United States Attorney you were and how hard you worked to keep their blow rare and expensive."

Jo kept scribbling away at her yellow pad, but Deaver was on tirade, he was in the flow.

That's why he became a trial lawyer, so he could talk without ever being interrupted.

He continued, ignoring that he was being ignored, "But even if you lose, you win. If you lose out, you don't have to try this dog again. Double jeopardy attaches and you can shitcan all the evidence. You will never have to defend the validity of the conviction to the Ninth Circuit Court of Appeal—you know the Ninth Circus, to a bunch of geriatric leftist, law professors with a very weak grasp on reality from deciding, no the jury instructions were wrong, the statute, the law itself is wrong, they will legislate from the bench, and throw your ass right back to the place you love least, before the throne of McJustice to try the case again." When he finished this sentence, he paused for air. Thirty-five-year-old Dylan Deaver, took off his wire glasses, wiped them on his Brooks Brothers rep tie and continued: "It all boils down to a very simple rule of success Jo, try the case, be fair, and be professional. And don't worry there will be another case like this.

This is not Judgement at Nuremberg." Jo set down her pen and stared at Dylan as he emphasized his lecture by slamming his ham-sized fist into his large palm. "Jo, let me just be clear, McJustice is a lunatic, to the immense misfortune of the people of San Diego. Some President I think it was Nixon, gave this guy a lifetime appointment to the federal bench, our defense bar is rabid, and the Court of Appeals have burned out their collective minds on acid. But we have one shield, the United States Constitution. It upholds the dignity of every person who has the distinct privilege of entering our borders."

"Nice Speech, Dylan," is all Jo said. "Are you running for Congress?" Dylan shook his head no, and glanced at his large digital watch, "No, I am just being Irish." Jo smiled.

"Jo, in spite of all the garbage, the heart palpitations, the hand wringing, there is something so vital here. It tears out your guts to be an authentic courtroom prosecutor, doing the right thing for the right reasons. Taking the high road always, even when your bosses are incompetent assholes." Dylan walked up to the desk and leaned his powerful frame, placing his long arms across the desk, until he was inches from Jo's face. "Jo, get out of here while you are young, make some money because the Mexican border will still be around in five, ten, hell, fifty years if you ever decide you want to pin a badge across your chest again. Make money, and come back, and buy yourself the job of United States Attorney, and then you can make a difference." Dylan finished the lecture by throwing his heavy torso into the chipped wooden guest chair facing Jo's work desk.

Jo inhaled deeply, and playing office poker said flatly, "Thanks Dylan, but I am working the instructions for tomorrow as ordered by McKinley L. Mack. I will see you tomorrow." And she returned to writing intensely at her yellow pad. She rose to walk to her bookshelf, and pick up a small red soft cover book entitled "Pattern Jury Instructions for the Ninth Circuit." Dylan heaved himself out of the low chair, turned towards the door, and then swung around to look at Jo. "Break a leg," Dylan said, as he slammed her office door shut.

23

CONSEQUENCES OF HARD WORK

JC MADE THE PHONE CALL FROM THE PAY TELEPHONE AT THE upscale bar adjacent to Horton plaza, Jamison's it was called. He had been escorted by Jose, who as promised, was at his side at all times. JC thought at first, he would just make the call from the courthouse lobby, but Jose´ persuaded him, emphatically nodded his head "no," when he picked up the black receiver in the courthouse telephone booth. Jose´ handed him the two quarters. "Hello, yeah, we found the short-haired girl. She does not know about the product, so it's all good," JC said.

"Sit there, until you see Carmen," El Chiño said and slammed the receiver down. Idiot.

JC closed the telephone booth metal accordion door. He found Jose´ sipping beer with a twist of lime at the bar. "We stay," JC told Jose. With an expectant grin, JC caught the eye of the twenty-two-year-old cocktail waitress. She approached and hovered inches away. "Two tequilas please," JC said tenderly to the young woman.

HUNCHED over her desk in the U.S. Attorney's Office, Jo scribbled away for hours, sifting through the reports, and evidence. She wrote notes on top of her stack of papers. She wrote a story and a theme from a seemingly random crime. "Trial work is therapy, performance art, and a blood sport," Heidi told her at their first meeting.

The long summer sun dipped into the ocean and day became night. Jo looked out her window. There were no pedestrians, no cars, no staggering sailors. "Time to go home," she declared. Jo grabbed her keys, her U.S. Attorney Creds, and her Velcro surf wallet. She shut the door, and walked into a dark hallway that smelled of stale coffee, and fermented politics. Jo dashed out of her office, and made a quick escape. She zoomed home in minutes to her quiet neighborhood, and cozy home. She parked her convertible in the driveway, and tiptoed into her dark home. She threw off her clothes, not bothering to hang them. Jo face threw herself down on her double bed and immediately fell asleep. Carmen rolled over to a hold a strand of Jo's thick hair.

The blare of the electronic alarm clock split Jo's REM slumber. She was drooling into her pillow. With reluctance, she opened one eye to peak at the insistent red numbers flashing. "7:10, how do I sleep so late!" Jo jumped out of bed. Her panties were indeed in a bunch as she had but fifteen minutes to get clothed, to pull on those unfamiliar nylons, skirt, and race downtown. This was the first full day of the actual trial. She had to be in Mac's courtroom before 8:00 a.m. She was not sure what time zone actually ruled for Judge Mack but it surely wasn't Pacific Coast Standard, more like the Bermuda Triangle. If her butt wasn't planted in the ancient counsel chair by 7:45, she was toast. A fate so terrible, she focused on pulling on her clothes and jumping in her car. There was a set of three edicts applicable to every prosecutor in every situation:

1) be in court on time, 2) appropriately dressed 3) and if you say anything intelligent that would be extra credit.

She had no time to dwell on philosophy, she threw on a white blouse with a ribbon tie, a blue pin-striped skirt suit that she had added last night on credit card. Next, she grabbed the shoebox holding her brand new black pumps.

Jo took one half second, and paused in self-preservation to stare into the mirror. She looked tired, but her thin, tanned face, showed twenty-nine years of healthy living, with nary a wrinkle. She winked at those blue eyes, revealing more than a glimmer of intelligence and insouciance. She liked what she saw.

HEIDI VANDEWEGHE WALKED COIFFED, cool, and calm towards the United States Federal Courthouse. She was there early, not only to impress the judge, but also to organize her exhibits, and defense file. As she entered, she thought she heard a familiar voice. She turned to see that once in a purple moon occurrence that demands a pause. Heidi removed the designer sunglasses from her face in disbelief, and stared. "Why Josephina Gemma, you shouldn't have," Heidi quipped as she gazed at the young prosecutor decked out in a skirt suit, panty hose, and shiny black high heels, with a pink ribbon bow tie. Sweetly and softly, Heidi confided to Jo as she took up the prosecutor's arm to escort her into the courthouse "You know Josephina, you are a very attractive woman." In response, Jo blushed. She had to admit, Heidi was a shameless flirt.

The two women were waved through the court security as regulars and punched the elevators for a precarious ride up to the top floor. They entered the courtroom together. Heidi entered first, she smiled widely at the Deputy United States Marshall in a blue suit and a wide red tie. The wire of his security feed was exposed on the trail from his muscular neck to his ear. He was always ready to call in the artillery.

Heidi placed her thin notebook down on the extensive defense counsel table, a heavy oak flat top, decades old, somewhere between an antique and an albatross. The clink of metal on metal betrayed the imminent arrival of her client.

Heidi's very own Sancho Panza, the private investigator she retained on all cartel cases, entered the courtroom and dumped ten pounds of case material on the table in front of the unoccupied chair. He claimed his family name was IlDefenso. She never had that verified as she always paid him directly in cash.

"Perfecto," she chimed. He handed her a pink can of carbonation, masquerading as diet cola. Heidi responded with a broad smile. She pulled open the tab and daintily guzzled a can full of saccharine. She was going to need that, and charm to circumvent the law and evidence. Heidi knew, it could all be done with mirrors.

Across the cavernous courtroom, which could house a full basketball court, Jo teetered in her new black patent leather pumps. She too was setting up and getting organized. She had the burden of proof. She had a lot on her mind. Closest to the jury box, she sat at the table reserved for the prosecutor. By hallowed tradition, this was her table. Was it written anywhere? Not that she knew. One of the traditions of the law, or at least of the prosecution, was to defer to the might of the tradition.

A trial, like a sports competition, came down to synchronicity. And so, knowing that discretion was the better part of valor, Jo glanced at her watch, observing the law school graduation gift from her papa Detective Giacomo Gemma of Chicago's finest. Her wrist watch that allegedly had a quartz crystal, which read 7:47 while the courtroom clock said 7:59.

"Note to self" Jo said loudly, hoping her words would travel across the expanse of the courtroom to draw a chuckle from Heidi, "The courtroom clock is 12 minutes faster than the outside non-legal world." Jo wobbled closer to Heidi as she saw the corners of Heidi's mouth curl up in a grin. Jo reached the defense table and cupped the microphone at the defense table which was there to amplify the comments of counsel for the diminished hearing of the aging judge.

Just as Jo delivered this witticism, the judge's courtroom deputy clerk, Mrs. Littleton heralded the incoming judge. Mack said as he ascended "I see you are nearly punctual, Miss Gemma. You look well in a dress." Jo tried to smile. She turned and saw Carmen sitting in the front audience seat on the prosecutor's side of the courtroom. Jo smiled wider.

Mack said, "We are now on the record. Your appearances please."

Jo rose up to a standing, really a swaying position in her unfamiliar pumps and said: "Good morning, your Honor, Josephine Gemma, for the United States." Judge Mack answered, "Why Miss Gemma, and good morning to you, don't you look splendid in your finery."

Heidi rose smoothly, and sang out "Heidi Vandeweghe for my client," she said, staring with maternal tenderness at her client. Garuda was trial ready, beefy head held high, his face adorned by a large scar over his left eyebrow.

Mack nodded and intoned," As always, a pleasure to have you." Mack continued "Ladies, I am now reviewing your proposed jury instructions. The Court will announce its decision at the morning break. Be prepared Miss Gemma, to stand and deliver as soon as we have one dozen warm bodies packed in the box." Mack then barked to Amber, the court reporter, "Please note we are now off the record." That was the order from the federal district court judge, that there would be no more typing, and that what was about to be said by anyone present would not be recorded for the annals of history, but would instead slip into the forgotten mists of time.

"Ha! Mrs. Littleton," Mack savored in a hearty voice, "I am so beating Judge Flynn. I might indeed have 50 trials by the end of this year, or is it sixty, I have to get our law clerk to count them up again. A record, I tell you." Mrs. Littleton who served at the pleasure of Mack, nodded agreeably to this victorious announcement.

Jo glanced at her wrist watch and then again at the dissonant court room clock. On top of all her other distractions, Jo noted that she had to perform arithmetic in order to determine first the time, and then interpret Mack 's pronounced schedule.

"I give up," Jo said without emotion. Capitulation came fast after that. She pulled out the knob on her watch, and made the first step into the dystopia of that courtroom. "There, the clocks run fast, my watch runs fast, and Justice has been entirely deleted in the interests of expediency" Jo said. The Courtroom Clock read 8:20 a.m.

Mrs. Littleton, formally pronounced in a loud voice: "All jurors for United States versus Garuda Cordero, follow me." One by one, the twelve, and one retired Navy Chief, the alternate filed in where they sat in the jury box, unamused.

Heidi scanned them all, and smiled her best smile. These were to be the savior for her client, but for her career as well. A not guilty verdict on a drug case this big was so valuable as to be unquantifiable. Heidi viewed these citizens with hopeful eyes. The potential jurors included a wealthy widow who trial lawyers colloquially categorized a Coronado Island Blue Hairs. Represented also were retired U.S. Marines with their erect posture and salt and pepper buzz cut along with the occasional University of California San Diego undergraduate, with the telltale red eyes of a pothead. All citizen representatives of America's Finest City.

Utilizing the skills of a ventriloquist, Jo wisecracked to Jacobo. He maintained the silent decorum at the prosecution table. "We have to find a way to get a conviction from this lot," Jo said.

For her part, Heidi smiled as wide as she could, stretching the muscles of her lips, and standing immediately as the jurors walked in the courtroom. With all assembled, Mrs. Littleton again heralded the entrance of the judge.

Garuda Gordon Cordero, Jo's Defendant sat, confident, and respectable in a sober, blue suit recently purchased for him by Heidi's investigator. Cordero stood stiffly as the jury filed in, he looked each one of them straight in their eye, silently arguing his innocence. He was, like all present, a proud professional.

24

A NUMBERS GAME

THIS WAS FEDERAL COURT, AND EVERY SINGLE ONE OF THE jurors had paid a very stiff price for admission, a lifetime of taxes. "Miss Gemma, call your first witness," Mack said, and the substance of the trial began.

Jo rose, aware that the jury's only access to truth was what she would present in this trial. They would never see what Jacobo had found. In her skirt suit, and obscenely uncomfortable high heels, she was part of it, the prison industrial complex. There were few victims in federal court. The victims' place was across the street. In state court, where the ravages of violence, child neglect and drug abuse were played out daily.

"Tell the story in simple words," Jacobo advised before trial. Jo flushed, her head was pulsing, her breathing came quick, like she was doing a swim sprint. The courtroom lights penetrated, to the vision she had when she opened her job offer letter to work for the Government. It was a job that she loved and hated at the same time.

The routine interspersed with the most remarkable,

poignant and disturbing events, excavated from the filthy crevices and back alleys. She adjusted her jacket, she traversed the five feet to the podium, and placed her yellow pad, filled with her script on the stand. She cleared her voice, carefully to sanitize her Chicago accent, into the flat mumbles of San Diego.

She took a moment to look again at the list she had written out late last night. Summoning a voice from a region deep in her diaphragm, Jo loudly said: "The United States calls as its first witness, United States Customs Inspector, Sean O'Connor."

Agent Sanchez strode to the rear of the courtroom and within seconds, a rotund man with yellow eyes, yellow teeth stepped into the courtroom.

O'Connor raised his right hand and with half closed lids grunted when asked if he would tell the truth, by an impassive Mrs. Littleton. With more than a little suspicion, O'Connor said. "I do."

Gripping the sides of the podium for stability, Jo threw a soft ball to the witness, to help him steady his nerves. "Good morning, Officer O'Connor," was the opening pitch from the home team.

Jo watched him inhale, and then began in earnest: "Directing your attention to March 17, 1988, were you on duty at the primary inspection at the Tecate, California Port of Entry?"

O'Connor answered robotically, without pausing to compute, "Yes ma'am. And that is still my shift."

Jo led him through the night's events, exactly as recorded in his report from that day.

"Jo then then smiled, and looked directly at the Honorable McKinley L. Mack and said, "I have no further questions, your honor." Protocol always trumped substance in the courtroom, per the explicit direction of McJustice himself.

Before Jo had stepped away from the lectern, Heidi was standing by her side.

McJustice, absorbing the delights of Heidi in full trial regalia, smiled broadly, exposing his over-sized predatory teeth.

He nodded his head towards the vivacious defense attorney and boomed, "You may cross examine the witness."

This loud announcement from the bench, caused the front row juror in the Sea World T-Shirt to lift his head up, and wipe the spittle from the corner of his left cheek.

In her sweetest tone, Heidi beamed "Thank you," and looked gratefully up at Judge Mack. Slowly, and with unnecessary gyrations of her hips, she traversed the twelve feet from the defense counsel table to the lectern. She then paused, and smiled for a few seconds, sweetly, and demurely right at Inspector O'Connor.

"Good morning, Inspector O'Connor," she said.

"Good morning, counsel," O'Connor answered.

"Were you aware that the Southern District of California shares a 140-mile border with the Republic of Mexico," Heidi said.

Out of the gate, this was not the type of question that O'Connor was expecting.

"It sounds right," O'Connor said, a bit off balance. "So that's a yes," Heidi said flatly.

"Yes," O'Connor answered obediently.

"St. Patrick's Day was on your mind on March 17th, 1988, earlier this year, is that also right Inspector O'Connor?"

Without pause, he said, "Yes. You know that's gotta be my favorite holiday, of course."

"Of course," smiled Heidi. "You testified you were getting off and then going to have fun?"

"Yes, that was my plan," said O'Connor.

"Officer O'Connor, did you put the plan into action on Saint Patrick's Day".

"Objection," declared Jo, jumping to her feet.

McJustice also enjoyed that holiday as a time-honored custom of law enforcement. O'Connor said "Of course, I did." "So, this incident that you just testified about, it occurred over four months ago, isn't that correct?"

"About that," O'Connor said. "And you have been on duty six days a week since that time?"

"Yes, that is true, we are a small port, and we have a small staff, and it has to be manned 365, 24-7, "said O'Connor.

"So, it would be fair to say you've worked about 100 days since this incident?"

Yes, I have, Ma'am," O'Connor said proudly.

"And you have worked other seizures, narcotics. Seizures of narcotics in addition to the one you are testifying about today?" Asked Heidi.

"Sure have, Ma'am."

"More than 10?""Oh yes," said O'Connor.

"More than 40 in these last 100 days?"

"Oh, easily more than that," said O'Connor with pride.

With a tone of surprise, Heidi than asked "More than one hundred seizures, in the last one hundred days, Officer?"

"Ma'am we have at least a seizure a day, and most days, yes, I get involved," said O'Connor.

Heidi shared a coy smile with McJustice, following that answer by the Government witness. Turning back to inspector, Heidi asked "Officer O'Connor you had about a two-minute interaction with my client, Mr. Garuda Garrett Cordero."?

O'Connor answered, well I did not time it, but that sounds about right."

"And Officer O'Connor, as the primary inspector at the Tecate Port of Entry, you have had interactions with all of those 100 people, who were involved in the 100 seizures that you have participated in, true?"

"Yes," O'Connor said, nodding.

"And you are asking questions of all of those at least 100 people who came from Mexico into the United States?" Asked Heidi. "Why yes, of course," said O'Connor.

"You do not have an independent memory of this case, now do you?"

O'Connor took a moment and stared into Heidi's pretty face, her red lipstick, her sweet questioning eyes. He listened to his heart beating, before he replied, "Nope, er No."

Immediately, Heidi followed with the right hook, "In fact, you do not remember, whether your conversation with Mr. Garuda Garrett Cordero was in English or Spanish, do you?"

O'Connor shook his head. "Mr. O'Connor, is that a no?" Asked Heidi.

"No," O'Connor stated.

"You do not speak fluent Spanish, do you Officer O'Connor?" Heidi asked.

"I do speak some Spanish." "Officer, your Spanish is not fluent, is it?"

"Well, no, not fluent," O'Connor answered.

"Thank you, Officer," Heidi said with a wan smile.

"Your honor, I have no further questions." She picked up

her yellow pad and red Mont Blanc, sat down, crossed her legs, and glanced over to the prosecution table, to punctuate the termination of her cross examination.

Jo called the rest of the witnesses, who had been lined up outside the courtroom. She knew of utmost importance was the fast delivery of the witness to the stand, to keep the pace moving, moving, so McJustice, could have justice served fresh and hot, regardless of quality. As her final witness, she called Jacobo Sanchez.

Of course, Jo had saved her best witness for last. It was Special Agent Jacobo Sanchez. Although no man-lover, she glanced at him with admiration. The guy was built, and he knew how to accentuate every inch of his tall and powerful build. The experienced agent strode across the courtroom. As Jacobo Sanchez raised his right hand to take the oath of a witness, all eyes were upon him, his 6'2" frame, his three-piece suit, his U.S. Army tie pin, and erect military bearing which promised disciplined strength.

Jo eyed him, and understood she could do worse. Jacobo held his right-hand steady, believing in this oath, and all the oaths he ever swore. In his own eyes, Jacobo was a real man. He swore to tell the truth, as he fixed his dark gaze on the jury.

Jacobo and Jo together told and retold the tale of the importation of 2000 kilograms into the United States from Mexico. Heidi did not object a single time. This unnerved Jo. Jo liked Heidi, but viewed everything that a defense attorney did as somehow sinister and underhanded.

The Government rested. Heidi rose, and very slowly, she turned to the jury, and said "The Defense Rests."

Judge Mack was satisfied. "It is now 6:00 p.m. The court will recess for the night. Jurors are ordered to return at 9:00

a.m. Lawyers are ordered to return to my courtroom at 8:00 a. m. Everyone is reminded that all admonishments are still in place."

25

TOO EARLY

Wednesday July 20, 1988
7:52 a.m.
Federal Court San Diego

FOR THE ENTIRE PACIFIC STANDARD TIME ZONE, IT WAS 7:52
a.m., for the courtroom of McJustice, it was 8:02 a.m. The
prosecutor was late for his court. "Find AUSA Gemma, and
bring her in.," Judge Mack told the U.S. Marshall assigned
to his courtroom. Immediately, the U.S. deputy marshal
exited the courtroom doors, in search of the tardy
prosecutor.

The U.S. Marshal observed two young women speaking
together at the end of the hallway. He walked quickly
towards them, his well-worn wingtips slapping the linoleum
floors with a "whap, whap." Deputy Marshall Slaughter,
soon recognized AUSA Gemma as the prosecutor in the
case and a younger, Mexican woman dressed in a short tight
fighting red skirt, extremely high stiletto heels, and a sleeveless white blouse. He tried not to glance too much at the
cleavage waving at him, and instead directed his greeting to

the prosecutor. "Hey there, excuse me," Slaughter said, who had played the offensive line for the University of Alabama, "but Judge Mack sent me out here, to locate you, and you probably do not want to keep Judge Mack waiting." Jo turned away from Carmen and gave the Marshall a frosty stare. She had some good conversation going with Carmen, she was feeling it, and she still had a few minutes until she had to enter Mack's tomb.

"Really Deputy Marshall? It's 7:52 a.m. I have at least 7 minutes of great conversation with my cultural consultant Carmen Cortez."

The handsome Marshall held out his hand, and said, "Miss Cortez, a pleasure."

"Likewise," Carmen smiled exposing her teeth and biting down her Spanish, "enchanted."

Marshall Slaughter touched Jo lightly on the elbow, "Judge Mack," he said "his time reads 8:05 and he is calling the courtroom to order. Really, he will put stuff on the record with or without you."

That was it. Jo had to tear herself away from this delicious banter. She picked up her briefcase, jury instruction book, Federal Code of Criminal Procedure, and gestured with her head for Carmen to follow. With the Marshall in the lead, the three entered the courtroom.

Carmen sat in the first row of the courtroom gallery, careful to cross her legs in the tight skirt.

She did not want the jurors getting a free peak. Carmen looked up and saw Jo walking quickly to a large table closet to an empty jury box.

The old man on the high bench snarled, "Nice of you to join us, Miss Gemma. You are tardy, no doubt adding on the final bits of your rebuttal argument, correct?"

Heidi did not listen to a word McJustice had uttered. She

was transfixed by her client's fascination with the pretty young Latina who had followed Jo into the courtroom. Heidi leaned in. "That's Carmen, I have seen her at carne asadas with JC and Ramon, in Tijuana." Cordero tilted his head even closer, "Yes, Carmen Sophia Ruiz de Quintana." Cordero confided exhibiting his expertise at associating names with faces. "I never forget a name or a face. You never know when you are going to need it in this business."

"Don't say a thing, don't look at her, who knows why she is here. We'll talk later about this after this trial. Wait until we are out on the street." Heidi smiled sweetly, and turned away from her client to stare at Jo.

Jo waved genuinely. She liked Heidi as a woman, though probably not as a person. Heidi was pretty, shapely, an outrageous flirt, most of the time to men, but practical enough to flirt with Jo, if it helped her client. Heidi would try anything at least once, and seemed not confined to convention nor middle class values.

Before Mack could growl another insult at Jo, Cordero elbowed Heidi. Together, they watched JC and Contreras enter the courtroom, selecting seat a few rows directly behind Carmen. Apparently, JC in a few days' time had failed to recognize Carmen's ass. They sat there staring at the back of her head and thought nothing of it.

"This is the last time you will be late to a federal jury trial Miss Gemma, I assure you," Judge Mack stated with obvious delight. "Call the jury."

Twelve people plus one alternate, filed in and took their seats in the jury box. "Ladies and gentlemen, you have now heard all the evidence. I am going to provide instructions. I will pre-instruct. You will then hear the arguments of the lawyers. You will not be permitted to leave the courtroom during these instructions."

Judge Mack then ordered the U.S. Marshall to lock the doors of the courtroom. Everyone inside was literally forced to sit, and listen. Death or loss of consciousness was the only escape from the drone of McJustice.

Judge Mack at last said "You will now listen to the arguments of counsel. Remove these arguments. Arguments are not evidence. What the lawyers say is just their spin on it. Miss Gemma, the Assistant U.S. Attorney will go first and the defense, finished up with the prosecutor's rebuttal."

Jo rose, smiled at the jury. She picked up her yellow pad with the outline of her closing argument. She wobbled in the direction of the jury well, and when she was parallel with the podium, she paused. Her swimmer's heart was pounding. She felt the weight of two strong fists punching her insides. Jo swallowed, remembering. The hardest part of a swim meet, was diving into the cold water. She opened her mouth and plunged deep.

For closing argument, she ignored everything she was taught in the Federal Prosecutors Advocacy Training Course. Instead, she relied on her love of literature, competitor's ethic, and her survival instinct.

She took a moment, just to look at those twelve people who would decide the next many decades of this man's life. "Ladies and gentlemen," she began "the evidence is clear: the Defendant is guilty of importing cocaine into the United States." With that, Mack, poured a tall glass of water for himself from his cut crystal water pitcher. A gift from the San Diego Bar Association, where he had served as President. He was quite the task master when it came to planning official banquets, and that logistical mastery launched him up to his storied career on the Federal Bench. He hummed quietly to himself until he heard his line "Thank you for your time and attention," uttered by Gemma.

Jo sat down. She knew she would have to bring this case home with her rebuttal argument. She looked over to see Jacobo enjoying the show, confident of the conviction. "After all, the guy was caught in the driver's seat," Jacobo had shared with Teeter.

Heidi rose. She had rehearsed for Garuda Cordero, and now she gave the final performance. She walked to the podium. She then slowly walked within three feet of the jury box. She smiled, opened her arms wide and said,

"Agreement. We agree! Mr. Garuda Gordon Cordero drove into the United States from Mexico at the Tecate Port of Entry. The Government had the burden to prove beyond a reasonable doubt that Mr. Garuda Garrett Cordero had actual knowledge of cocaine.

There is nothing," and Heidi lowered her voice dramatically.

"There is nothing to show knowledge. Period. Nothing. All the Government and all their many witnesses have is value. Millions of dollars. They gave you a number, a number based upon their best guess.

Is it reasonable that the owner of the cocaine is Garuda? Millions of dollars and driving that truck?" Heidi shook her head emphatically no.

"Is it reasonable to believe that the owner of that cocaine, would put himself in the driver's seat in the riskiest part of the whole business, as you heard the government's own witnesses, the point where the drugs cross that border, and double, and triple and value, to go up ten times as that cocaine gets cut into a street use amount. Is it reasonable that they would go through the effort to build a special compartment if the driver knew there was drugs? And then leave the cocaine there to be delivered? Let's go back to the burden of proof ladies and gentlemen. We are talking about our Constitution. The hallmark of our American Freedom. The hallmark is a level playing field. That is why Mr. Garuda Garrett Cordero walked in here presumed to be innocent. The Prosecution has all of your tax dollars to investigate this case. They came here, today, one card short.

They brought in a trailer full of suspicion. But ladies and gentlemen, they have proved nothing." Heidi walked over to Garuda, and stood behind his chair. She gripped his left shoulder and he turned towards her, also turning to face the jury as well. "We are talking about our Constitution. Mr. Cordero, who you met two days ago on Monday, walked in here innocent.

The explanation is never for Mr. Cordero."

Heidi walked across the cavernous courtroom. "Ladies and Gentlemen," Heidi said, standing right behind Jo, "The explanation must come from the Assistant United States Attorney, Josephine Gemma." And Heidi pointed at the back of Jo's head, as the prosecutor's face bloomed pink. But, Heidi was not done, and McJustice was delighting in every tasty morsel of patriotism.

"It is the duty, the sober, weighty and difficult duty of the Assistant United States Attorney to prove *beyond* A reasonable doubt. We have 2000 kilos of cocaine, but not a single gram of evidence that my client Mr. Garuda Gordon Cordero ever had knowledge. You have one choice consistent with the laws and the evidence. The only just and only fair and the only right verdict and that is not proven and therefore not guilty."

Heidi sat down, and whispered in Spanish into Garuda's hairy waxy ear, smiling "Sweetie, we are going to take the Constitution for a long ride, your tribulations ends here. El Chiño will come through, right?" Heidi smiled ice, to let him know this was business."

26

2000 KILOS OF GUILT

McJustice looked at the courtroom clock. "You have fifteen minutes counsel."

Jo knew the courtroom world was form over substance with consequences that could last for decades. She rose again, this time focused on negating every punctuation mark and thought delivered by Heidi with passion and skilled artifice. Jo had learned "that anything dogmatically asserted could be taken as true" in the eyes of a juror, that was her watchword for closing argument, and she found it to be a valuable adage in living her life, and particularly for her love life.

And she was going to do everything in her power to make sure the guilty guy got convicted, and she knew there was a beautiful woman who was watching every move she made. She wanted Carmen to want her.

Jo stood and cleared her throat. She contorted her face into a pleasant bland, half smile. The clock in Courtroom Ten said 9:30 a.m. The true time was a matter of conjecture.

Jo continued walking towards the jury. She turned to squarely face them. This was her parting shot:

"The Defendant was in the Driver's Seat. With a tractor trailer full of cocaine, 2000 kilograms. The evidence has shown he was not duped. He was in the driver's seat. This was a crime that has been proven. It was a crime that was carefully, skillfully, and professionally planned. As a professional truck driver, this Defendant was an integral part of this plan. The Government in the course of this trial has met its burden beyond a reasonable doubt." Jo walked to the evidence table. There were ten bricks on the counsel Table from. The description of the Inspector Connor of how the bricks were packaged in the trailer portion of the tractor trailer rig.

There was a diagram depicting the special compartment, with dark rectangles represented behind the sketch of the false wall in the trailer. Jo picked up a brick, looked at it, showed it to the jury. She said nothing. She picked up a second brick, looked at it showed it to the jury.

McJustice didn't bother to look at the prosecutor. He was staring at his watch, waiting for the interminable fifteen minutes to elapse. And such was the life of a judge. Counting time, like a highly elevated competition time keeper. He noted the time, and stopped the game when the time had elapsed. "One, two, three," Jo finally said. She walked over, and picked up the third brick and put it down. She picked up another and said, clearly, slowly, and methodically: "Four, five, six." She held up each brick and then "seven, eight, nine and ten."

She paused. The jury looked confused.

Jo shook her head up and down in a "Yes," gesture. "These are ten reasons to vote Guilty. Guilty beyond a reasonable doubt. But there are more bricks then ten. There are 200 bricks.

That's a lot of work. Does the same boss who put all that

effort to bring all this in, to package it and then give it to somebody that has no idea?

This, ladies and gentlemen is an unreasonable explanation. Let's do some basic math. Don't worry, it won't be any more advances than what we all learned in fourth grade. She walked to a large blackboard she had placed in the center of the courtroom.

You heard the testimony of Special Agent Jacobo Sanchez, with his one dozen years as Federal Law Enforcement Agent, a designated narcotics expert, according to the Honorable McKinley L. Mack. "So, let's review this profit:

When cocaine comes into our country, it is about $20 a gram, 100 grams would represent $2,000 dollars. One gram is equal to 1,000 milligrams."

Jo paused "Are you still with me? We are near the finish line, I promise."

Jo continued: "But you heard from Special Agent Sanchez, of these 1,000 grams of cocaine sold on the streets of San Diego or LA is filled with about 250 milligrams of filler stuff, only about 750 grams are actually the real deal, the real dope. That changes the price then, the price of cocaine if you factor out the filler. Is actually $133 dollars a gram. 2000 kilos of cocaine then equal $133 times 200,000 grams, that equals over twenty-six million dollars. But this cocaine came from Mexico.

That's 26 million dollars for 100 kilos. Then multiply that times four.

You came in here to do a job. You raised your hand and swore to follow the law. Both the law and the evidence complex you to make the Defendant accountable and lead you to the only verdict compatible with both. Both the law and the evidence compel you to vote Guilty. Thank you."

Jo sat down, and poured herself a full Dixie cup full of

foul tasting water from the plastic pitcher on her prosecutors' table. Urban legend held that this very pitcher had been filled with the backed-up water system from the federal jail holding facility for inmates. This story ran that when the jail sewer system backed up, it fed into the drinking fountains located in the courthouse, which is why all the federal judges, very noticeably, had bottled water delivered weekly to their chambers.

HEIDI SQUEEZED Cordero's left arm with that happy memory. Cordero knew the deal. He whispered, "I hope you get that extra $100,000." He believed. His carotid artery pumping, Cordero stared down at his sweaty palms. Oh, he was so guilty. Not just this once, he could not even count the times he had crossed. But this was not reality. It was theater, and comedy, and a sex show. Heidi had been told by the voice in accented English, "Do not cooperate Cordero to the AUSA, and that is $100,000. You acquit, and I head back and you get an extra $100,000 in cash. In the trunk of the blue El dorado the day after the trial, parked in the valet parking lot of the Hotel Del, in Louie Vuitton Bags. "He stared at his hands. The booming voice of McJustice, caused Cordero to raise his head as the court interpreter translated the judge's words.

"MY LAW CLERKS will now escort you to the jury room. He will deliver the exhibits. You will not receive a copy of these jury instructions. If you wonder what was said you can request that we reconvene. And the court reporter will re-read this transcript. This may take hours. And further delay the process of deliberation." Agent Jacobo elbowed Jo, with his eyes he directed to look up at the bench.

Jo had been daydreaming. She held nothing but contempt for that black-robed tyrant. Who were the puppeteers anyway, who passed these laws, who really controlled that border that kept out nothing, and only raised the price of drugs.

She thought of the beach, of the surf, of the girls, of the sandpipers searching for sand crabs. Jo smiled slightly at those thoughts. Jacobo elbowed her again. "Jo," he whispered with an edge to his voice. She turned, nudged out of her daydream of surfing. Jo glanced to her left, to the defense, and saw the coiffed and composed Heidi Vandeweghe, erect and smiling a millimeter from the Defendant. She was so close physically to the corpulent man, that the two were almost cuddling. Jo nodded at the duo, and just as duplicitously commented to Jacobo under her breath, "Oh, brother." The self-serving treachery that occurred in the courtroom however, was nothing compared to that which was committed daily by her bosses in the Criminal Division of the United States Attorney's Office. Lowering his voice to the deepest and most magisterial register, Mack decreed "The jury is now excused to deliberate."

Jo, Jacobo and Heidi jumped to their feet while the Defendant remained seated after a wary stare from the menacing U.S. Marshall. Deputy Slaughter did not want Cordero going anywhere, he told him before the trial. "When the jury files out, you keep that butt in the chair, got it?" Cordero had waited so long, and he had a feeling, Jesus Christ, he had a feeling. Jesus Malverde came to him in a vision, while he was laying on his jail cot, or maybe it was just the fine cocaine he had snorted, smuggled into the

MCC. It was an ethereal and brief high just like success. So, he sat obediently, for now, and watched the rest of the court-room stand. Cordero watched the jury grab their purses, and crumpled Union Tribune Newspapers and file out of the courtroom.

Jacobo had other thoughts. "Ready for something deli-cious to eat?" He asked Jo as soon as the last juror had left the court room. The courtroom clock said 12:25 p.m., who knew what time it really was, but it was roughly lunchtime in San Diego.

"Let's grab some sushi at that cheap place up the street, Sushi Uno," Jacobo said to Jo. "Yeah, I think it's some kind of dog, but absolutely not chicken," Jo replied. Jacobo looked at her stunned.

"I'm kidding, but I can't eat anything, my stomach is knots." They looked at each other, like weary soldiers, happy to have the experience over with for now, having lived through a short, intense, memorable, well, trial.

Jacobo said, "I am done with that evidence. I hope the jury gets high really high, but not so high that they would not render a verdict." The evidence was being guarded by the U.S. Marshalls now. He could relax and enjoy lunch.

Jacobo looked to the front of the courtroom, and saw Mack tapping his gold pen on the solid mahogany of his judge's bench. It looked like he was thinking. What a concept.

"Stay close counsel," Judge Mack growled. "I want you within twenty minutes of my court room."

"Of course, your honor," Heidi agreed.

Jo tried to unclench her teeth to answer the bully in the black robe. She almost said "asshole" but managed to say "Yes, judge."

Saturated by his own brilliance, he had experienced

enough, and the judge trotted out of the courtroom. The trial was over. Another notch.

With this job for life, Judge Mack enjoyed his high station and the authority to over-rule even the President of the United States while his own indiscretions remained unchecked by a deferential legal system.

27

TIN FOIL ANSWERS

A MATCHING PAIR OF IMMACULATELY GROOMED AND BURLY U.S. Marshalls walked forward to menace and manage Heidi's client. "Let's move," they told Cordero. He complied and walked forward towards the holding cell that smelled strongly of ammonia and despair. He shuffled forward, knowing in his gut, that this time, his freedom had been won through Heidi's sweet smiles. Cordero sat chained in a small turquoise room, smaller than his bathroom in Ensanada. He blinked at the fluorescent lights, visualizing the clean blue waters of his seaside home, and the tasty corbena he would be catching so very soon, off the white sandy beaches of Baja, California.

Stupid San Diegans, they had no idea how clean and empty the beaches of his country were, and filled with fish. He knew either way, he won. He had been the good worker, the responsible follower, he kept his mouth shut, and took the case to trial, like a real man. He took the risk and trusted the lawyer they provided would work hard for his innocence and not his conviction.

He enjoyed the trial. He had seen firsthand the American justice system. This education was on the job training. He liked it when the old gringo judge yelled at the dyke prosecutor.

He enjoyed glancing at the jury. Heidi told him not to stare at them, because he was a scary looking man, so he glanced out of the corner of his eye. He would sit transfixed at the Cathedral de Nuestra Senora Guadalupe, right off of the boulevard.

He closed his eyes, and remembered his padre's face, and he molded his face to that expression. Cordero was no saint, but most of the time he was a damn good actor which is how he came to cross so many loads of drugs over for so many years without getting caught or even sent to secondary inspection at the port of entry.

What Cordero liked best about the trial was the grandeur and ceremony, so much like the Church. As he was reminiscing over the events of the trial, the steel door unceremoniously opened, and a guard handed him a plain, slightly wrinkled brown paper sack. Cordero grabbed the bag wordlessly.

Cordero opened up the bag. The cartel had advanced his bonus. He carefully removed a bologna sandwich on white bread, fruit punch, and his favorite and new acquaintance, a foil wrapped ding-dong.

Cordero was raised by a strict mother and an indulgent father. His mother never let him eat his cake first as a boy. Cordero was no boy. He leisurely unwrapped the smooth foil surrounding the ding dong pastry treat. He daintily bit in, and pulled from his mouth a bit of chocolate cupcake, and inside the cake was a tiny plastic bag. He wiped the small plastic bag on the brown paper bag and revealed a white powdery substance.

Cordero tilted his head to the fluorescent light up above

and whispered to his unseen benefactor and snorted the potent whiff of that precious Columbian elixir. With equal care, he removed appropriately enough the top sheet from the paperwork Heidi had handed him. He folded the paper in half then in half again and ripped the small square. With great care, he formed the paper into a cylinder and then into a straw. He tapped the white contents with meticulous care into his palm, and sniffed the powder up his flared nostrils. He licked his hand, and rubbed the residue into his gums. He threw the straw and small bag into the toilet and flushed.

He laid down on his wooden bench, and smiled broadly. He knew the truth. He was the winning matador, he had slain the American justice system in the grand arena. This gift was the signal that $1 million dollars had been deposited in his account. That was for his family, for keeping his mouth shut and it was independent of the verdict. He too, enjoyed his job.

JACOBO AND JO walked together to Sushi Uno, one block from the courthouse. The restaurant which served cheap and plentiful food was jammed with a lunch hour crowd of clerks and cops. When the punk-rock waiter asked for their order, Jo ordered only tea. "The jurors are going to eat. We can be back in court in ten minutes. I will pay the bill if you have to run. Please relax, you are giving me a heart attack," Jacobo said.

I'll try," Jo said as the waiter dumped their small order on the large table. Jo grabbed a piece of eel rolls while Jacobo picked up a crunchy shrimp roll.

"You have good taste," Jo said, pointing a chopstick at his selection.

"That is what the girls tell me," Jacobo responded. "How's the food," he said.

"Sweet and spicy, like you know, Carmen," Jo commented between bites. "I just really hope this is eel and not escargot," she added with genuine concern.

Buzz, buzz emanated from below the dining table. Jo flinched. Jacobo, to determine the source of the electronic vibration, slapped his own right front pocket, but his pager was silent. Buzz, buzz, buzz persisted beneath the tables. Jo choked the sushi down and retrieved the small black pager.

"Jacobo, I have to go. It is the court. Please pay the bill, I will pay you back."

Jacobo stood, and touched her hand, "Jo this one is on me, I will be there as soon as I get the check."

"I know you well, thank you Agent Sanchez." She left Sushi Uno, and squinted out into the blazing sunlight. She walked quickly in the direction of the federal court house.

She flashed her U.S. Attorney credentials at the court security officer and was admitted to the courthouse. Jo punched the elevator button and smiled weakly at the other elevator passengers. The elevator stopped, the doors pulled open, and Jo lunged forward, only to have her unfamiliar high heel fall into the crevice between the elevator floor, and the courthouse.

It was a wide crack, which separated the elevator from the floor of the building. Jo could not move her foot. This was an unfamiliar event, as unfamiliar as wearing high heels. The doors began to shut.

Jo quickly bent down, and lifted her foot out of the stuck high heel, and then pulled the shoe wedged in the gap between the elevator shaft and the floor of the courthouse. She grabbed the black, and now scuffed high heel. She hobbled forward, like a modern-day Cinderella. She grabbed the missing shoe so she could retain the pair for trial. But the level elevator was plummeting down, away from her destination. These were precious minutes, and she was imprisoned with no escape in an elevator traveling in the opposite direction. It did always seem that the more she hurried, the more some intermediate force intervened to impede her forward travel. The elevator slammed open. She had descended to the basement. She was six floors away from the verdict.

She stepped back to allow the new passengers to have a place in the small elevator, in time to see the manacled Defendant shuffle in. He was dressed in a well-tailored, conservative suit, complete with a wristwatch, and set off by shiny leg irons, and matching cuff links, that were in reality handcuffs.

"Counsellor," the United States Marshall greeted Jo. He smiled as he saw Jo in her stocking feet, carrying her high heels.

From the basement to floor five where Mack's courtroom was a long smelly journey, like taking the local train from mid-town Manhattan to New Jersey, thought Jo, who had worked in NYC one summer in law school.

Despite her mishaps, Jo had beaten McJustice.

The party could not start without her. She seriously hoped that Mack would at least wait a moment for the prosecutor and the main subject of the trial. The Defendant, Garuda, glanced right into Jo's eyes, and smiled. Jo turned away. She did not feel lucky today, she always felt a bit oppressed in Mack's courtroom.

This defendant looked giddy, and looked like he was high on cocaine. Seriously, is this level of irony even possible? Jo pondered. "Ding."

The mechanical noises of the elevator signaled that

the elevator had ascended and they had reached their destination. "Penthouse," the Marshall said. The second Marshall held the elevator door open with his large forearm, and Jo deliberately stepped over the gap in the elevator floor and the courthouse floor, still in stocking feet.

She stopped for a moment, to stoop and place her high heels on her feet, as the two Marshalls strode by with the Defendant, who craned his neck to smile broadly again at the young, not unattractive prosecutor. He would see her again on the street. He would remember that face and that name.

Jo ran ahead, she was not going to be beaten by a man in chains. She pulled open the heavy doors into the courtroom. Did this door separate truth from reality, pretense from hard facts? She could hear the clink of the Defendant's chains. She looked straight ahead, and saw a person on a raised platform, attired in a black robe, cloaked in authority. McJustice was waiting. He was not happy. He pointed silently at the wall clock, as if that meant anything, as his clock was not the correct time.

Judge Mack then nodded at Heidi. "Well Miss Gemma, I see that you elected to attend the trial. The Court thanks you for your presence." Jo noted, yup, he speaks of himself in the third person, always a sign of a tenuous grasp on reality "The jury has a question Counsel. Madam Clerk please call the case, and then read the question, "Mack ordered.

She obeyed and read: "We would like to view the tractor trailer rig. We have questions after seeing the photographs."

Judge Mack loudly cleared his throat and then said," Ladies, the jury would like to go on a field trip. Intrigued no doubt by both of your arguments and presentations, or maybe just plain confused, they want to see for themselves. Ms. Landwehr, what is your response?"

"Fine with the Defense," smiled Heidi. As usual, Heidi was all smiles, perfume, curtsies and pleasantries. Yes, she knew how to kill, and mortally wound with actions mistaken for kindness. "Rather than have the jury endure the journey out to Tecate, it is so hot, especially in July. Why not just ask our Government agents to bring the evidence- here for efficiency," Heidi said in a light and playful tone. Heidi had last seen the truck in the impound lot in a highly dismantled state.

"The Court hereby orders the Government to produce the tractor trailer rig forthwith, and by 9:00 a.m. tomorrow at the latest. The vehicle will be parked in front of the old Federal Courthouse. This way it will be a short walk, in sunlight to view the subtleties of the evidence." And McJustice, was done.

28

KNOCKOUT

Jo burst out to the hallway, she barreled directly into Jacobo, who had swung the courtroom door pulled by a courtroom spectator, a witness to the unfolding courtroom drama.

Jo looked up, wobbling on her high heels, when Jacobo grabbed her firmly by the arm, and the scooped her waist with his other arm. He held her with real concern.

Jo pulled away unnerved by her momentary vulnerability, and his closeness. She smelled his sweat and his aftershave. She felt his strength and gallantry. She did not want this man's help. Though surely, he saved her this time from another hard, painful fall.

"What's up counsellor," Jacobo asked. "While you were enjoying lunch, the jury was up to its usual hijinks, thinking up stupid questions to waste our time, and defenses that not even Heidi thought of," Jo said.

Jacobo shrugged, unimpressed.

Jo, continued, "The jury wrote a note to the judge and asked to see the tractor trailer rig."

"Are you kidding?" Jacobo said.

"Judge Mack impartial arbiter of justice, immediately ordered that we have that behemoth of a truck here by 8:30 a.m. tomorrow.

"It's in Tecate, and I'm not sure it will even move If we can't get that engine started, it will be quite the towing job."

"Listen, Jacobo, it is already 1:30 p.m. Why don't you go to Tecate now? Check out the tractor trailer rig, and see if we can get it out here by whatever means necessary. "

Jacobo raised his thumb to show he had it covered. "I'm going to gather up all the photos from the initial seizure. No doubt, there are discrepancies between what the truck looked like on the day of arrest, and now, after the truck has been torn apart to find the drug load," Jacobo repeated. "I am going to call the lot right now Jo, the impound lot, to tell them to expect me. I will get the truck and trailer here, even if I have to personally drive a tow truck. I will page you at 5pm tonight to give you a status."

"Jacobo, I will be at the office," said Jo. "I will call you when I leave, and then next when I have the whole rig, parked in front of the old Federal Courthouse. We will get it here tonight, and then guard it. They just do not pay me enough for this," Jacobo said. He thought the trial was over, and now these stupid questions.

Jo reached out, and shocked Jacobo's hand firmly. "Agent Sanchez, thanks for catching me. You are a good man. Take good care of my evidence Special Agent."

Jo picked up the yellow pad where she had placed it on the old carved courthouse bench. She walked towards the stairs. After this afternoon's adventures, she was not going near those elevators in the heels she was wearing. She wanted the exercise. She took the door labeled exit, and chose the solitude of the staircase to the crowded court-house elevator.

Alone in the narrow stairway, she kicked off her painful shoes, and trotted down with a smile, like the endurance athlete that she was. She did not want to see Heidi until tomorrow.

As she descended from the top floor to the street, she reviewed her own performance; she had given it her all. She was doing the best she could do, and usually that was good enough for a victory, for a guilty. Hopefully that would be good enough, and there she was on the ground floor, pushing open the glass turnstile door to the searing sunlight. She squinted, in the bright sun, ever reminded she was in a strange half-baked town with nothing but third-rate law schools. This created a bacteria-rich petri dish even in this dry border town.

Jo stared down the city street. Somewhere up the coast, her raucous friends were catching a wave. Was Carmen with them? Now? Surfing with any one of those predatory lesbians she surfed with? This did not comfort her racing mind, but it served as a distraction from planning her presentation.

Jo dug into a cardboard file box filled with all the evidence from the case.

She glanced out the window to see Heidi emerge from the building she owned with her husband. Yes, a structure that drugs and crime had built, a truly impressive achievement.

"Crime pays, and well" her father would never acknowledge this axiom.

Was there something more personal, more critical to this trial for her? Jo was giving it her all. Heidi seemed to be laughing, flirting and smiling into a life of maddening ease, luxury and fun at society's expense. She could not be mad at Heidi for profiting by the rules, exploiting the system that begged for exploitation. Not everybody could be an idealist.

Jo grabbed the stack of photos and shoved them in a large mailing envelope. She placed the bundle in her briefcase. She saw that it was 5:00 p.m. There were waves to catch, and still a bit of summer to enjoy in San Diego, and maybe even some fresh sushi to taste. She had missed lunch again. She needed a break, after going all day in the courtroom. Maybe a clearer head would give her that final push she needed to go for victory.

She shoved an office chair under the doorknob and closed the drapes on her ceiling to floor office window. With the practice of too many one-night stands, she ripped off her clothes just slowly enough to insure she did not shred her nylons, pop any buttons, or burst any zippers. Yet in less than 60 seconds, she was standing in her bra and panties, nearly naked Justice. She was many things to many people, but of all things, Jo strove to never be a hypocrite.

She abided strictly to the sixty second rule which provided that, once sexual activity was begun, the clothes came off as soon as possible. She peeled off more than her work clothes, you shed her prosecutors' skin, and became a civilian lesbian surfer pulling on worn jeans, flip flops and a loose-shirt. After a trial, she tired of the confrontation and arguments. She needed a job where she could get more hugs and accolades. She climbed down six floors of cement steps and out into the San Diego sunset.

"Maybe," she said to herself as she walked to her car,

"Maybe I can just be kind to people." She fumbled for her keys, those car keys in her jeans pocket, this is such a small town where who you know seems to be so much more important than what you actually do. Jo's head was buzzing as she walked from the bright sun into the dark parking garage, descending deeper in thought, and down cement floors filled with fumes.

A rough hand grabbed her, as Jo was walked down a staircase. She was held her by her throat. A husky voice laughed in accented English: "Where is she?"

"What?" answered Jo, trembling but holding it together. Pops, the detective had prepared her for this, but the big man held tight.

The attacker continued jeering "Carmen-Yes?" Jo did not respond. "Where is she?" The burly man said. JC stood silent in the shadow of the steep stairwell and nodded yes, to the much larger man. He cold cocked Jo in the face, and she fell unconscious to the parking garage floor. Nonchalantly, Contreras and his friend strolled out to the sunlight once again, and slowly slid into the backseat of the waiting black Chevrolet Suburban.

Jo sat up, disoriented. It was dark, and her head hurt. Jo blinked to clear her eyesight in the dim surroundings.

The home telephone rang. A voice shouted out from a few feet away "I'll get that!" A woman's voice shouted. Jo looked around. She was at home, in her own bed, apparently, hours having elapsed. She had no memory of getting home, of going to bed of anything. In a moment, she remembered the questions in the parking garage stairwell, and the sudden burst of pain. "How? "Why" was her only thought.

She felt the softness of her worn white satin sheets, that of late, had experienced more than a taste of nocturnal gymnastics. She identified the silhouette of her coffee mug on her rickety wooden bedside table. She glanced at her window, with the opaque curtains, and yes it looked to be very dark outside.

Rosie, round and wide, called from the hallway into Jo's bedroom. "How y'all doing, counsel?" Rosie drawled.

"I'm alive, I guess," came Jo's all too uncertain response. "Did anybody call?" Jo added.

"Are you expecting a message from the Lord?" Rosie said.

Still lying in bed, Jo plopped her head back down on the pillow. "Rosie," she whimpered.

"Jo, you need to get yourself a safe job, like gang detective or fire fighter, these desk jockey jobs are just too dicey."

Jo sat up again. Rosie walked towards her and turned on the light at the bedside table.

"Let's take a look at that head of yours," Rosie said. "They found you in the parking garage sprawled out, with a nasty, well Jo, you got quite the blow to your head. The Doctor said to watch you, and to bring you in the morning. You were conscious when I came to get you around 7 p.m. Remember?"

Jo shook her head, "No,." But Jo clearly remembered the moments right before. The rough hand, the questions about Carmen. And when she woke up, she remembered feeling in her jeans front pocket. There was a number, a local number and the name: "Jacobo."

Jo got up on one elbow- so far so good. She found a small scrap of paper written from a yellow legal pad with a number very neatly written on it. She squinted and read the name Jacobo, in clear block letters.

In her t-shirt and underwear, Jo shuffled to the rotary telephone hanging on the kitchen wall. Her head was spinning a bit, and her mouth was dry, but her athletic reserves carried her the fifty feet from her bedroom to the telephone.

Jo had the yellow sheet clenched in her left hand, and

read the numbers as her temple throbbed. She dialed the number on the paper. "Hey Sanchez, it's me."

"Duh," came the answer. "My wife is sleeping alone again tonight, thanks to some crappy AUSA who is running my ass off." "Ha, ha such a comedian," Jo responded flatly.

"Josephina," Sanchez said in his deep voice "the engine turned. Yeah, we got some help from an old grease monkey named Mike. He said he's always happy to help the Good Guys. The hundred dollars we gave him was all the incentive he needed. Anyway, we'll be driving this land ship across the desert to San Diego tonight. I just wanted to confirm that with you, McJustice's evil plan to scuttle our prosecution has once again been foiled."

"I sure appreciate your overtime work Agent Sanchez," Jo said earnestly.

"Are you being snide again?" Sanchez said.

"I guess, you can call that unrecognizable sincerity," Jo replied. "I can lose my habitual Chicago sarcasm."

Jo said nothing about the attack in the parking garage, since it was not related to the Garuda case. She told everyone she fell down the steep stairs in the parking garage. Jo had been a federal prosecutor for 3 years. She had been told the bad guys south of the border would not have the nerve to smuggle their violence north from Tijuana to San Diego. If they did, the border could be shut down. Jacobo had said, if they ever dared, "We would shut the border down. They need dollars more than we need Kahlua."

"Is that the purr of an engine I hear," Jo asked. "Teeter's behind the wheel, so I better get back before we have any more damage to the evidence," Jacobo said "I have to turn down the blaring Country Western station he's set on the AM radio."

"Sanchez, I hate to tell you at this point, there really are worse things, but what security did you get for our evidence?" "Teeter and myself are going to park the rig near the old tax building on E street and maintain security through to midnight, then two agents from my group will take over till morning, so I can look so suave for the trial," Sanchez said.

"Thanks, Sanchez," Jo said with genuine gratitude

"And no matter how much he begs, do not let that judge behind the wheel of the big rig," Sanchez added.

Jo laughed, until she cried.

"Bye," Jo said and replaced the black rotary phone to its cradle.

Jo wandered back to the bathroom and against the stark white tile of the bungalow bathroom, splashed her face with cold water from the faucet. She reached into her dark hair, and felt for the sizable but unseen bump on the side of her skull. "Good," Jo said aloud, it was a doozy but completely hidden by her thick hair. Carefully, she felt the bump right above and behind her right ear, measuring both its outlines and its tenderness. She gritted her teeth, quieting her instinctive "ouch" which she emitted as a whisper. Jo stared into the bathroom mirror at her own deep blue eyes, looking for the answer on whether she should report the attack to her boss. She had to just finish the interminable trial.

She was going to beat them, them, meaning those unnamed co-conspirators who payed Heidi's paycheck. She had no idea who there were, that's why they remained unnamed. She had a hunch they were connected to her assault. She blinked, the decision was made. She splashed more water on her tired face and turned off the tulip lights.

Jo walked back to her bedroom, and rummaged about

until she located the backpack she had managed to haul back home despite the violent interruption. She unzipped the backpack and dumped the white envelope stuffed with photos on the round crochet rug. She kneeled down next to the jumbled pile of unmarked evidence. Jo sat down beside the pile and began to squint at each photo, determining if any of this would help the jury "pull the trigger" and vote guilty as charged.

A knock on the door was followed by Carmen's quick entry into the bedroom. The slim woman stood over her. Jo looked away from the photographs and into her face. The simple adjectives were true, Carmen was young and beautiful. She was dressed for the summer evening, in a shear gauze sleeveless top, and cutoff jeans, ending an inch below her crotch. Carmen's hair fell across her bare shoulders.

"I just wanted to check in on you Jo," Carmen said flatly. Carmen stepped closer and then kneeled next to Jo, staring at the pile of photographs on the rug.

Jo turned, touched Carmen's exposed shoulder, and then pulled her close, dropping the photograph in her hand, for an open-mouthed kiss. "Business and pleasure," Carmen teased. They disrupted the photographic evidence. The chain of custody was not on Jo's mind. The earlier violence in the parking garage was soothed by Carmen.

Zing! The electric alarm sounded. Jo woke up startled. She remembered what she had spent the night forgetting, that this was hopefully the last day of trial. Coating her nerves was the sticky memory of the night with Carmen, first on the floor, then on the double bed.

In her hurry to undress, Carmen had thrown her clothes all over the photographs.

Jo smiled, as she picked up the discarded panties and bra from photographs of pallets of cocaine. Still naked, Jo got down on her hands and knees, collecting the photographs of the loaded tractor trailer rig. Jo stacked the two dozen photos together, and carefully returned them back in the envelope.

In the dark, Jo put on her trial uniform: a blue skirt suit, panty hose and high heels. She tiptoed next to the bed, where Carmen remained deep in sleep. Jo leaned over, and paused to admire her bed-mate's curves. Was this her lover? Or just a one-night, two nights, three-night stand? On impulse, she kissed Carmen's soft cheek. She uttered the words, unheard "I love you." She tightened and was relieved to see Carmen's eyes were still shut. She was intimate with Carmen's body, but had no idea about her values. Once in awhile, Jo reasoned, it was permissible to dive in head first as long as the water was not too shallow. She hoped with time, Carmen would appreciate her own depth.

Jo stepped into the narrow hallway leading into the rectangular dining room. The sun was already up, and she glanced over to the large picture window that overlooked the rear of the house. Sprinklers had transformed the back-yard into a green well-groomed garden, complete with kitchen herbs. A frantic humming bird insistently probed a honey suckle. Its wings a blur with movement, as it was drawing sustenance from what was imperceptible. She watched as this same bird succumbed to the easy pickings of the hummingbird feeder. The bird, enticed by the ruby-colored liquid, chose a belly full of sugar water, instead of a thimbleful of concentrated to goodness drawn from the flower. "Just like me and Carmen," Jo said under her breath to no one in particular.

Jo dropped the envelope filled with the selected photographs for the trial on the dining room table. She glanced at her watch, it was 6:00 a.m. She made a quick cup of coffee, and sipped her hot brew, as she carefully opened up the white business envelope and scrutinized each photo. She pointed with her finger at a photo showing the "space discrepancy." She slipped on her flip flops, grabbed her high heels and keys, and drove the five minutes downtown federal building.

29

OFFICE OBFUSCATION

July 21, 1988
Thursday
Federal Courthouse

FOR THIS DAY OF TRIAL, JO PARKED ON THE STREET, AND DID not enter the bowels of the parking garage, to be certain should could be done with the trial. She went straight to Courtroom Ten, to meet with Agent Sanchez on the bench outside Mack's courtroom, Jacobo held two Styrofoam cups of coffee. "Thanks, Jacobo," Jo said. "You know, in the 20th Century, nobody believes in the Tooth Fairy, or Santa Claus, but still the fable of the infallibility and wisdom of judges persists." Jacobo ignored Jo. They emptied their cups and entered the courtroom.

Jo glanced over at Garuda, who was chained to his chair, dapper in his pressed suit and snowy white shirt. Jo focused on stacking metal paper clips to new heights, and arranged yellow sticky notes on the counsel table by size and color. She was waiting for the show to start. Silently, Mack had glided in.

Startled by his appearance, Ms. Littleton rose to her feet and announced his presence. Reluctantly, Jo stood. Heidi was not in the courtroom.

"Miss Gemma!" Mack's bellow was further amplified by a microphone. This is totally unnecessary, noted Jo. Saliva fell from the corners of his mouth as he carefully chose his next words, as clearly the absence of the defense lawyer was yet another prosecution deficiency.

They were so close to finishing this trial. Come on, she could make this. "Yes, judge," she answered.

"Miss Gemma, I am directing you to find Miss Vandeweghe and bring her to my courtroom so that we may conclude this trial in a timely fashion."

Jo nodded "Yes." Jo slumped down next to Jacobo and through a clenched smile, whispered "Are you kidding? I have absolutely no idea where she is. They call Reagan the Teflon President, but she's gotta be the Teflon Attorney." In compliance with the judge's order, Jo and Jacobo left the courtroom.

They stood outside the courtroom in the hallway, when Jacobo heard the click-clack of high heels approaching in their direction. Around the corner came Heidi, grinning. Never one to tip her hand, Heidi scurried down the hallway ahead of both of them, carrying nothing but a narrow, maroon briefcase.

She spoke first "Hi, Josephine, were you waiting for me?" Jo was unable to parry this passive challenge. She could not imagine her fate if the tables were turned.

McJustice, who was staring at door to his courtroom, watched as Heidi, Jo and Jacobo entered. The judge turned directly to Mrs. Littleton and ordered, "Call in the jury."

Eight men and four women, and the alternate were shepherded to their jury box. "The jury is now present, madam clerk may the court be handed the note received from the foreperson at 4:50 p.m. yesterday evening," Judge Mack said.

The clerk rose slowly and handed the note up to the judge.

With a wide gesture, and a guttural cough, Mack tilted back and read:

"We the jury believe we must view the tractor-trailer rig, complete with special compartment, itself without deliberating further. Thank you, Foreman Forrester."

Mack then placed the note carefully in front of him on the judge's broad desktop. He stared directly at the jury box: "Mr. Foreman, is this your note," he asked.

"Yes, your honor, it is," said a 55-year-old barrel chested man with salt and pepper hair, cut closely to head.

Mack then motioned with his right index finger and said, "Counsel, approach. "Heidi and Jo sprung up and complied "Ladies?" Mack greeted them, "Any objection to this viewing."

"None," Jo said. Heidi could feel the heat of Mack's scrutiny on each curve of her taut body, undesirable as it was, it was definitely beneficial to her client. She walked closer to the bench, so he could stare right down, and get a more revealing view. She smiled "We're good with that, the defense fully agrees with this jury request, as we indicated via telephonic communication last night." The court reporter Amber stood by holding her stenography machine, taking this all down.

Mack shook his head and said "Fine."

Mack turned to speak to the jury once again. "My two law clerks will escort you across the street to view the special compartment, and the tractor trailer rig. You are instructed to remember all of the other admonishments, rules, warnings and guidelines I have already conveyed, I will also be providing further instructions at the end of the trial." Led by the two law clerks, the twelve jurors were escorted out of the courtroom, and into the hall, and then down on to the street, to be guided to the tractor trailer rig.

After pushing the elevator buttons, the jurors descended to the street and then quickly crossed the street where the truck was illegally parked in the red zone in front of the old courthouse. Heidi, Jacobo, and two U.S. Marshall's firmly escorting the Defendant, Jo and then the judge followed.

The jurors, one by one, took a turn in the driver's seat. The most irreverent one honked the horn, and bounced on the seat. They flipped on and off the lights, slammed the doors, kicked the tires. Jurors were helped up to the cargo portion to see the dismantled false wall. Within the hour, the trial was re-assembled and back on the fast-paced schedule set by Judge Mack.

After the viewing of the rig, the jury was escorted back to the deliberation room. With the jury in the deliberation room, Jacobo and Jo returned to her office. "Coffee?' Jacobo asked. "Oh, I'm good" came the response. "Now they need to do the right thing, and convict," Jo said.

"Jo, you did your best," Jacobo said. Her large rotary tele rang loudly.

Jo stared as Jacobo, "I've got to get this," she said. Jo picked up the telephone and said, "This is AUSA Gemma."

A soft women's voice responded, with an accented tease: "Well,' and after a pause "hello-Jo." Blankly, searching to place the voice, Jo was at a loss, "Hello?" She questioned not sure of who this could be.

"It's Carmen, I miss you Cariño." Jo felt light-headed, "How's your head, your bruise?" Carmen asked with concern.

"Oh, hi Carmen,"

"What are your plans for the rest of the day?" Carmen whispered, careful to have the inflection rise at the end of the sentence, inviting a desired tryst.

"I am chained to my office phone or pager-I'm waiting for the jury," Jo said.

"What are your plans, though?" Carmen repeated, not understanding.

"I have to be here." Carmen drummed her fingers at the pay phone while the legal lecture continued. When there was a pause, she inserted "Cariño, I think we have just enough seconds to sneak home," she giggled, and placed the heavy receiver of the black pay phone back in its metal holder.

Jo knew the jury would have to take some time. She wanted to see Carmen. It was only fifteen minutes door to door from her Hillcrest house to the courtroom. She could do that. She had never met anyone like Carmen. If not, there would be sanctions, but then again, she always had hell to pay from her boss.

She stopped thinking, and acted. As a prosecutor, she had learned the power of words. From Giacomo her Dad, she had learned the potency of action. She left a note across her desk in thick permanent marker "verdict pending" in case anyone from the office came looking for her. She shut her office door. She ran down the side stairway, avoiding the usual office crowd, to her car.

Her heart pounding, she jumped out of her car, leaving it unlocked in the driveway. She knew her garage was filled with Carmen's Chevelle. Jo did wonder why Carmen never drove that car, even after spending all that money to fix the flat. Carmen was such a pretty girl, Jo focused on ways to spend more time with her.

Jo jogged to the front door, and Carmen was on the landing, she was warm and welcoming. Jo embraced her, and in her right fist was the damned court pager. She did not love the law, but she had an animal fear of McJustice.

The bell of the noon mass from St. Michael's around the corner punctuated their afternoon of sticky connection. Jo smiled, safe in her carnal crime. This treat had been worth the risk.

Jo stroked Carmen's hair, and whispered "Carmen, I have to get back."

Carmen lifted herself up, and patted the bed, "Oh come back, whatever it is, it can wait."

Jo looked at the gorgeous woman in front of her, and paused, enjoying this one second of indecision. With genuine regret, Jo shook her head. Silently, she blew a kiss, aware that one step backwards would unravel her promising future.

As she approached the front door to her house, she turned around, and walked back to the bedroom.

"Do you want to come to court, Carmen?"

Carmen had a bad feeling about this, but it sounded fun, and interesting, and she responded with a quick "Yes, just give me a second."

True to her word, Carmen was swift in moving from complete nakedness to fully dressed. Never again in her life, would she ignore her very feminine intuition.

THEY DROVE BACK to Jo's office to wait for the verdict. As the two women passed into the federal building, a group of impeccably dressed men exited onto the street through an adjacent door. Reeking of expensive cologne and machismo, they too were awaiting the verdict, with different hopes for the outcome. They had bank rolled the defense, and they came to see, if their financial contributions yielded the same results that it did in the south.

Secure in the knowledge that they had the best defense in this case that money could buy, for this judge, the men strolled down the hall. This very same operational plan they carried out for all of the "organization's" "investments." It was the same for race horses, apartment buildings, maquiladoras, as that of an integral employee like Garuda. These same men so enjoyed opening day at Del Mar in the Winner's Circle. Today, they came again to see a win.

After such days, there would be poolside top shelf tequila, a hand-rolled Cuban cigar, and a shapely 19-year-old co-ed. All such expensive commodities included as pay offs for their high-risk enterprise.

———

TOGETHER, Jo and Carmen walked across the shiny floor to two gleaming glass doors with a large gold-embossed seal of the United States Department of Justice. The large seal of the Bald Eagle, in color, with his fierce peak outstretched and his sharp talons clenching arrows. This vigilant icon always impressed Jo. When Jo first met Heidi at this entrance, Heidi had pointed to the DOJ Seal and said, "I like your Paper Tiger."

Jo led the way back to her desk, and shut the door closed. She taped a sign to the door, "Office Meeting, privacy Please."

"Jo, I want to see the view," Carmen said as she entered and firmly shut the door behind her.

She walked up to the floor to ceiling window, and stood

facing the street view with Jo standing next to her. Carmen, in her heels, stood eye to eye with Jo. She closed the distance between them with a full mouth kiss. It lasted the length of Jo's passion. Carmen pulled away slowly, looking directly at the open button on Jo's blouse and said, "Nice view." Carmen unbuttoned remaining buttons on Jo's pressed blouse. She softly touched Jo's firm breast. Jo shuddered with delight. Suddenly, Carmen sat down in the office chair, breathing hard. She said, "What do we now?"

"You can have fun, relax, go surfing with Rosie," Jo said in a sad tone.

"I have to stay here, and wait, and wait. Prison is not just for the defendant, but also for the lawyer, and I guess," Jo paused and laughed, as she said the words "even the judge.

Standing, Carmen said "It's not a crime if no one knows." "Come again?" Jo said.

Jo stepped very close and said softly "I do know what I want. But I am not a mind reader." Jo stared directly into Carmen's eyes, and squeezed her hand. Jo pulled Carmen to her, and Carmen stepped into her arms. "It's OK, Jo, I will stay with you."

"What if the jury can't decide?" Carmen asked. Jo pivoted. Hearing no apology, Jo said, "I do not like talking about this, maybe it's superstition, but a hung jury is the worst thing for a prosecutor, I never want to case again, like throwing away the trash, or breaking up with a girl. Once I get the balls to do it, I don't want it coming back. Like a burial. Or last night's tequila. Some things just need to be final."

Carmen said nothing, not knowing what she had done to tick this woman off. She tried to just look pleasant. Jo continued "A hung jury is where all twelve jurors in a criminal case cannot reach a decision, cannot decide all together unanimously for guilt or for innocence, so it is a case that just has not been decided."

"What does that mean, I mean what then happens?" Carmen asked.

"Well in most cases, then the jurors then write a note to the judge, and say something like-

'Judge we can't agree, we can't decide.' Jo said.

"Can the judge learn anything more," Carmen said.

"That depends, which side you are on," Jo said.

"The Defense loves hung juries, because they think and often they are right that if they can stop the prosecution from getting a conviction in more than one trial this will help them."

Carmen stared, Jo continued, "Defense will try anything that delays the prosecution, costs money, makes the government jump through hoops."

"So, for not guilty-what's that?" Carmen asked. "All jurors say not guilty-all twelve. So far I have not had that in my career."

Carmen paused, and said with emphasis on the final word "You must be good."

Jo said softly, "Why don't you tell me, Miss Cortez. Am I good?" Jo walked to where Carmen was seated and bent down and touched her cheek trailing her right hand to dive deep into Carmen's cleavage. Jo pulled off Carmen's bra and blouse. "I want to go back to where we were," Jo said. She threw off her own clothes. She was careful to hook her suit and blouse on the coat rack in the corner so that they would not wrinkle. Jo was careful too with Carmen. She eased her onto the sturdy old desk and guided her shapely legs wide into "v." Jo dropped Carmen's panties and nylons onto the office rug. She knelt down and showered Carmen with gratification with her tongue. Carmen twisted in pleasure and threw her head back. Her long hair brushed the jury instructions onto the floor. "Aah," Carmen moaned. Jo moved to introduce two fingers upwards into Carmen. Both women sighed in pleasure in unison. Carmen felt a connection and affection for this American. She opened to her touch.

The door knob to the office twisted, and the door was pulled open from the outside. Before a word was emitted from either woman's lips Jacobo had entered the office, and was inches from where Jo had knelt.

At this point, Jo was seated in a swivel chair, completely naked, and Carmen was sprawled across the large wooden office desk.

"Good Afternoon, ladies," he said, showing no surprise. He turned, with a military about face, and shut the door. "I thought we could use some privacy," he added, and walked out and stood in front of the closed door.

After three minutes of hurried dressing, Jo opened the door and motioned for Jacobo to enter. Extending his right hand, "Good to see you again, Carmen," he said. He noticed that her hands hand displayed no jewelry. Clearly, she was a lady who did not commit. Matching both his sangfroid and good manners, Carmen riposted with impressive composure "Nice to see you again." She showed no embarrassment.

Carmen prayed that this Sanchez had not bothered to investigate her. This trial should be keeping him busy enough, and she did not want to make this guy overly curious.

Jacobo stepped back, wondering what in the world these two naked women were doing during jury deliberations. It didn't take a lot of imagination. Easy enough, Jo would spill details after some tequila shots at the trial victory celebration tonight. He was not surprised at all. In the Army, he had seen tension and fear lead men and women to hop from bunk to bunk.

Jacobo understood that a few days ago, Carmen was a stranger with a flat tire, and now she was butt naked in the United States Attorney's Office. She was Jo's latest squeeze, not a witness or a suspect, so he didn't give it a second thought. They had a defendant to convict.

Nonchalantly, Jacobo threw Carmen a pair of stilettos, instinctively understanding they could not belong to Jo.

"So, ladies, I have a great hotel room across the street on Broadway. I have a San Diego per diem for food and fun. They can take their time, those jurors. I feel great, but geez, my nerves are shot. I am ready for the verdict," Jacobo said.

Carmen now fully dressed, approached the door that Sanchez was blocking. "It was good to see you again, but I have to run," she waved to Jo and Jacobo opened the door to let Carmen out of the office. Jo rose "I have to escort the guest out," she said and followed Carmen down the long office hallway.

With Carmen ahead of her, Jo leaned into Carmen's back, and said softly "I'll see you tonight at home," and she squeezed her shoulder as Carmen exited out of the main office reception area into the federal office building hallway.

"Thank you for lunch, it was delicious," Carmen said and she licked her lips, with what appeared to Jo to be genuine satisfaction.

Carmen pushed the down button of the elevator. She glided out of the federal building and into the afternoon sun.

30

COLLISION

Carmen walked up Front Street towards Broadway on her way to Jo's house. As she looked straight ahead, she saw a group of men in shirtsleeves, and ties walking toward the U.S. Courthouse. The men walked fast, and the couple of yards, soon became a matter of feet. Face by face, she recognized each of the men. This recognition transformed Carmen's increasing discomfort into animal fear. Before she could even think of what her next step might be, JC dashed to her, and pulled her to him, kissing her powerfully and fully on the lips. Carmen remembered, it was just minutes earlier that she had been with Jo, and this calmed her momentarily.

This kiss was an act of both possession and aggression performed for the other men, and also a warning to Carmen. He had her. No more evasion. He would get the car within the hour, and all would be right again carne asadas, Cadillacs and fucking.

The other men in the group, stared at JC in admiration and approval. Yes, ardor with a promise of ruthless violence, was a way to keep a girl in line.

As a group they pulled the doors open and strutted into the Federal courthouse. They did not bother to remove their designer sunglasses. The cartel had purchased the best justice that money could buy. When the group of men, and Carmen arrived outside the courtroom of McKinley L. Mack, El Chiño motioned to JC and said, "Go in and talk to the clear," he instructed. "I will watch the girl," El Chiño added and grabbed Carmen's upper arm with a venomous smile.

Carmen could feel the bruise forming as his large, ringed fingers grabbed onto her upper arm. It was no loving touch.

Carmen remained passive and calm. She felt pressure and pain, but she showed no emotion, because she did not want to give that fat sadist a hard-on. She understood if she could survive this, she could win, and win big. She knew that she had mind over muscle. She submitted for the present, but of all places, this cartel, El Chiño, was powerless in this precise building.

JC emerged from the courtroom's double doors and motioned to the assembled men. They walked into the courtroom and filled the back row of seats. The deputy marshal standing near the rear door, touched his fore finger to the corner of his eye. JC followed by the rest of his comrades with almost military precision, removed and pocketed their sunglasses, in compliance with the non-verbal cue. JC had observed that decorum trumped decency in the U.S. court of law.

Mrs. Littleton, stood to start the court proceedings. "All Rise," bellowed the court clerk as Judge Mack entered.

JC, Carmen, and the entire narco group rose respectfully, without their sunglasses. Never one to miss a correction, taunt or disciplinary action, Mack noted there was one recalcitrant sunglass wearer in his courtroom.

The judge motioned to his clerk, who in turned summoned a U.S. marshal. The deputy marshal confronted the largest, fattest, and clearly most fatigued member of the El Chiño group. The marshal shook the violator from his slumber, and through pantomime, insured that these sunglasses were also removed and pocketed, however slowly.

After all, rules were rules. Mrs. Littleton, her important work done, sat quietly on the alert, at the feet of the austere and vigilant purveyor of Justice.

McJustice smiled slightly. His expression broadened as Heidi Vandeweghe entered the courtroom, as it was opened by the deputy marshal guarding the door. Jacobo Sanchez, turned at the sound of the courtroom door, and caught Heidi entering. Mack scoured the courtroom for the prosecutor-he did not see her. His stare turned stony, the lines around his deep eyes tightened.

Breathing heavily, for in fact she had been running, Jo rushed in, almost colliding with Heidi and pivoted to the right and stood behind the prosecutor's table closet to the jury box.

Jacobo put his head down to hide the fact he was laughing uncontrollably to himself.

Carmen sitting in the middle of the hulking group of men, now with JC's tight grip on her left forearm was not seen by Jo as she dashed into the courtroom to face the very apparent displeasure of the perennially irritable McJustice.

"Nice of you to join us Miss Gemma." Jo glanced at her wrist watch that showed 12:53 p.m. To the side, she saw the courtroom clock hit 1:03 p.m. "We have been waiting.

Marshalls you can now produce the defendant," the judge pronounced.

Garuda Gordon Cordero was brought into the courtroom, as he jingled and jangled his manacled legs and arms to the center of the courtroom, he lifted his head and smiled at Heidi Vandeweghe. A deputy marshal with a red-crew cut, and freckles, quickly unlocked his shackles, and handed them to a third man in a blue uniform to stow for the remainder of the trial. The red-haired marshal then took a seat directly behind Garuda. Heidi touched Garuda's shoulder and whispered very softly into his ear. As she talked, she continued to rub his back in soft circular motions. Mack stared at this process of Defendant and Defense Counsel for some moments. Abruptly, he bellowed "Madam Clerk, please call the case."

The court clerk complied with equal pomp "United States versus Garuda Gordon Cordero, day three of trial. The judge unfolded a note, and ostentatiously followed the lines on the paper with his right index finger, while mouthing words to himself. He refolded the note with some care and precision, and folded his hands together. He then cleared his throat, and with a noticeably light air, addressed a courtroom, crowded with attentive narcos, U.S. Marshalls, court staff, and of course, the attorneys and defendant.

"It seems, lady lawyers, we have a verdict. Madame clerk, please show counsel the note that the court has just received from the jury."

Heidi and Jo approached and were shown the note. Heidi nodded and smiled. Jo nodded solemnly. She had been an observant Catholic for most of her life, and she knew how to mindlessly follow the ritual, independent of her beliefs, and emotions.

"I will read the note for record: "Judge, the jury has a verdict," signed Vincent G. Foster, Foreman."

"The law clerk will now advise the jury they may enter the courtroom to proclaim the verdict, "said Judge Mack.

From a side mahogany door, twelve jurors and one alternate filed in and took their seats in two rows of six. They had been strangers on Monday, and now they had more than enough of each other, and the criminal justice system. The foreman, stared at Heidi, and then at Garuda, and he smiled.

El Chiño, who focused on small details, observed this exchange, and noted with his developed expertise, that this was indeed a good omen. He elbowed JC and whispered in soft Spanish: "This is an NG." JC nodded.

"You grab the chica and I'll take Garuda. We'll meet in Ocean Beach by 4:00 p.m." JC shook his head in agreement. Carmen heard only the murmur of El Chiño's deep voice.

Judge Mack coughed, once all jurors were seated, motionless, and silent. "Ladies and gentlemen of the jury, do you have a verdict?" he asked. The foreman stood, and said "Yes your honor, we do." The note was in turn handed the note to Judge Mack. He quickly unfolded it, and impassively read it, and then handed the form back to his clerk.

"Counsel and defendant, please stand. madam clerk, you may now read the verdict," Mack said in his deepest voice. Jo looked down at her breast, she thought her heart was about to blast out. With disappointment, she saw her body was still intact.

Heidi reached over toward the grizzled, Garuda Gordon Cordero and took his rough left hand in her right hand. She him a gentle, loving squeeze, as the court clerk inhaled, loudly.

Mrs. Littleton pulled up her rhinestone silver reading glasses, and read in a loud clear voice:

"To count one, Importation of 2,000 kilograms of cocaine, we the jury find the Defendant: not guilty."

Jo looked up at the court clock. Time stopped. Now. She was dead.

But the court clerk kept on reading, and the red hand on the courtroom electric clock was running its circuit around the numbers on the clock face.

The clerk read: "To the Indictment Importation of 2,000 of kilograms of cocaine, we the jury find the Defendant "not guilty."

Jo could not move, stunned. She stood frozen. All her hard work, for weeks, the culmination was humiliation. She flushed red, and then despite digging her nails into the palms of her clenched fists, she frowned. In her raw anger, and racing pulse, she could not see the faces of the jury. She just hated them for their stupidity, for their focus on trivialities. This was more than about Garuda, about a stat. This trial was about, the violence, and destroyed lives. This was about turning their faces on all that made life, society, civilization good and beneficial: order, peace, respect for the law.

Jo under her breath, pronounced the first word that came to mind: "Imbeciles." She turned to Jacobo, who tried to shake his head "No" But Jo said it anyway "Maybe they or somebody in their family, their son or daughter would be crime victims because of this stupid verdict." Jacobo shot back his most threatening stare.

"Don't talk," he ordered her.

"They would understand, when their child O.D.s." Jacobo stroked his lips with his left hand, a gesture for Jo, to knock off the talk.

"Ladies and gentlemen, the court would like note for the record what an unusually pleasant and attentive jury you have been through these long days of trial.

Jo's eyes filled with tears, and she tried to cough them back and force a stony look. Heidi beamed. Standing erect, her shoulders back, she tossed her head, as each of the sanctified dozen from the jury filed past the defense table to the freedom of the hallway, Heidi whispered a throaty "thank you" to each juror.

Jo rigidly pushed by the cluster of buzzing jurors, with Jacobo by her side. Jo shared her thoughts with Jacobo as they were out of earshot: "There is no point in talking with a losing jury. "Do you want me to go back and talk with the jury- to see, to hear how they let that dirt bag off?" Jacobo asked.

"No, let's just get out of here. If I talk to them, I will even get angrier. I don't want to see their faces, I just want to get out on the street."

"We'll see Garuda again-don't worry Jo- driving another load, maybe tomorrow," Jacobo said. "Great thing about this business, it's a revolving door," Jacobo said trying to lighten the mood. And the more darkly, "Don't worry, the odds are in his favor, you know, he'll do it again."

As Jo was processing Jacobo's incantations, she saw a young Mexican woman quickly escorted through a side exit door in the courthouse. In a flash, she thought it might be Carmen, but she was not so sure. The stairwells were steep, and narrow, and rarely travelled. When she wasn't burdened by trial materials, the exhibits, the heavy laws books, and anxiety, she would sometimes choose the stairs, and she would never see "a civilian" that is just a member of the public, somebody not part of the downtown legal and law enforcement crowd.

Jo and Jacobo, walked together down the steep court-house steps.

They were passed on the stairway, by an impeccably dressed and groomed, man, reeking of aftershave. Jo ignored the man, still smarting from the defeat. "Well, Heidi just made this week at least twice what I make in a year," Jo said. Jacobo twisted the knife further, adding:

"And no doubt the cartel adds a Not Guilty Bonus." "Jacobo, will you walk me back to the office?" Jo asked, "I need some back up when I tell my boss John Lucerne, the bad news."

Jacobo shook his head slowly, "You bet Jo," he said.

31

BUSINESS FIRST

IT HAD BECOME SO ROUTINE FOR JO TO OPEN THE DOORS OF power every day, and then throw the book at some poor jerk. Now the jury just threw that proverbial book out the window, and in record time.

Past the security guard, past the rows of typing workers, the ever-present crowd at the water cooler, Jo and Jacobo lumbered to the doorway marked "John Lucerne, Chief Border Crimes."

Lucerne was shouting on the phone and dropping a large chunk of ash from his unfiltered cigarette into a large red ashtray emblazoned in gold with "Tijuana, city of enchantment."

Without removing his scowl or lowering his voice, he turned his head and said seemingly to no one, "Sit down." Jacobo and Jo, did not move for a few moments. Jo entered first, and sat in chipped wooden office chair. Jacobo remained standing.

Lucerne continued to shout on the telephone. As he did so, he swiveled back and forth in a large office chair. Lucerne hung up at last and turned to present the full effect of a large jowly face topped with thick white hair, and a pompous sneer. He had spent close to 37 years as a San Diego prosecutor. He enjoyed it. It was him. He liked to see the squirming and pleading. He could bring the charges. As a supervisor, he could shit-can months and months of a subordinate's break-ass work, simply with a thumb down like a Roman Emperor. A staunch believer in past lives, he thought he resembled one of the great ones. He also relished using his width and height to make others uncomfortable. For this reason, he was a close talker. He knew how to throw his weight around.

He assembled files, and maintained index card vaults of secrets and indiscretions. He kept the box in nightstand. Reviewing it prior to bedtime, made his sleep easy. Knowledge of another's embarrassing past was useful. Some might call it extortion.

First of all, there were the defense lawyers, then there were the Ivy Leaguers, and he saved his special venomous retribution and put downs for the girls who refused to flirt with him.

He loved the DOJ. The Department of Justice. He had such a wonderfully secure job without any adult supervision and he had complete latitude to prosecute and settle cases. Dozens of years, or millions of dollars. Ultimatums were the sweet elixir that made life worth living, in the legal maxims composed by Border Crimes Chief Lucerne. This had been a busy few years for Lucerne prosecuting the border. He had been with the office for years, and things were getting busier in all areas. Illegal Alien apprehensions in the San Diego Border Patrol Area rose from 100,000 in 1973 to 250,000 by 1976. In 1986, San Diego Border Patrol Area recorded its highest number of apprehensions for illegal aliens in in its history for one year,

628,000. These big numbers meant more cases, more prosecutors and more resources for Lucerne to deal out as he chose.

Lucerne fixed his gaze at Customs Special Agent Sanchez, completely ignoring Gemma. He stuck his large and fleshy hand out with a gruff "I'm Larry Lucerne, Gemma's Supervisor."

He continued, "I think we spoke on the phone a few times, you know authorizing the additional costs on obtaining some expert witnesses, and so forth." "Right," Jacobo said, sizing the guy up for himself. "Has the jury spoken?" Lucerne asked Agent Sanchez again, still ignoring the presence of the subordinate attorney. Silence filled the room, and that was the answer.

The lack of an answer was not wasted on Lucerne, who made up with animal instinct what he lacked in intellect and industry. "Gemma, what is the verdict?" he said. Jo answered, "Not Guilty." Always quick to the put-down, Lucerne said "Well, you're going to have a late one tonight, writing your failure memorandum to the United States Attorney."

Jo did not rise to the bait. She was mad at herself. In this office, she felt like a prisoner of war but Lucerne's comedy routine was just getting started. "It's not every day a Federal Prosecutor manages to let a crook of the hook, who smuggled 2,000 kilos of cocaine. Nice job Germa," Lucerne said intentionally mispronouncing her name.

This was enough for Jo. Unsteady in her pumps, she walked to the door. Over her shoulder, she called, "I will get you that memo." Jacobo was fast to follow her out the office door.

Back in Jo's office. Jacobo broke the silence, "Do you have any tequila in one of those drawers? For the record, Jo you did a good job." Jo sat at her desk, and said nothing as she stacked the papers from the trial.

A tall, bespectacled man in a rumpled grey suit stepped into the office. "Hi Dylan, I'd like you to meet Special Agent Jacobo Sanchez," Jo said introducing the two men. "Good to meet you, wish it could be under happier circumstances, I'm Dylan Deaver, I have the office next to Jo's." Dylan coughed and placed his hand on Jo's shoulder. "Jo, this is the sign I told you to look for. It's time to write the next chapter in the Book of Jo."

"Dylan, I caught a bad break it was the dynamic duo of Heidi and McJustice." Dylan walked towards the door. "Sorry about the verdict but remember what I told you, change can only come from the top. Get out of here and go out and become a million-dollar litigator. Don't come back until you have the juice to break this broken system."

"Look, tomorrow there will be another load and we'll convict another asshole, OK?" Jacobo put on his sunglasses, and stood in the entryway to her office. He removed his tie and his suit jacket. He was ready again to get back to the street and the chase. He would try tomorrow to cut the head off the snake.

Jo closed her office door and kicked over her meticu-lously prepared trial exhibits. She walked to her floor to ceiling office window with a birds' eye view of downtown San Diego. She looked down on the tourists enjoying the delicious sun.

The scenic view did not mitigate her mood. She had failed. That not guilty was not going to pass away soon. Her stray thoughts of the day led back to what she had seen in the courthouse, right before leaving. "Carmen," she said aloud. And then again, "That was Carmen, or was it?"

Jo walked back to the large window, and then walked

back to her large desk and pulled out her set of binoculars she kept in her office drawer. Jo could transform anonymous pedestrians five floors below on the street to known personalities. This was a big, very small town, especially downtown. As a prosecutor, and a very single lesbian, she liked to keep tabs on people. Who lunched, kissed, or dated.

Through the binoculars she saw a slim woman with long hair being pulled by two men with short dark hair. She zeroed in on the lady as they walked up a street, adjacent to Heidi's office. "It's her," Jo said in disbelief. She looked back again and it was clear. Spread across her prosecutor's office was the tumbled contents of the crime, photos, legal briefs, transcripts, and federal codes. But there was something else being committed right now, not many feet as the crow flies, right in front of her. She had tried using her intellect. Now she just had to move.

Moving with the speed and coordination of a college athlete, Jo picked up the debris of her failed prosecution and threw it back in the cardboard box, a jumble.

With her back against the office door, she removed her heels and pulled on jeans, and sneakers. She ripped a yellow legal sheet and in very large letters wrote:

"GONE SURFING"

She taped the note to her computer keyboard. She grabbed her wallet government and car keys, focused on now what she really wanted, and ran down the exit.

She might never go back to that office, but she would find Carmen, now. Right now. She had just seen her. Jo walked down towards Heidi's office, on instinct.

Jo ran up the three flights of stairs to Heidi's suite. Catching her breath on the landing, Jo waived at the attractive young receptionist in the office space and dashed towards attorney's office, not pausing to ask permission.

"Hey" was the receptionist's only attempt at decorum and order.

Jo had not been in this building before, so she searched for Heidi's name on each name plate on the hallway. She paused and heard the sound of Heidi's unmistakable soprano. Jo stood before the office, when Heidi opened the door.

"Hi counselor," Jo managed.

"Madam prosecutor," Heidi piped out.

"Sorry to barge in here," Jo apologized.

"Well, you don't have a warrant, copper," Heidi laughed.

Jo stayed the course, not smiling back, quiet and intense. "Heidi, I don't have a lot of time here. After the trial were there were some men who stopped by your office, two especially hefty, well-dressed guys from south of the border, with a very pretty woman, long dark hair?"

Heidi said, "I couldn't say."

Jo put her hand on the door knob, and whispered," Heidi, this is not a case, there will not be charges against your client. This is my life, my connections. Please, I am asking you as a person, as a woman, just tell me, if you know."

Heidi paused, and put her hand on the top of Jo's hand.

"Come in Jo, close the door, and lock it," Heidi said. She stalled for a few moments, and then walked over to the coffee pot and poured a cup of coffee into a mug emblazoned in blue with Columbia Law Review. Heidi extended the dark beverage to Jo.

"Oh, you went to law school?" Jo said, instead of thank you.

"Jo, listen, I'm a defense attorney."

"Oh!" Jo replied.

"I can't tell you, of all people, about who comes and

visits me. Of course, you are curious, staring down from your office, looking at my entrance. I have a responsibility to my clients. You know Jo, attorney-client privilege, they covered that at your law school, didn't they?"

"Heidi, it's not about the case, it's personal, it's about a woman, her name is Carmen Cortez- I think, I think that's her name."

With the mention of the name, Heidi raised a plucked eye brow. "Carmen Cortez?" Heidi asked.

"That's right, Heidi. I know she came to your office. She's not a witness. She's just a human being, a beautiful woman, I am interested in her, socially, and also romantically. On a girl to girl level." Heidi did not respond. "Heidi, please, I am asking you, please tell if you know, where did she go?"

Heidi's ubiquitous smile was gone. Her eyes watered, and she bit her lip. In a quiet monotone, Heidi said,"Jo, I can't help you. You've always been square with me, been good with providing exculpatory evidence. I'm a professional, this is business, my business, and I'm a lawyer first."

The federal prosecutor rose in her running shoes, and squeezed out of the leather chair.

Jo gave voice to her inside thought, to her fear based upon all she had learned in the last few years, and the hundreds of cases she had personally touched at the United States Attorney's Office. "Heidi, I just hope, you didn't put a financial arrangement in front and before Carmen's very life."

Heidi pursed her lips, and said nothing.

Jo went to the entrance and pulled the knob, with Heidi following. Jo turned suddenly, to speak. "Heidi, as always, thank you for your professional courtesy. Please keep in mind, it is always reciprocal." And Jo, flew out the door, seething.

Heidi locked her office door and then sat at her desk.

With her Montblanc pen, she wrote her to do list for the next day. At the top of her yellow legal pad she wrote:

Contact Carmen Sophia Ruiz de Quintana aka Carmen Cortez.

JO NOW KNEW. She learned what she had tried not to even think, or guess at. What Heidi didn't say and wouldn't tell was the answer and the fulfillment of all of her initial doubt. Carmen had been to Heidi's law office. Carmen was part of the organization, the drug organization, Jo surmised.

Jo reviewed all that she had seen. The case, Garuda, the weird, intimidating posse in McJustice's courtroom sitting at the back, the rush to put the case on, and finally the acquittal. This was all connected. Jo shook her head, and said aloud: "Carmen is the linchpin." Jo wished she could talk to Jacobo about this, to stack it all up, with the elements of proof and charts, together they could make sense of it all. He was driving somewhere now, or at his kid's baseball game.

Jo did what she did when she could do nothing. She walked to her car and drove home. As she turned the key to her home, the gals were hanging out watching the daytime soap operas, eating Rosie's unsurpassed salsa and chips and swigging beer with a slice of lime. "What's the party?" Jo asked. Rosie said, "It's surfing time."

32

DANGEROUS SUSHI

Jo climbed into Rosie's van. She just wanted to feel and taste the good in San Diego, and her smiling friends. She was numbed by the Not Guilty verdict. She didn't want to think about this bad guy on the loose, his creepy cartel friends, the War on Drugs, or her venomous boss. She shut her eyes to switch scenes. To gulp down her feelings, with the sensation of the smooth, Mexican beer. She opened up the window on the freeway to feel the hope of the summer afternoon.

"Judges!" spat out Jo, somewhere between a complaint and a curse. "They are just peons with powerful friends." Rosie parked. Jo hopped out and hooted- "I will race you to the sand with a surf board. "You are so on!"

"Beat you- screamed Rosie over the roar of the waves.

Jo's reply was suffocated by the power of the roiling white cap. Soon, Jo was astride her bouncing board beyond the breakers, waiting for the big one.

The AWOL prosecutor pulled out to position herself perfectly like the adept swimmer that she was. She caught the wave in the moment as it crested in a pause of perfection and power. She had thought she could conquer justice and Carmen. And in a breath, the wave smashed the surf board and Jo onto the wet sand.

The serendipity of a perfect ride buoyed Jo's spirits. She jogged up to her board, finding the hope of triumph and absolution in the salty Pacific. She wiped the sea off her face with a towel. The not guilty verdict stung more. She smiled, feeling only the constancy of the moon as it reigned over the ocean, a consolation after McJustice. She was an adroit swimmer and this brought comfort. So, Jo swam beyond the breakers waiting for Carmen to come or maybe just another perfect wave.

"Hey. Pussy!" Jo turned to see Rosie laughing, her pink, burned face, matching her hair color of the day. Jo snapped out of her focus on the wave pattern.

"What did you say?"

"I wanted to make sure that I got your attention."

"No Matter."

"Want to hit Cuervo's in a few?"

"How about Dangerous Sushi" instead?

Jo jogged up the wet sand, and toweled off her thick short hair. It was a soul filling view, the ocean at sunset, the waves, the horizon reaching West endlessly and then there was Rosie. Whenever she saw Rosie's face, she visualized Baby Dumbo - the flying elephant of Disney fame. Rosie's sticky layer of naïveté and humor stood out. Big personality, fit Rosie. She was a woman ravenous for food and love.

"Hey Rosie," Jo said. "This afternoon's surfing adventure was exactly what I needed after...." Rosie did not hold back. "Oh, don't I know Jo. After your not guilty, the cartel goon on the loose and your tanked record as an Assistant US Attorney." Jo looked at her roommate and nodded. Rosie put her arm on Jo's shoulder. She then slapped Jo on her black wetsuit rump. "Better idea, toss me a beer and we'll get some pussy at Dangerous Sushi," Jo said.

"Hey Lady, don't be messing with my job! As a serious chef- I follow the Sandwich rule- I never get my meat or Sushi where I get my bread," Rosie said.

"I want to celebrate. They haven't fired me yet, it may be my last night as an employee- because I might be making history: A federal employee who managed to get herself fired," Jo said.

"Jo, you are a riot, but before you get yourself fired, you need to cough up this month, and next month's rent, so I can find myself a new and fully *employed* Lesbian roommate." Jo chuckled in response.

Rosie stopped smiling, and touched Jo's shoulder. "Listen Miss Lawyer, I never joke about money. Love, surfing, lesbian love- but never money, because money don't buy ya love but listen when I tell you sista girlfriend it buys me freedom." Rosie paused swept back her pink crew cut and continued:

"Like no kidding - I want $2,000 cash from you tomorrow half for this month and the other $1,000 for next month when your unemployed ass is going to ask for some special Catholic dispensation, but I say I got to live, and I am on track to buying my own restaurant and your war on drugs is not going to fry my dreams of restaurant freedom. Capisce?"

Jo nodded in agreement. "Rosie, my stomach is doing the talking tonight, the sushi and sake is on me, let's celebrate!"

Jo ran to the van, and was in street clothes, revving the anemic engine, by the time Rosie caught up.

"Let's move it chef, or should I call you jefe? I got sushi to meet and swallow!" Jo tossed Rosie a worn beach towel.

Rosie grabbed the towel, and ripped off her wet suit in the parking lot. Buck naked for a moment, she used the parking lot as her dressing room.

Rosie lifted her pink hairdo with an afro comb, threw out her arms in best Broadway style confiding to Jo: "Let's hit the town." Jo screeched to a stop. Rosie leapt in, the car pulling away with passenger door still open.

"Next stop, sushi" Jo declared, and floored the gas pedal, screeching south out of the beach parking lot and onto the Pacific Coast Highway towards succulent raw fish.

Windows open, the freeway blow dried their wet hair. Jo screeched to a halt in front of Dangerous Sushi in a faded red zone. Rosie tugged at her pink crew cut and jumped out of the hemorrhaging van. She landed on a cracked, uneven segment of sidewalk. She used her surfing skills to stabilize her heavy Doc Martens brogans as they slid her heavy torso towards the bar door.

She dug her heels back and extended her arms, and by a few inches, she missed careening smack into a slim woman blocking the entrance to Dangerous Sushi.

Rosie took a moment to check her shoelaces, looked up for a moment as she tightened the double knot. She inhaled loudly and blew out oxygen through her mouth. "Car- men?" Carmen gestured with her head at the well-groomed Mexican man who held her tightly on the upper arm.

"Ay, Rosalina," Carmen exclaimed

"No Dicks are allowed in this Bar- Señor whatever your name unless you are gay." Rosie said in a menacing way with a big smile. "Confused? Well, so am I" added Rosie, not giving JC a millisecond to respond to the lethal attack on his machismo.

JC eyed the fat dyke with disgust. In another setting, he might have slapped her hard across the face, or directly in the face with a tightened fist, like the man she so pathetically tried to ape. Instead he just laughed in ridicule and disgust, for in reality, she was beneath contempt to him.

She had no use except to serve.

JC responded wordlessly, pulling Carmen tightly to him and then tugging her away from the door. As he did this, the rest of the syndicate stepped up.

Rosie, utterly unaware of JC aside from his maleness acted fast. She waded into the roiling breakers of roaming lesbians. Rosie shouted out to a throng of beer regulars of her teammates from the Rugby "Red Tide" as were pouring pitchers of Budweiser into Frosty Mugs. Taller than a head, Rosie elbowed her way to the sticky bar top. The spike headed baby Butch bar back handed her a chilled mug. Wordlessly, a pierced and tattooed barmaid filled Rosie's mug to the top, skillfully limiting the foam. Rosie read the purple ink declaring "<u>girls</u> rule!" on the barmaid's back. These words were visible in the gap between her spaghetti-strapped tank t-shirt. "girl's rule!" Rosie softly repeated the declaration aloud, each time a bit louder. Repetition of this phrase inspired Rosie to action.

"Hey!" Let's get rid of those Dicks," Rosie sloshed her beer mug in the direction of JC. These words were pronounced with perfect balance of determination and sportiness. Like the 3-point shot or the end run, skill and risk-taking had a big upside. Fortified by beer, the ladies of the Red Tide Rugby Club rose to their feet, teammates and allies.

"Sometimes," said Rosie, "you have to wait your whole

life to taste your dreams. That's want my Mom says. You know what I say- it if smells good, why not take a taste?"

"Hey bud" Rosie greeted JC, spilling her beer foam onto JC's brown leather jacket. Why are you in this girl bar? Why don't you go somewhere where you can find women who actually like boys because this is a lesbian bar? We like girls not boys. Comprendas?"

JC turned, feeling the reassurance of his trusty Glock 19 9mm semi-automatic pistol in the interior pocket of his leather jacket. This big dyke had to be taught a lesson.

He knew he needed some back up, and he motioned with his left hand. Three hefty men stood up from a cocktail table and flanked JC. JC muttered in Spanish and Jose lunged and twisted Rosie by her wrist. Rosie crashed down from pain. As she did so, JC was soaked by her beer. JC, encouraged by the overwhelming odds, backhanded Rosie across her face, slapping a large gold ring into her jaw.

Rosie crumbled now on to the bar floor. "Call the police, call Border Patrol!" rang out from the crowd.

Rosie did not get up, nor did she smart off with any further lesbian lip service. JC tightened his own grip on Carmen. "We are going there. You understand?" JC said to Carmen through barely parted lips. The female crowd stared from a distance of a few feet at the three large men, and JC forcing Carmen towards the Dangerous Sushi Dead Fish sign gleaming in bright pink at the entrance. JC looked around, and saw the bartender making her way to the telephone and pick up the red receiver and say: "Bar fight at Dangerous Sushi: woman down and bleeding: yeah she's breathing," the bartender said in an unperturbed Southern drawl. "Yeah, we are at the corner of 8th and University right next to Yummy Donuts- ya'll should know that place they are open later than we are... Ok, can you hurry-," the bartender said loudly staring directly at JC. "It looks like that the Dudes are leaving...you bet Ma'm - I'm staying on this damn phone and not getting off, if you hear the phone go dead you'll know those bad dudes did it- please send a cruiser," the bartender gripped the telephone receiver like a choke hold on a softball bat. With her right hand cocked like a gun, she growled at JC "Cops are on their way."

JC returned the glare of the barkeep and tugged Carmen by her left wrist as he wiped the dripping beer off his clothes. JC pulled Carmen with him toward the exit, trailed by the three men who had entered with him not 15 minutes before.

Jo walked into the dim entry way to Dangerous Sushi. She smiled at the neon display sign of a bloated fish with an "X" over each eye socket and the caution "Dangerous Sushi!"

JC charged forward, maintaining his grip, on Carmen as she slammed into Jo. Jo lost balance and paused. Immediately, she observed JC's tight hand pulling Carmen away. The rugby captain in the back called for help from the rear of the bar "JO! Rosie's hurt- I think she has a fractured jaw."

Just a moment was needed, and JC made it out the door to the waiting black Suburban. Jo made her choice in the moment, and pursued Carmen.

JC pushed out the door, Jo followed five steps behind, and was staring down the sidewalk just in time to see a dark-suited man with dark glasses jumped out of a black Suburban and opened the rear car door for the departing couple. She ran closer as she saw a sinewy man release Carmen only to force her down into the back seat.

"Hey, hey Carmen are you OK, hey Carmen come out!" Jo called. Jo dashed to the Suburban, but JC hopped in the car and slammed the door.

The driver skidded out from the curb, flooring the gas pedal, as Jo stepped back, focusing on the make, model and year of the car. She grabbed a pen from her pants pocket and wrote the three final letters on her hand WXN.

"'86 Black Suburban."

Jo stood silently on the busy sidewalk, and stared Carmen was swallowed into the tide of Hillcrest traffic.

Jo hustled back into inside Dangerous Sushi. There she saw Rosie on the floor, holding a bag of ice against a swelling jaw. Jo came up, and put a palm softly on Rosie's broad shoulder. "Hey- I am here for you lady." Rosie just nodded. "How's that jaw?" Rosie held up her fist and made a thumbs down. "OK, let's get you to the ER." The Veronica, which was how the Rugby Red Tide Captain demanded to be addressed, stepped forward. Red-headed, freckled, and bespectacled Veronica said, "Rosie, me and the team are going to take you to the ER now to get that jaw of yours looked at. That narco dude slammed you bad."

"Did you get the plates of the thugs that hit Rosie?" Veronica asked.

Veronica tugged at Jo's form-fitting knit black shirt. "Jo, you didn't see this. I did. Those guys who hurt Rosie, they are the real deal. I think they are Mexican, and I am pretty sure I saw guns underneath their leather jackets." Jo nodded. Veronica continued, "Look Jo, we are taking Rosie to get her jaw wired or whatever - I have seen worst things in Rugby- but you take those plates and your connections. You have to find out where those guys took that fine-looking woman."

Veronica and two other ladies eased Rosie up to a standing position. "Rosie, the team is taking you to the hospital," Jo told her. "Did you see anything with Carmen tonight?" Jo asked. Through her tears, Rosie mumbled.

"They dragged her I recognized her." Rosie paused to grab her left jaw and nodded her head, "Then, boom, right in the face."

Veronica and the rugby team escorted Rosie to a team-mate's truck. Rosie hid her face in the bar-towel wrapped over ice and cried.

33

OUT OF ORDER

THE EVENTS OF THE DAY SWIRLED THROUGH JO'S MIND. THIS loss was hitting her hard. She had grown accustomed to the callousness of the prosecutor who views crime, tragedy and calamity as career opportunities- not traumatic, life-changing events for the victims. Sure, her Dad was a cop, but as a teenager in the 1970s, it was the strategy, the competition that pulled her. Not the hand holding, not the hugs, not even the thank you notes from families. It was winning, beating the dude and watching him wither. As a girl with short hair and glasses, she liked to beat the crap out of bad guys with words, preparation and persistence. Today, those words had not been enough.

Jo asked the bartender "So, you got a phone, I need to use your phone." The bartender gestured with her hand. "You can't use our phone. I am waiting for the cops." She smiled suggestively, sizing up the tanned athleticism of Jo, set out with such style by her tight-fitting jeans. "They have a pay phone by Yummy donuts, if you need one," said the bartender. Jo ran out the door to get help.

Jo found the promised pay phone, and found loose

change in her pocket. She pulled out two quarters and a torn bit of paper with the words "Jacobo "She read the number from the yellow legal paper in the light outside the 24-hour donut shop.

"Jacobo" she announced definitively, as she pushed the buttons on the pay phone after hearing her two quarters register, and the chime of the dial tone. She bit her lip in annoyance as she heard the unmistakable beep of the Federal Pager Service. She peered at the pay phone and quickly punched the numbers, deliberately repeating them aloud to insure accuracy. She pressed the pressed the number sign to send the page. She looked at her watch and hovered near the phone. She waited. She needed his muscle.

Jo looked at her watch again two minutes! Would Jacobo return a call to an unknown number? Jo watched the pre-weekend party scene from her sidewalk stance. Drunken gay boys staggered past. She stared at them fiercely, protecting the sanctity of what she now considered to be her pay phone. A woman dressed in a knit dress slowed down to gaze at the donuts visible through the window. She inhaled, "Ah, smells good. Ever have one of these donuts?" the woman asked Jo. Jo took a beat and glanced at her, did she know this lady?

"Amber?" Jo tentatively stated. "Amber Larsen?" Jo asked again. The woman in red flinched. Encouraged by this obvious recognition, Jo continued "you're the new court reporter for McJust-, Jo snapped her fingers, I mean Judge Mack- "at first I didn't recognize you with your hair down and without your glasses"

"I get that a lot," Amber said, tossing her long honey-blonde hair. "Well, I know you are so not celebrating," Amber added directly with a faint smile.

"Ya think?" was Jo's playful response. "You got a thing for donuts?"

Amber rejoined, "Ms. Gemma, I think I should turn that question on you as you are the person who is loitering on the premises of a Donut-ery."

"I'm waiting for a phone call and fighting crime- see that's my day job and my night job."

"Josephine Gemma," the court reporter flatly announced- "let me buy you a donut.

"Until, I get that call, I am all yours." Jo said as she held the heavy glass door open for Amber.

"So, I never knew you were also a Thespian," Jo said, waiting for a reaction.

Jo stood close to Amber as she caught the eye of the thin middle-aged proprietor. "I'll have the pink with rainbow sprinkles, and Madam Prosecutor?"

Jo paused and chose -"That big, fat, oozing apple fritter, and a cup of Jo." Amber chuckled and paid for the bounty.

The two women sat down on a crumb-strewn table together. Jo chivalrously swept the assorted crumbs off the table and onto a napkin, which she then tossed into a waste bin.

"What a day," Jo declared. "Was it?" Amber answered.

"Well, you do remember that verdict. I am not feeling terrific."

"Nothing like a donut to cheer you up," Amber said. "And yes, I am very much a Thespian."

"A donut, correction, the right donut is the answer to the seeming futility of our efforts." Amber held out her hand in the universal symbol of the traffic cop for STOP. As a court reporter, she had heard enough of long winded young lawyers.

"I think you are reacting to the trial, the Not Guilty."

"Oh Amber, that hurt," Jo said. "Maybe if I had a fair judge, they would have pulled the trigger."

Jo took a large bite of apple fritter, and of course, the payphone rang. Choking on fried dough and a canned apple slice, Jo sprinted to the phone.

"Hello?" She shouted into the phone.

"Jo?" came Jacobo's pleasant tones. "Thank God it's you!" Jo said with real appreciation.

"How quickly can you meet at Yum-Yum donuts in Hillcrest?" She asked.

"About twenty minutes, "he replied.

"I'll be here Jacobo, this is truly an emergency." "In the meantime, can you run these plates, this model and make Suburban?" And Jo gave Jacobo what she knew about the black Suburban.

Jo went back inside, "The Calvary is on it is way," Jo explained.

"In the meantime, then," Amber said drolly, let's enjoy our donuts. And share our Thespian interests."

34

SUBURBAN CRIMES

JC SMILED IN THE BACK SEAT WITH CARMEN. IT WAS ALL GOING to be good, He had Carmen. Carmen had the Chevelle, and soon, El Chiño would have his Cocaine. And then, he would sleep with Carmen in Coronado, party on the beach, only A few things unexpected things had happened. But now, everything was good.

He squeezed Carmen's hand. She did not respond. She had the key to the Chevelle. He had his own key. But they needed the car. She gave the driver the directions, they were so close anyway.

JC touched Carmen's cheek. She pulled away. Annoyed, he grabbed her breast hard, and twisted.

"Oh Carmen, you are mine," he said for all to hear in the car. "Where is my gold medallion, chica? I don't see it on your neck," JC said.

Coolly, Carmen answered, "I left the Jesus Malverde medallion with the cocaine for his protection and luck."

Carmen gave directions to the Chevelle, in the peaceful neighborhood. "Park here, it's this house, the dark one, with the entry light." Carmen surmised correctly that no one was home, as Rosie was at the ER with a broken face, and Jo was on a mad goose-chase to find this black Suburban. Carmen hoped she would soon be rescued from these brutal men.

JC jumped out of the car as soon as the Suburban came to a stop in Jo's driveway. He eyed the padlock on the manual garage door. "It's not locked, just pull it off," Carmen suggested.

JC saw that she was right, and he swung up the old creaky single car garage door.

It was dark, and he walked to the wall and flipped on the fluorescent light.

She was beautiful and safe, thank God. He loved that incredible '66 Chevelle. She was there, he knew it, she had been waiting for him, sleek, clean and perfect. As JC stroked the car, he ordered, "Hold the girl."

JC pulled his key from his pocket, and turned the ignition. For the first time in a week, his asthma did not trouble him. JC took a deep breath of relief.

"Leave her here," El Chiño ordered. Carmen said nothing. Men, so arrogant, so sure they knew it all. JC gunned the powerful V-8. Finally, he was inside her. Carmen stepped aside.

The Suburban backed out of the driveway, and El Chiño slid into the passenger side of the Chevelle. El Chiño withdrew his Colt Combat Commander and undid the safety with his thumb.

"Follow the Suburban," he said. JC obeyed.

Carmen sat on the stoop and watched the two cars drive out of the cul de sac, and get lost into the foggy night. "Good luck, Cariño," Carmen said to the departing Chevelle, not clarifying if she meant the car or the lover.

The Suburban drove east for two miles, out of the quiet neighborhood, to the outskirts of the Marine Corps

Training Center. Immediately outside the entrance to the Base, stood a series of train trestles. The railroad bridges hid much, and were host to hobos and homicides. The Suburban parked in the dark shadow of a large railroad train overpass. El Chiño, motioned for JC to get out of the Chevelle.

"Friend, it is time to deliver. Pop the trunk and we'll confirm delivery," El Chiño said.

JC swaggered to the rear of the Chevelle, placed the trunk key in the lock, and expertly revealed his treasure. At last, he could put these annoying days behind him. With business taken care of, he could turn to his attention to his many pleasures. He triumphantly ripped back the gold trunk upholstery expecting the tightly packed white bricks. He pulled up the felt with a stiff jerk, and saw a vacant chamber. His jaw went slack. This could not be. He ripped open the entire trunk area, and it was completely empty.

El Chiño, despite his size, sprang out of the Chevelle. He slammed JC into the Chevelle side panel, denting the car, and causing blood to pour from JC's newly disfigured cheek. Grabbing JC's shirt collar, El Chiño simply said: "Where is it?"

"A simple question, where is it?" El Chiño restated.

Bleeding, and shaking, JC, for the first time in his life, told the truth. "Jefe, I don't know." JC held his breath in fear. Today he would be a man. He did not breathe a word about Carmen. He had no idea what happened to the cocaine. It might be with stupid sunburned gringo at the Tecate gas station. He would be the sacrificial lamb. JC bit his lip. The delicious sensation of grabbing Carmen's breast flashed across his mind. Surely his uncle could buy just a few hours' time to clear up this confusion.

El Chiño smiled. JC smiled. JC lifted his hands up

exposing his soft palms. All was good. He broadened his smile. El Chiño took out his shiny Colt Commander and shot the trembling man through the stomach.

JC screamed in agony and horror. In this desolate place, the screams did not procure a helping hand. JC knew all too well what would come next. This knowledge was a greater torment than the pain that radiated throughout his bleeding body.

El Chiño kicked JC in the stomach, and the fallen man whimpered and sobbed. More of JC's blood marked the parking spot. "Maricon!" El Chiño spat down.

"Throw him in the Chevelle trunk, "El Chiño grunted. They dumped the body in the faultless trunk. JC's muffled cries continued.

Jose' jumped in the driver's seat, gunned the V-8 engine, and blasted the radio. He enjoyed driving the lovingly restored '66 Chevelle, even for such a short ride. JC did not lie; this car drove like a dream. The Suburban followed close behind.

The two cars were across la linea in fifteen minutes. Five minutes later, they were parked in Tijuana Auto Repair. Both the body and the car were expertly processed by the same chop shop.

35

BETTER THAN DONUTS

"WE MEET AGAIN," JACOBO ANNOUNCED HIS ARRIVAL AS obviously as possible. He figured, it wouldn't be the last time he interrupted Jo on a date. Jacobo used police privilege to park in the red zone in front of the donut shop.

"Do I have time for a donut?" He asked half in earnest. "Not tonight, Jacobo," Jo said. Amber and Jacobo nodded recognition at each other. "No luck Jo," Jacobo said to Jo's questioning eyes. "Your partial plate info was not enough to get a match," he said.

"How about I drive you home?"

Jo said her good bye to Amber, and climbed into Jacobo's truck.

"Where to ma'am?" Jacobo asked.

"You can't find that Suburban?" Jo countered.

Jacobo shook his head "We can do a lot, but telepathy, and magic have not yet been mastered by the United States Customs service," Jacobo said. "Yet."

"I wish we could find her, to maybe we could put a look out for Carmen Cortez." Jo continued.

Jacobo, kept his left hand on the big steering wheel, and

pounded his big right fist on the dash. This made an impressive thud.

"Jo, you don't want to do that. She's gone, probably in Mexico by now. Regardless of the verdict, you are a federal prosecutor, this light-hearted romance you had with her, this could mean ten, twenty years in prison for some creative conspiracy charge-I'm not talking about Carmen. I am talking about AUSA Gemma, Josephine Gemma. My mama has a saying, "Sleep with pigs, and you are going to get dirty. She is a beautiful woman, and fun, I don't doubt that Jo. But you have to stay away. Have another donut, another night with Amber and drown your heartache in deep fried foods. It's a lot safer, than trafficking in cocaine. You know the score."

Jo clenched and unclenched her fists. She said nothing.

"Heidi can flirt with estas personnas but not you, not me, not our team. It's about integrity. Not easy to describe, but like attraction, and character, you know it when you see it," Jacobo said.

"Make a left here," Jo said.

"You've got your Detective Papa. You need to call him to talk about this. But he is in Chicago. It is up to me to drive you home. It's been quite the day. I have been up for about twenty hours, and I think you have been up too and it might be a good idea to sleep. Sleep Jo, and do not do any more stupid things. Believe me, she's in some mansion in TJ now, sleeping with her boyfriend on satin sheets." Jo stared at Jacobo. She sat silent.

"If you remember one thing from this whole flat tire, stranded damsel, escapade, remember the distinction between nice and good. Remember also that choices have consequences."

Jo gave directions to her home. Jacobo pulled over to the

curb. Jo hopped out, shivering in the mist of the fog of the coastal night. "Jo, promise me, you'll just go to sleep." "Thank you Jacobo, thank you for everything, go back to your family." "Promise me, you will just go to sleep," Jacobo cautioned out of his truck window. He then drove out of the cul-de-sac, and back to his wife and kids in Chula Vista.

Jo swung open the waist-high gate from the sidewalk to her entry walkway. She closed the gate and started up the path. She looked up, tired, wrung out, and she looked up at the front door and fished for her front door key. It was time to go to bed. She did not know if she was going back to her office tomorrow, or ever.

To the right, in a dark section of her front porch, she saw a silhouette of a person dozing. Jo approached with careful steps, unsure.

"Jo, you do take your time, don't you," a woman's voice said.

36

THE FRONT PORCH

CARMEN SPRUNG TO HER FEET AND HUGGED JO. SHE WAS GLAD to see her.

She needed a ride on the Surf Liner. She remembered, it left at midnight.

If she got Jo, to move they could just make it. She needed to be out of here. She knew she would never see JC again. At least not in one piece.

"Sh" Carmen said, as Jo opened her mouth to speak.

Softly, Carmen placed a finger over Jo's lips. She kissed Jo, hard, thrusting her tongue in, and grinding hip to hip. The prosecutor submitted to delight, sensations erasing Jacobo's lecture in a millisecond. Jo was too eager, always, with any woman she met in a bar, to throw off her clothes and jump into bed. It was a thrill to meet a girl, a woman, and then see her naked. Jacobo had warned her. Her sexual curiosity and hunger for Carmen put more than just her job at risk. Carmen held Jo by her Achilles heel, unchecked lust.

Jo started for the front door. She turned the key, opened the door, and flipped on a light. She turned back and was bathed in Carmen's beauty. Jo walked towards Carmen, not thinking just giving into feeling. She pulled Carmen to her. She was drawn to Carmen's skin, her smell, her unavailability. "We have now," Jo said.

The two women kissed. Jo tugged Carmen inside. Carmen kicked the door closed with her heel. "I missed you Carmen," Jo confessed. Carmen crumbled into the large easy chair in the entry. Jo straddled Carmen in the chair, and kissed her again. Jo's lips followed the soft contours of Carmen's neck. With closed eyes, Carmen tossed her head back, her long hair falling down. She smiled at the now familiar pleasure.

Jo paused, to swiftly pull off Carmen's blouse and then her bra. "I am so glad I picked you up on Friday," Jo said. For the first time Jo did not have court and Carmen did not have JC. Jo touched Carmen's face and kissed her again. Jo felt light headed at her first touch. "Don 't leaves tonight, our one week anniversary is in a few hours, "Jo whispered. Carmen kissed back. Jo moved her right hand under Carmen's panties and between her legs. Her index and middle finger slipped inside to the smooth moist velvet within Carmen's thigh. Carmen sighed. "Carmen, we have something amazing. I feel your passion, I want you. I love you."

37

THE TRAINS I MISSED

Thursday
July 21, 1988
11:35 p.m.
San Diego

CARMEN COUGHED AND PUSHED JO'S HAND AWAY FROM HER
body. This was survival. First, she had to be safe. She had so
many men profess desire and love. Jo was simply the first
woman to do so. Carmen inhaled deeply and exhaled
loudly. "Oh no Cariño, I must leave. Now. You must take me
to the Santa Fe Depot now, there's a train at midnight. I need
to be on it." Jo looked at her and knitted her eyebrows.

"Oh yes, you want me on that train, or I will be in pieces
on the pillow by dawn. They have JC. Yes, you know the
young man, that man who grabbed me, and shoved me in
the Suburban. They have him, I am sure he is dead, or
bleeding to death now. You need to get me gone."

Carmen pulled Jo towards her convertible. Jo opened the
door, and Carmen slid in the passenger side. Jo drove

silently. It was three miles from Jo's bungalow to the Santa Fe Train Depot. Pressed for time, Carmen spoke fast, compressing her lifetime of silent understanding into words. "Oh Jo, I saw your trial, and I have seen others before it. The jury believed their story. We all tell stories to explain the inexplicable - our sad childhood, the evil men do to others. American courtroom stories are told about those charged with breaking law. Your American judges write the end to the story. Look at Judge Mack. More dishonest than a drug king because he calls himself good. Thank God, I was raised Catholic and I have faith - so I know He will make it right. Ay, Josephina. They have murdered my boy. He was a fool, he was arrogant, he thought only of today. I do not doubt that he is very dead. I do not doubt that he is most definitely not in heaven. It has been all of you, the Gringo drug users in LA who don't think." Jo did not take her eyes off Carmen. "Josephina, this border made of cheese cloth holds nothing. Stops nothing. You let it all in. It is a cat that kills only every tenth mouse, and lets the other nine infest the home," Carmen said. She brought her right hand to her eyes, and brushed the tears away. "I have not seen this. I don't want to remember. I want to laugh and drink Coronas and dance in the clubs. I want to study art and fashion. This filth is not me, it is not my life," Carmen said.

Jo said, "I know Carmen, I know."

"Nothing I can do can make this right never. Justice? Not in my lifetime. Not for Mexico," Carmen said.

Jo stopped the car, they had arrived at Santa Fe Depot, a glorious Art Deco building. It stood as the remnant of the marriage between unemployed Italian-American craftsmen and the Depression Era Works Progress Administration.

The two women left the small car unlocked. Jo and Carmen walked together to the only train on the track.

Carmen approached a uniformed train conductor and smiled. She was an accomplished flirt in every circumstance, it had kept her alive this long.

Ever practicing her most precocious skill, Carmen asked "Is this the train north, to L.A., Santa Barbara, San Francisco, Portland, and Seattle." The whiskered conductor grinned at her soft accent and said "Yes, Miss, it is, but if you are going further north than Seattle, you will have to get off and buy a ferry ticket to Vancouver." "Thank you, Mr. Conductor, "Carmen said with a giggle, "I'll just buy my ticket on the train." "Sure thing, Miss," he said. Jo stared at Carmen, knowing certainly, that it would not be the case.

Carmen walked to the train entrance and grabbed Jo's hand. She handed Jo a sealed envelope. In the dim light, Jo could only see that it was addressed to her. On the outside, it said "To Josephine Gemma, Esq."

Jo looked at her, and she said quietly, and deliberately, "I am here. I am not leaving. I am not letting this crime go unanswered, unpunished, forgotten. I do what I do to make things better - and now more than ever I want something more." Jo paused, and stepped towards Carmen feeling her warmth and pulling her soft fragrant form towards her for a long, deep embrace.

Jo stepped in for one more ephemeral kiss.

"Carmen, stay here. I want to make this town good and beautiful. I love Mexico, its culture, its passion, its history. These border crimes are not the real Mexico.

We've got it ass-backwards. Some say Hernando Cortez murdered Mexico, but from what I see, I know it's this War on Drugs," Jo said.

"Listen Jo, gracias," Carmen said. Finally, Jo said, "Carmen, don't leave. We can have something." Carmen shook her head and took a step away. She turned and said flatly:

"Adios. Hope a murder investigation doesn't screw up your career, Jo. Karma's a bitch, even when you can't see her."

Jo shook her head: "No, Carmen. Karma is a boomerang."

FREE ADVICE

JO DIDN'T WAIT TO WATCH THE TRAIN LEAVE THE STATION. With tears soaking her cheeks, she ran back to her convertible. She felt sick to her stomach. She felt the loss. She hurt from the loss at trial. She hurt from Carmen leaving. Jo sat alone in the dark car and cried. For those few minutes, she regressed to the motherless six-year-old girl in Chicago, whose mother had been killed. Just old enough to read and write, but not old enough to be told what really happened. She cried, she felt the loss of her mother even twenty-two years later.

Jo coughed, and picked up the crumpled jury verdict form balled on the car floor mat. She wiped her tears away with the discarded paper. Like a horse going back to its stable, she looked around to find the car had driven her back to her neighborhood. But she couldn't go home, and go to a bed that did not include Carmen. There was no chance of sleep now.

She made a sharp left, and drove down the steep hill, under a railway bridge, and to the gay bar Defcon 2. It was be sure to be open. It was practically Friday. She parked in the bustling parking lot out front. Patting her hair down, and plastering a wan smile on her face, Jo squared her shoulders and approached a sturdy woman guarding the entrance to the club.

"I am here to just look at the fish, I don't intend to eat here, or take out," Jo said.

"Huh?" the bouncer said.

"I just broke up with my live-in girlfriend of one-week and I need some eye-candy," Jo explained.

The husky woman glanced at her thick black wrist watch. "We don't close until 2:00 a.m. so you still have two hours to get a replacement." Jo sighed in response.

The bouncer looked around, and lowered her voice. "Look, we've all been there. Women are the worst and the best. I'm not supposed to do this. Go on in, the cover is on me. But let me add some free advice, don't get laid tonight."

Jo threw her arms up in a weak surrender and entered Defcon 2.

Father DiGiacco was right, Jo realized as she entered the smoky interior packed with sweaty, scantily clad dancers.

Sodom and Gomorrah definitely had its good points. She peered in the dark, looking for attractive women. Retracing her steps, from the previous week, she climbed up the bar's winding metal staircase to the second floor. She stood at the railing, watching young bodies move to the pounding sounds. A soft hand touched her shoulder.

Jo turned around. Jo tilted her head. Lana, from her surfing pack, was inches from her. Only tonight, high heels and a tight purple dress, replaced Lana's habitual beach sandals and board shorts. "Nice to see you tonight," Lana said, brushing her long blonde hair from her face.

"Even better to see you Lana," Jo answered.

"Where's Carmen?" Lana asked.

"She moved to L.A.," Jo said flatly.

"I'm glad, I never liked her," Lana blurted out.

"Really? Why?" Jo asked with genuine curiosity. "Because, I have always had a crush on you," Lana said.

Jo blushed, and took Lana's hand. "Lana, thank you, I like you too, but, I just need some time," Jo said. Lana held on to Jo's hand and kissed her full on the lips.

"I got to go wash my face," Jo said.

Jo walked down a dimly lit hallway. In a corner, was phone booth to make phone conversation possible. Jo dug into her tight jeans and pulled out a fistful of quarters. She dumped in eight quarters. She dialed a number she had known by heart for twenty-five years. After the first ring, she closed the accordion thick glass door and waited.

"This is Detective Gemma," the voice answered. "Hi Dad," Jo said.

"Josephine, it's after 3:00 a.m. Are you calling to tell me you just won the Publisher's Clearinghouse grand prize?"

"No Dad. I just wanted to talk."

"Seeing as I don't have to get up for three hours, I can listen," Giacomo Gemma responded.

"Dad, I just lost the biggest case I've had," Jo said.

"I am sorry Jo."

"The guy was so guilty, and we just got a bad deal the whole way through," Jo explained.

"Jo, I hear you, you must feel bad."

"Dad, I do. Really bad. I don't want to go back not now. I need a break. And I need some answers."

"Jo honey, so do I. I have been working at this damn city job for 30 years."

"Dad, I am being real," Jo said.

"Sure Jo. You can come to the Albany Park homestead. Nothing's changed."

"Dad, I have to ask you about Mom. And how she died. I remember some things. I feel more. Especially, when things in my life aren't working. I just need you to help me figure this out."

"Jo, honey, I wish, I could replay that night. I wish I could protect you from the unknowable evil with a night-light and hug. Or even a snub-nosed Colt, but I don't know."

"Dad, I love you." Jo sniffled.

"Jo, you gotta decide for yourself. Do you want to win or do you want justice?"

"Dad, I will see you Saturday night, or earlier."

Jo hung up, crying.

The pay phone rang. Jo picked up and listened as a high-pitched voice said "Please deposit $1.75 for the last call. Again, please deposit $1.75." Jo dug through her pants and wallet. She found $2.00 in loose silver coins. She dropped the coins in the slot at the top of the payphone.

Jo returned to her convertible. She picked up the pink envelope Carmen had handed her at the train station. She carefully lifted the sealed edges with her finger and exposed a greeting card. The outside of the card depicted the silhou-ette of a couple walking on a beach. Jo opened the card. In a neat cursive handwriting was a short note: "To the only girl I love, Carmen."

Jo felt better. She had hope.

39

SPARE KEY

THE VERONICA AND OTHER MEMBERS OF THE RED TIDE, escorted Rosie back home. They rang the doorbell. Nobody was there.

"Good thing your jaw was not actually broken," the rugby captain said.

They called out, and rang the doorbell a few more times, but nobody answered.

After some minutes waiting, Rosie mumbled out through a cracked and swollen face, hey let me grab the spare key from the garage. Rosie opened the door adjoining the small detached garage, and stumbled on a loose board. She retraced her steps to hit the fluorescent light on the wall. Rosie looked again down at the board that had caused her to stumble. There was something, a package or something in the old oil pit. She kneeled down to get a better look.

"Hey Rosie!!" You OK? "The Veronica roared.

"Yeah, one sec!" Rosie said.

She knelt down, and pulled a second, then a third, then a fourth loose board. The oil pit was filled with packages.

With bricks of something. Carmen's Chevelle was gone too. Rosie had learned a lot from Miss Fancy Pants Gemma, about cartels, and bricks. Rosie bent down and picked up one of the packages wrapped tightly in silver electrical tape.

With a trained chef's attention to detail she turned it in her hands. She rose to her feet, and grabbed an awl from the toolbox, and poked a hole in the silver package. A white powdery substance slipped out. Rosie was no stranger to the party scene. She put her right index finger in her mouth, moistening it, and dabbed a few grains of powder and put it her nostrils. Rosie's eyes lit up.

40

GRAND OPENING

January 7,1989

"ROSIE!" THE VERONICA LED THE CHEERS OF THE RED TIDE.

Veronica handed the microphone over to the large woman with pink hair.

"Thank you to the Red Tide, and everybody who has been a part of celebrating our grand opening. Welcome to Cafe Madame Defarge," Rosie announced. Rosie winked at an old girlfriend standing in the soft warm light of the January afternoon. To soothe her agitation, she fingered the 24-carat mustachioed saint wedged between her voluptuous breasts. Under her breath, Rosie whispered "Gracias, Jesus Malverde." Unseen by Rosie, the gold pendant winked back.

AFTERWORD

The War on Drugs was launched over thirty years ago. If you want to know how we got here:

Follow the Timeline Started in the 1980's

- **1984** United States Sentencing Guidelines Enacted into Law
- **1985** Kiki Camarena, a Federal Special Agent with the Drug Enforcement Agency, was murdered by narco henchmen at the behest of the Attorney General of Mexico
- **1986** the U.S. Congress enacted 5, 10 and 20-year mandatory minimum prison sentences for importing drugs
- **1988** the Chemical Diversion and Trafficking Act (CDTA) gave DEA the authority to regulate chemicals and industrial machinery used in processing cocaine
- **1988 to 2017 Price of Cocaine Decreases 80%** -1988 $300 per gram / 2017 $60 per gram

- **2017** Drug overdose deaths kill over 60,000 people in the U.S. More than four times the rate of gun homicides.
- **2017** U.S. has the largest prison population by percent with 1 in 100 people in prison or on probation, half of them for drug crimes, 2.2 million people in prison or jail
- **2017** War on Drugs Annual Cost -$51 Billion

Thank you for reading my book.

As they say in Narcotics Anonymous, to do the same thing over and over again and expect a different result is indeed, Insanity.

Join me at AlDeNovabooks.com, and please share with a friend or loved one. If you enjoyed my book your book review and comments on Amazon would be most appreciated.

A.L. DeNova
December 2017

ABOUT THE AUTHOR

A.L. DeNova has worked in law enforcement for over two decades protecting the Southwest Border between the United States and Mexico. A.L. DeNova is a pseudonym. The experience is real.